SPIRIT WALKER: A CHEYENNE SAGA

SPIRIT WALKER:
A CHEYENNE SAGA

RUSTY DAVIS

FIVE STAR
A part of Gale, a Cengage Company

GALE
A Cengage Company

Farmington Hills, Mich • San Francisco • New York • Waterville, Maine
Meriden, Conn • Mason, Ohio • Chicago

LIBRARY OF CONGRESS CATALOGING-IN-PUBLICATION DATA

Names: Davis, Rusty, author.
Title: Spirit Walker: a Cheyenne saga / Rusty Davis
Description: First Edition. | Farmington Hills, Mich. : Five Star, a part of Gale, a Cengage Company, 2020.
Identifiers: LCCN 2019015466 (print) | ISBN 9781432860110 (hardcover : alk. paper)
Subjects: | GSAFD: Fantasy fiction.
Classification: LCC PS3604.A9755 S65 2020 (print) | DDC 813/.6—dc23
LC record available at https://lccn.loc.gov/2019015466

First Edition. First Printing: January 2020
Find us on Facebook—https://www.facebook.com/FiveStarCengage
Visit our website—http://www.gale.cengage.com/fivestar
Contact Five Star Publishing at FiveStar@cengage.com

Printed in Mexico
1 2 3 4 5 6 7 24 23 22 21 20

This book is dedicated to the men, women, and children of the Northern Cheyenne Indian nation, who wrote one of the most courageous and tragic chapters in all of North American history during the Cheyenne Exodus. To face death in the name of a dream; to prefer a grave on the windswept prairie to life on a reservation; to walk a thousand miles for freedom, in rags, through the cold of winter in an endless valley of hate: this is heroism shot through with tragedy that is the hallmark of the story of the Plains Indians. This is the story of that miracle when The People and their spirits lived out a broken-hearted quest that should never be forgotten.

CHAPTER ONE

December 29, 1890, Wounded Knee Creek, Dakota Territory
The wheeled guns sent their hot breath of death whistling past Rides a Crow and over her head into the camp where the Indian women and children were gathered.

Moments before, from the camp where ranks of blue-clad soldiers faced down thinly-clothed warriors feverish with a dream the Ghost Dance had instilled in their heads, a single rifle shot had barked. Then another. Then a splattering of rifle fire erupted. Then a volley.

As the women sought to find their children and to gather rifles they had hidden, the soldiers had acted as they had of old—killed women, killed children.

Rides a Crow had come from the Northern Cheyenne reservation on the Tongue River weeks ago, leaving behind The People as they tenaciously held land they feared would be swept from them once again. She was known as a Wise Woman among her Northern Cheyenne. Her Lakota cousins were trying to discern if the Ghost Dance would bring the end of the whites and return them to the days when the plains were black with buffalo and free from the soot of the railroads. She doubted a new war would do anything except kill more of The People. She'd planned to return home but had repeatedly delayed her departure, because within her there was a spark of defiance that wouldn't die, a hope that, if the spirit triumphed once when it should have been quenched, it could triumph again.

Then Sitting Bull was killed, new fights flared, and any pretense of friendship ended. Her cousin's band of Minneconjou Sioux fled into the Dakota winter for fear that to stay was to die. But flesh could bear only so much. Spotted Elk, known to the whites as Big Foot, had finally brought his band to surrender, fearing the worst but unable to resist any longer as winter gripped the land under lead-gray clouds.

On this day, Rides a Crow could all but feel the ring of evil tightening its noose around the camp. She had heard Custer's former troopers were manning the guns to ensure that, if the men fought back, their families would die.

Death was no stranger to Rides a Crow. It had ridden with her for fourteen years, since the Night the Dead Rode with the Living, since the slaughter at the Pit. She would not run away today. As another blast from the terrible guns-on-wheels erupted, she ducked back into her tipi and reached in the blankets for the old rifle she had brought with her. If the soldiers meant to kill them all, they would pay dearly.

Then she froze. She heard within her the only voice that could make her change her mind.

"Stop."

She turned, her braids bouncing off the Ghost Shirt she wore in defiance. There was no one there.

"The People need you," came the voice in her head. "The Ghost Dance is not of the spirit world. It is the dream of men. It is the death of men. Save who you can."

Gunfire raged again. A shell tore through the tipi.

"I shall never surrender," she said aloud. "They are killing The People. I did nothing when Dull Knife's people were slaughtered like this! Dead Face fought. This time I will fight."

"You cannot save children from the grave, foolish woman. You cannot lead The People from a pit of the dead. It is not your time to join him!"

The loud gun's roar was followed by new screams. Rides a Crow emerged from the tent with her rifle, stepping around the body of a Lakota woman who yesterday had been nursing a child.

Her rifle had only four bullets, but four soldiers were better than none, if all the women and children were going to be killed. A soldier, face disfigured by hate and rage, closed in on a toddler standing in place, watching, crying in fear amid a world of fury. The soldier's rifle descended, with its bayonet fixed.

The Hotchkiss guns thundered then, and the smoke obscured what came next. As the smoke dispersed, she saw the child still crying by the torn, bleeding body of the soldier. *He* was here! She looked but could not find him.

Around her, women were plucking children and carrying them to any form of safety they could find on this day of murder.

"They need you. Go!" she heard his voice say.

A scream tore her ears and soul as a horse galloping into the maelstrom registered pain. The coal-black mare's muzzle showed red and raw from a shell that had exploded nearby. The horse stared at Rides a Crow with imploring eyes: leave now or die!

Rides a Crow fired her four shots into the mass of soldiers, then tossed the rifle aside. She gathered up the crying child. Blue figures with guns emerged from the swirling haze of smoke. A bullet pierced her side. Unbelievable agony coursed through her. She turned to fight her way through what now seemed to be a wall of soldiers. The knife she threw vanished into the dimness. A second bullet plowed a furrow along her face as the soldiers closed in for the kill.

As death came to claim her, she set down the small Lakota child, hoping a Cheyenne blessing would be good enough on this day of killing. While slaughter and blood-madness flooded forth from the wave of soldiers descending upon the camp,

Rides a Crow sang her death song.
Then she charged.

CHAPTER TWO

August, 1874, Tongue River Valley, Cheyenne Indian Nation
Dark Hawk looked out across the Tongue River Valley but was untouched by its richness and beauty. A great sadness was upon him. Tendrils of evil were slowly forming around The People, known to the ever-growing mass of white settlers as the Northern Cheyenne.

Men who coveted their lands, who sought to destroy their ways, and who wanted the Great Spirit to turn His back on their souls were working, day by day, to accomplish their goals. This land had been the Cheyenne homeland for generations, but the white newcomers had already named it Montana Territory, as though the right of naming it was theirs.

At first, white people brought their religion, which taught little The People did not already know and do, but now they brought their dark spirits to wrest from The People everything the Great Spirit had given them.

It was six years since the Treaty of the Powder River, signed in the year the whites called 1868, had given the Cheyenne, the Lakota, and the Oglala a victory, halting the flood of the white settlers, supposedly forever. Yet the dam had cracked. First a trickle, now a flood rendered the words on the paper as insubstantial as smoke from a fire.

The People were divided. Many wanted to fight to the death, believing they could turn back the whites forever, even if the sacrifice would be beyond imagining. Others argued the white

11

menace was too vast and too strong. No matter how many soldiers and settlers died, others took their places. The People fought when they could, temporized when they needed to, and every day grew weaker.

Word had reached Dark Hawk that Indian Hater Custer had proclaimed gold, the metal for which whites would kill even one another, existed in the Paha Sapa—the Black Hills. This would mean a new flood, and no matter how much even well-meaning white men talked, the army would break every treaty and take from The People everything they'd been promised. That was the only lesson to be learned from years of dealing with the soldiers.

He knew the spirit world also cried out, because those who would bring foul and evil spirits to the lands of The People were among those trying to take the land. As a man who had been given a slight and distant glimpse of the world of the spirits, Dark Hawk knew troubled days lay ahead.

He accepted the limit already cast to his days. He was a warrior, and it was his fate. In a recurring dream about Custer, he watched from his journey to the next world as the Indian hater was surrounded by The People and killed. He accepted this as a prophecy of what would be, and it did not trouble him, for, if his death also meant the end of the soldier who hated The People, it would be a good day to die.

What concerned him was the fog of uncertainty around his daughter, Rides a Crow. He knew she was destined for more than the life of another member of the Northern Cheyenne. Although the signs were clear she was a Spirit Walker, her path would not be easy. The way animals all but spoke to her showed she was deep in the spirit, but her indifference to the way a young girl should act—she wore no beads or bracelets and accepted none as gifts—made him worry about her future. She was independent to the point of being more contrary beyond that which most husbands would tolerate, yet her judgment was sure and her heart true.

"Great Spirit," he began, "The People cry out. The days of trial we face are nothing like those to come. Let not The People be scattered like dead grass. Raise up for us a champion from your realm of spirits, send to us the spirit guides of our ancestors, so that The People who cry out to you, O God, to live in peace with all You made and all peoples will not fall into the fire and be burned to ash and scattered to the winds forever more. Only the spirit world can save The People from destruction at the hands of our enemies."

He did not know how long he waited for an answer. His eyes burned, and the sun danced. For a moment, he saw a place of despair and death. Then a woman wearing a cloth of red around her hair and holding a rifle began speaking to The People as they gathered in a place he knew was the Tongue River Valley. Dim spirits stood behind her—horses, a warrior, and a wolf. His vision told him this was his daughter; this would be her fate. Then the vision was gone, leaving Dark Hawk wishing the spirits had said more. Like a feverish man clutching water, he held to the hope the vision was a glimpse of what was to come and not the imaginings of his troubled soul.

Sand Hills, Nebraska, October 1876
Amid desolation and beauty, the Outcast greeted the day. When the sky became light, crows would come and, later, songbirds. If he was lucky, no men, unless those who passed for friends, the ones people called Northern Cheyenne, would pass through again. They lived as he did, lightly and quietly.

Although he had long ago stopped tracking days, he knew time to be near the month of October in the year of 1876. Two years since the day that changed his life, unless one counted being born what he was as that day.

13

He leaned on the buffalo gun. A massive rifle, he had mastered it in his time alone. Rifles had come quickly to him, other things less easily. So adept had he become as a hunter, visitors from the north, the Cheyenne, had come to call for his help when they hunted the ever-scarcer herds of buffalo. Whites killed for sport; he condemned them. Killing was easy. The Northern Cheyenne killed for survival.

With them he had forged an odd trade, for they taught him about the land, about their ways, and their spirits lurking at the edge of human awareness—but not his. He might see ten visitors a year by choice. All were Northern Cheyenne, for he had come to think of them as friends. One warrior, Dark Hawk, seemed to understand he was more than met the eye, but nothing was said, for the language gap between them was too great to bridge.

Dawn wind fluffed his long hair and unkempt beard. His collection of cowboy, soldier, and Indian clothing was a testament to his indifference about his appearance. He wore a cowboy-checked shirt over cavalry pants that flopped in the wind above his moccasin-clad feet. Gray was gaining in its race to dominate his head, with stubborn islands of reddish brown in his beard refusing to give way. His wind-worn face bespoke a life outdoors. The only feature easily visible above his beard except for a pair of dark, piercing, uneasy eyes that studied everything, whether it moved or not, was his prominent nose. His small frame was a study in tension when he scanned everything he could see, and then he relaxed.

The sun now peeked over one of the mounds of what they called the Sand Hills, land where no plow would run and no crop would grow because the soil was sand instead of deep Plains dirt, making it a safe place for the birds, for the big cats, for him. The sun rose past small trees. No buildings cluttered this place they called Nebraska. No smokestacks, no cloud of grit from the coal of the city.

And he thought, once again, about Jenny Blue Eyes. She had been perhaps eight, or perhaps not, since truth and age were both flexible assets for a blooming London pickpocket and accomplished beggar.

He would never forget the day. She wanted to see where the toffs lived—the rich of London whose lives were so near theirs, yet so far above. He'd been spending much of his time in Whitechapel, much of it in his least favorite haunts, as he tried to learn the ins and outs of the vast city where his clan made its home and its living. Jenny had seen him wandering, lost, one day and adopted him. Theirs was a curious friendship, but nonetheless real for all the differences between them.

On the last Sunday in October, in that fateful year of 1874, for a reason he could not fully understand, he led her from the warrens of Whitechapel out past Westminster. She marveled at the sight of a sky without soot. She pleaded, and he allowed her to beg outside a church. She knew churches were where toffs gave money, not in the city during the week. In the city, they threw their hatred against the world and everyone in it in a hurly-burly to survive.

He had waited beside some trees. He was always careful in those days.

Lord Gerard Entwhistle had come out from the church. The Outcast could still hear Jenny's voice in the little song she sang asking for a penny. Then she started coughing. Lord Entwhistle had roughly pushed her away, knocking her down.

Jenny Blue Eyes then let him know in her vast Whitechapel vocabulary what she thought of toffs who assaulted girls after going to church. The Outcast had not caught all the words of the toff's reply, but he called her a series of names that were not the stuff of Christian charity. She rose to do battle with the knife no Whitechapel girl ever forgot.

The battle ended swiftly. The lead-tipped, silver-headed cane swung once; Jenny Blue Eyes fell, never to sing or cough again. Carriage drivers then surrounded the scene—a wall of servants he could not break through. Lord Entwhistle escaped, but only for a time. As the rich man hid—for he had his own secrets—the Outcast sought absolution through violence for the guilt he felt for the girl's death. Vengeance became his only reason to live.

Luck was with him. The engagement party of Simon Cawthorne and Philippa Entwhistle was proclaimed in the society pages. The Cawthornes, rooted in American banking and the Entwhistles, English nobility dating back to the Wars of the Roses, represented a fusion of the new and old worlds. A society centerpiece, the event had a guest list so long it would be easy for the Outcast to slip in. He looked at the words of the newspaper clipping in his hand, words he knew by heart.

Lord Entwhistle rose for a toast and waited with an impatient eye until conversation stilled and all attention featured on the host, a man whose reputation for dabbling in dark arts was better left unsaid and untouched. At his feet stood a huge, mangy, skinny dog, rust-colored, with mud and filth all over its few patches of what might have been white. His Lordship asked one of the staff to have it killed and thrown out. The dog clawed his leg. The animal dropped a rolled-up piece of paper on His Lordship's chair.

His Lordship, intrigued, set down his glass and unrolled the paper until he saw the portrait of a girl known to have been called 'Jenny Blue Eyes,' which police later learned was painted by a man in Whitechapel who forges art for his mean living. The lord's visage drained of blood. Then it suffused with red, and he cursed at the mangy creature, which sat on the floor at his feet in perfect attention.

His Lordship was in the act of drawing the pistol he always kept in his coat when the animal sprang. Before the bejeweled guests could even scream, the creature's teeth had done their work. Lord Entwhistle wobbled, dripping blood, as his eyes shifted and lost focus, and he toppled onto the table, tipping it over and starting an endless chorus of screams as the noble and important personages in attendance perceived that the animal had ripped His Lordship's throat to pieces.

The animal then calmly walked through the transfixed crowd, seemingly having done what it had come to do, until the police guarding the event against agitators were called to kill it. One shot hit the animal, whose howl of pain and rage was the one thing everyone attending agreed upon. Police and guests closed in. The animal fought back. Gunshots and teeth left five people dead and three dozen wounded.

The estate's staff told the police they watched the bloodied, injured animal with fear as it limped across the manicured lawn and into the trees. Their tales left the believable behind, and the servants claimed the creature transformed into a man as it moved over the high wall. Police say they will round up anarchists, devil worshippers, and those seeking to overthrow the government.

The Outcast recalled what came next.

For weeks, London newspapers went wild with headlines about werewolves. The government organized a roundup of stray dogs, none of which proved to be the animal in question. Men matching the description of the man the staff said they saw climbing over the wall, and the one whom the Whitechapel artist said ordered him to paint the girl's picture, were brought in if they showed sign of recent wounds. All of London's high society begged for police escorts to and from their gala functions, but as days turned to weeks, and weeks to months, escorts proved needless. The sensation faded as fast as a November frost. Everyone only knew that Lord Entwhistle was killed, and that a portrait of a little beggar girl with the word "Justice" written in red had been found on his body. Police raided those who dabbled in the arts of sorcery, which Victorian society denied existed even as its members experimented with evil as though it were a toy. Many were arrested, but few detained.

A rogue to begin with, exile for the Outcast soon followed.

"You have endangered us all," the clan chief, Rheged, told the Outcast. Rheged had hunted him down in the hovel where he had hoped to escape notice until his leg wound healed. "It is bad enough you left our ways and the old religion and adopted theirs. Now they know we werewolves are here. Worse, Lord Entwhistle was a friend to our kind. He used his powers to help build our power, and now that this has come to light, we are being hunted."

"He was an evil man whose death I do not regret."

The Outcast and Rheged stood nose to nose, the hate between them alive and raw.

"They are clumsy in their hunt, but, if they are lucky once, we are all finished," Rheged said. "I should kill you now, but the clan wants you given a chance. Skellig remains soft on you, and others follow her. She will learn. You have one week. After that, there will be a bounty to kill you if you are seen or heard of again. I hope to collect it."

There was nothing to keep him in London. From the day the Outcast had been stopped by the street preacher who gave him a Bible and showed him all creatures were children of God, he had grown distant from the clan, which believed itself spawned by other forces.

He took ship the next day. He gave himself a new name—Hunter—and headed west when he reached America, until he reached this spot, where he stayed. He built a shelter for the worst of the days, and, for the rest, God provided, with help from the Northern Cheyenne, who showed their white visitor ways to survive the winter, a courtesy he repaid by helping them hunt.

And now? The Outcast thought—no, he knew—his idyll was ending, for he felt hate flowing after Custer-the-hero led his men to their deaths. The winds that blew a gale around him would soon envelop him in a terrible pattern he could not yet discern. He would never walk properly again, thanks to the bullet in his right leg that would remain until the day he died. But he could walk as far down the road as he had to walk.

He looked at the paper in his hand—brittle and yellow; barely legible. He crumpled it and threw the pieces to the wind, wondering yet again if the feeling at the edge of his mind was the same evil he had felt in London, clinging to him like smoke. Or was it evil closing in on those who called themselves The People as they tried to live in a peace with white settlers who refused to allow them to do so?

He watched the fragments of paper hang for a moment and then drift to the northwest. A wind from the southeast was the rarest of all winds on an October day. It was as close to a sign as he was likely to get. He would go where it led him.

Fairfax Ranch, Colorado, October 1876

Morrison Fairfax walked into his trophy room looking at the framed photograph in its place of honor, as if it oversaw the work of his life. As always, when entering the room, he saluted the photograph.

John Chivington's name should have been praised in every corner of the land. Instead, Chivington was reviled, maligned by those without his vision. The 1864 attack on Black Kettle's village at Sand Creek in Colorado should have wiped out the Southern Cheyenne tribe forever. His men had killed women and children beyond reckoning on that day. Fairfax recalled the day as a shining moment of glory when he rode with a man he worshipped, doing the holy work of ridding the world of Indians. If the government had followed that glorious day with the kinds of blows needed, the Plains would now be rid of the Indian menace.

Fairfax had done his part. He'd served Chivington at Sand Creek, killed more than his share of women and children then and afterward, and supported his idol when the whiners and coddlers criticized their progress. In time, he'd built this room to the glory of his work. His collection had grown. Relics of every Indian he had killed—and he had done all he could to kill everyone within reach—were displayed here. His only regret was that there were not more of them.

He had used his determination to build a massive ranch now sprawling along eastern Colorado. Some of his range was in Kansas and Wyoming, in lands no Indian dared set foot upon any longer. Fairfax wanted more: an empire running through eastern Wyoming into Montana. The Tongue River Valley was perfect, except that the government had allowed those Indians to have it!

Using his wealth, he paid rewards for scalps. His vast collection grew daily. It impressed visitors and had brought him to the attention of others who shared his feelings about Indians. He and they worked toward the same goal, although their methods were perhaps more subtle, if equally deadly.

Now in his mid-fifties, Fairfax was at the height of his power. A massive man, he stood over six feet tall and sported a rim of black hair, now peppered with gray, and a large bald spot. A prominent nose and a massive, drooping mustache adorned his face. His dark eyes glared at the world above dark circles and amid a network of lines earned from squinting at the books he acquired.

His revelation that he was not alone in his battle against

Indians had come to him via one of the riders he had fired. The man had allowed a Cheyenne woman to glean wood from *his* land for her fire! That woman had told the rider Indians could never be defeated because the Great Spirit protected them. Books on the occult soon began making their way to his ranch, because he would take any ally who would help him defeat the Cheyenne. Then came letters and meetings with those who performed rituals to combat the spirits protecting the savages. Proud to be one of its foremost members, he'd been amazed to find the extent of the network of hate against Indians that had developed over the years.

His first reaction had been to quail at the actions of these who called themselves conjurers, because he had been raised Christian. But then he saw the use of darkness to defeat evil as necessary, if it gave him what he wanted, which was access to the land within the Northern Cheyenne range. He also felt his own importance and power grow as he made common cause with others like him, and he soon became a leader in the work of using the spirit world to defeat the Indians.

The record of those who sought to raise spirits was impressive, but Fairfax was irked that, of all the tribes, the Northern Cheyenne were the hardest to crack, being so guarded by the spirits with whom their lives were entwined. As a result, some of his former allies faded in enthusiasm, trusting time to do its job as buffalo were slaughtered to feed a market they helped create. Many focused on the Lakota, guardians of the Black Hills and its gold.

The Little Bighorn fight in Montana, when that idiot Custer's column was mauled, proved the job was not finished. The fight had given Fairfax new energy to crush his enemy. Until Custer's fall, it seemed pacifists were winning, and that the Indians who deserved nothing but death would be allowed to live on land reserved for their use.

He had fired off letters to President Grant. As an important man in Colorado politics, he was a voice to be reckoned with. The Lakota and Cheyenne were out there! Grant's waning administration promised action, but the army was always making promises and rarely delivered on them.

In St. Louis, when he went to personally demand of the army's commanders that Grant act, he had encountered a friend who had told him about new weapons and new ways he could use to defeat the Indians.

The person this friend described as stronger than any other force of this world or the next was due soon: a personage who had recently come from London and was known to be a confederate of the late Lord Entwhistle, of whom Fairfax was aware through writings never meant for the public eye.

Fairfax was hopeful. He was convinced that the Indians had held the Plains through the spirit world, not just the world of men. With this newcomer's plan, he could crush the Indians in both worlds and then use his power to control as much land as he wanted, for as long as he wanted.

CHAPTER THREE

Red Fork of the Rosebud Creek, Montana Territory, November 1876
Rides a Crow had heard all the arguments for running away. She was ready to stand and fight, not that anyone would ask.

The People had made a strong camp. They had defeated Custer, whom she had heard talked about all her life. Still, it seemed from the way the elders acted, they were more afraid of the white soldiers than ever now that the one who hated them most was dead. Elders! They said there were more blue soldiers coming. Who would send more soldiers to die after those who were already dead?

She knew the white men were angry because the Indians had fought back, but what else should they have done when death galloped through a peaceful village? She wished she could have fought with them. She had seen one little boy—younger than she—grab a pistol and race to where the guns sounded. She should have followed the boy.

Why did white people believe they had a right to attack The People, when The People were living as they always had? If the newcomers did not like the fact that the Indians would fight for their homes, they could go back where they came from!

Her father, Dark Hawk, had told her before he left to join Crazy Horse in the spring that the white people who wanted more land were cursed. They would always want more and never be happy with what they had. Dark Hawk was among those killed when Custer charged the village—the village that was not hurting anyone. His body had not been recovered. Antelope Horn, her mother, had been wounded, too, but was brought back to where the Northern Cheyenne were camping that summer. She died weeks later as Rides a Crow held her hand and sang her passing song.

Now sixteen, Rides a Crow reached only to the shoulders of an average warrior. Standing straight, she had snapping black eyes that signaled a quick mind and—when called for—a sharp tongue. She wore her straight, black hair free when she could, but in braids when there was work to be done, as there was this day. She never allowed her hair to grow as long as girls looking for warrior husbands. She would hack it off with a knife from time to time when its length got in her way. Arranging hair was a time-wasting activity with which she had no patience.

The day was cold, but she was not. She was fortunate to have a warm buckskin shirt, skirt, and leggings, none of which she adorned. She wore no jewelry, because jewelry was a nuisance when she dwelled in the wild with the animals. She wrapped a blanket over her shoulders more from habit than the need for extra warmth, and she wore moccasins in the snow.

She should have been married that summer, but Horse Walking, the warrior her parents found for her, also died at the Greasy Grass. She mourned him distantly. He had been older, and was very polite when bargaining for her, but the marriage was from duty, not desire. She would have preferred to marry the warrior pledged to her when she was a child, but, due to hideous injuries he had suffered, he no longer rode with The People, and she knew Horse Walking to be a brave man. Another would come in time, she supposed.

Her grandparents had taken her in. The Northern Cheyenne traveled separately from the Lakota, although some were her cousins through the marriage of Antelope Horn's sisters to Lakota warriors. She had heard her genealogy so many times, it

seemed they were all one people—the Lakota, the Northern
Cheyenne, and the Southern Cheyenne, who lived so far south.
She had heard of death from the start of her life, since Dark
Hawk had relatives at Sand Creek, when the Southern Cheyenne
who wanted to surrender were butchered by white soldiers.
That had been long ago, but the dead were not forgotten by the
Northern Cheyenne.

Although there was nervous talk about leaving the camp site
and following Crazy Horse, she was not afraid. Crazy Horse's
band needed to be able to move fast, because the army would
seek them to avenge Custer. Women, children, and elders could
not move as fast as warriors. Although some said the camp was
not safe, others said that, if they could defeat Custer, the whites
would never dare attack them.

Rich in game, the camp here had not been used in many
years. The creek flowed clear. Rides a Crow was glad they had
decided to stay here. If soldiers came, they would lose, for The
People were strong. If there was a fight, she would play a part in
the battle, even if her brother tried to stop her. Long Knife
thought he was a warrior because he was a year older than she,
but he was more boy than man! If he was old enough to fight,
so was she, because she felt within her a burning need to do
more for The People than a young girl's lot allowed.

For now, she walked through the snow, picking the few berries deer had not eaten. The sun glinted off the flowing water.
Tonight, they would listen to Tame Deer's silly stories by the
fire, and, when the night became calm and still, she could walk
among the stars and ask the spirits about everything in her
heart. She'd felt ill at ease for no reason lately, as though some
incoherent but insistent purpose of great importance crawled at
the edges of her life.

A noise blared. As a volley of guns sounded, Rides a Crow

realized the noise came from a trumpet the army used to signal a charge.

She looked up to see troopers fording the creek. Bullets clanged off of the pot she carried, sending red berries scattering across the surface of the snow as death came for The People.

At the first volley, Rides a Crow sought cover, as she had been taught. When horses rode past her, she rolled into the thicket of bushes. She hollowed out a place and built up a mound of snow to make herself less visible, then listened as guns fired and men screamed. She could picture what would happen. The men would form the best line of defense they could to delay the soldiers. Women and children would run. Then the warriors would charge, and the soldiers would run away again.

But as she hid, she grew fearful. The size of the battle was unlike anything she had ever imagined. She rose up once from her shelter to look at the village. She saw blue uniforms, more than she had ever seen in her life. Clearly, the camp some of the elders had said could never be attacked was being overrun. For a moment she wanted to leave her safe place, find a weapon, and defend The People.

Then she recalled her father's admonition, his final, mysterious words as he rode off with Crazy Horse at the Greasy Grass. Her life had been given to her by the spirits to ensure The People would endure. It was not hers alone to spend as she wished. Therefore, she watched, before more riders coming near made her duck down in the thicket.

The largest flurry of shots was over. It seemed to last forever when it was thundering, yet, once it was over, she knew the attack had not even lasted the entire morning. Shots still rang out occasionally, but they were distant. The People must have returned to chase away the soldiers. And here she was hiding, thinking all had been lost!

She rose.

"Stop right there, squaw girl," came a voice.

Looking down the barrel of a rifle, she saw bloodshot eyes staring back. The trooper wore a thick hat, wool jacket and cape, and boots to his knees. She wondered how white men moved in such heavy clothes.

She had learned English from traders, soldiers, and missionaries. She was very good at all languages and spoke English as well as many white men. She stopped and held her hands out from her body.

"What do we have here?" he said. "That hair might fetch me twenty bucks back in Kansas." He scanned her over. "Rest of you ain't worth so much." He squinted. "Not pretty enough to risk a knife in the ribs for, girl."

He moved closer, his Winchester cocked and ready. He squinted at her. Judged her.

"Maybe, maybe not. Toss that blanket away and let me get a good look at you," he said. She waited. "Toss that thing away!" he commanded.

She took the blanket from her shoulders and flung it at him. Frozen feet betrayed her, though, and he was on her in twenty steps. He tackled her to the snow, rolled her over, and punched her hard in the face until resistance ceased. He then unholstered his pistol and pointed it in her face.

"Now, maybe you understand who the boss is here," he said.

A deep, throaty, threatening growl emerged from the bushes behind them both. The sound chilled Rides a Crow as it sent a thrill down her spine. Her attacker, sitting astride her, turned away to look.

Rides a Crow did not hesitate. The soldier's head was still in motion as she grabbed her knife and swung it blindly, knowing that whatever she cut would be a help to her. She nicked his chin, prompting a scream of rage and surprise mixed with pain.

She rolled as the pistol exploded next to her head and stabbed with the knife, feeling it connect. She pulled it free and stabbed again, then scrambled to get out from under his weight. As she turned back to him holding the red-bladed knife, he still knelt in the snow. Two red blotches decorated his chest. He looked at her, but she could tell he saw nothing.

Her first thought was to leave, but a rifle and pistol were prizes. She grabbed the rifle from the snow, but quailed from taking the pistol from a hand not yet dead. Her moment of indecision was almost her last. Two troopers who had heard the shot now approached. One of them saw her and sent a rifle bullet whistling into the trees. Rides a Crow heard the bullet strike the branches behind her as she dove to the snow in hopes of crawling through the thick bushes to safety.

The men moved together, fearful, covering both sides of the path with their rifles as they approached her hiding place. Coming ever closer, they would find her in a second.

One of them bumped into her and, looking down, kicked her angrily. "Get up, you . . ."

He never finished his sentence. A snarling, rust-colored wolf leaped from the shadows. Both soldiers fired their guns. Rides a Crow heard the rounds hit the trees. Then the wolf ran through the trail and moved left, right, left, as the guns spat and missed, spat and missed. The wolf changed tactics and came straight at the men, who stood shoulder to shoulder as the hammers of their guns clicked on empty—as if the wolf had spent a lifetime learning how to dodge bullets and also knew that guns ran out of bullets.

The soldiers grabbed for their pistols but never reached them. One man screamed as teeth sank into his leg; the other as a razor-sharp claw gouged the back of a knee and teeth sank deep into his thigh. Once the men were down, the wolf's jaws closed on their hands, until they screamed and whined in helpless rage and pain.

Riveted by the swift, brutal battle, Rides a Crow realized her chance to escape had come. She turned away from the spectacle, ran until she found more cover, and tried to hide under the leaf-bare network of branches in the thicket.

She could barely hear footfalls in the snow, even in the silence. She did not know if there was a bullet in the rifle she'd taken from the soldier, but she clutched it to her chest. No one would take her easily.

Something pushed her left foot.

She turned and cocked the gun as she had been taught by her brother, then almost dropped it at the sight greeting her eyes.

A thin wolf, a mix of gray and brown she'd never seen before, looked back at her, its head turning from side to side like a bird studying something with which it was not familiar. Blood flecked his gray muzzle. Rides a Crow felt power, danger, and awe, but no fear.

The wolf's eyes seemed more alive than those of any animal she'd ever known. It motioned its head to her right, then stared directly at her. When she peered behind her, she saw a thicker patch of bushes where, as the day faded, she would be far less visible than in her current hiding place.

"You want me to go there?" she asked the animal, unsure what manner of spirit being this might be.

The wolf's head nodded; at least she thought it did. She rose.

As she moved, she checked the rifle in her hands. It held no more bullets. She tossed it to the ground. She moved to the denser thicket, but, when she looked back, she saw nothing. Although she wanted to look for the wolf, she waited. The spirits had sent her a sign; she would heed it—for once without argument.

Hours later, freezing and frightened, Rides a Crow came out of hiding, her feet nearly frozen and unresponsive. The darkness was complete. The world smelled of fire. She left the thicket and walked clumsily through snow trampled by hooves.

Dark stains were visible in the white layer where the attack upon her had taken place, but she saw no bodies. She tried to make sense of the pattern of footprints, but there were too many of them.

Slowly and softly, she walked onward. She did not smell tobacco or the foul poison the soldiers drank, but the odor from fires and smoke almost overwhelmed her.

Finally, she reached a place where she could see without being seen. The soldiers had built an enormous fire. Many of them were drunk. She wanted to cry out, to run out, to stop them as they destroyed relics of The People. She saw some soldiers shoot objects—sacred objects—then throw them in a fire. Soldiers gleefully celebrated their victory.

Another fire was being used to cremate all The People's food. The stench of burned meat almost choked her.

The winter home of The People had been captured, and their shelters, their supplies, and everything else they owned! All or almost all of them must have been killed, or the army wouldn't hold this ground. If The People were all dead, she could strike one last blow. She started to advance.

A hand muzzled her mouth as a strong arm gripped her around the middle. She fought back.

"Hush, sister," a voice hissed.

Long Knife, her brother, removed his hand from her mouth.

"No noise," he whispered. "There are sentries."

Taking her hand, he led her on a route through trees and bushes that took them away from the ruined camp.

"Most of The People escaped," he said. "I can take you."

"How did you know to look for me?"

"Our grandfather said you were picking berries by the creek.

I knew you would wait. Now we must go. What is that?" he said, pointing at her footprint.

Rides a Crow had stepped on something that cut her foot, but she'd not felt it bleed. She had no idea where the moccasins she had worn were. A small dark circle now delineated every step she took. She and Long Knife peered back at their trail the moon illuminated in the white snow. Even in the dark, a white man could follow the trail.

"We need a horse," Long Knife said. "They captured most of our herd, but I think I can get one for us. Stay here."

"I can help."

"You can lead them to where we are. Do what you are told sister, for once."

She did. This once. For only a second, he turned to stare at her. The moon shone upon his face. "We shall reach The People, sister. We shall reach them."

Then he was gone, melting into the shadows of the leafless trees and scraggly undergrowth. She could neither see nor hear him, although she heard army patrols. Then she knew she heard a horse! Many horses.

Long Knife galloped hard. A rifle fired far behind him.

When he reached the spot where he had left her, he reached down a hand. "Now, sister, unless you aim to be lazy as usual!"

She did not need a hand to vault to the back of a Cheyenne horse, but he had stolen an army horse with a saddle that would get in the way. She reached up for his arm. His forearm was wet. Sticky. Blood!

"Brother?"

"Quiet, sister!"

He kicked the horse to start it running, then turned it to their right as more rifle shots came from their left.

The horse galloped for a time, then slowly reduced its speed as Rides a Crow hung on. She had ridden rarely and never this fast at night. At first, she felt relief when the horse slowed its dizzying pace. At times it seemed her brother could barely control the animal as it ran. Then she grew alarmed as the animal went slower and slower.

"Brother, we cannot go this slowly. Brother? Did you go to sleep?"

The animal stopped. Rides a Crow took her hands from Long Knife's waist to shake him. He lolled in the saddle. Fear flooded her.

"Brother?"

Shaking and talking were of no use. She touched the hand holding the reins. The stiff fingers possessed no warmth.

In the distance she heard voices. Soldier still pursued them! She struggled to free the reins from Long Knife's hands, but his fingers had frozen, and she could not move them. The voices came closer.

Despite the horse's restive protests, Rides a Crow crawled within the space of Long Knife's arms, keeping his dead hands in hers in order to hold the reins. She gave the animal the mightiest kick she had.

And the living rode with the dead through a night that would not end.

Enraged, Morrison Fairfax pounded the table as he scanned the white expanse of the December landscape. The telegram he held proclaimed a victory, but Fairfax knew that as long as the Cheyenne lived, they would be a thorn in his side.

"Why didn't they kill them all?"

"Relax, Mr. Fairfax," his visitor said. "The Northern Cheyenne are not like Custer, ready to be plucked in an hour of fighting."

"I heard there were hundreds who should have been killed! The Cheyenne will scatter!"

"All the holy relics of the tribe were burned, Mr. Fairfax. That was the real purpose of the attack. I led the soldiers there for that reason. All the things that made them think they were special have been destroyed. What does it matter if they scattered for now? The heart of the tribe was put to the fire. Their spirit protects them no longer. With the allies you are making in the spirit world"—the visitor stifled a sneer at this part—"you will soon be more powerful than they."

"Are you sure their spirit is broken?"

"With their relics destroyed, nothing protects them. Now they can be dealt with like mere men. Surely you know how to kill men? I would like to think that my work is to your satisfaction. Have I not done more in a month than others did in years?"

Fairfax grunted in grim satisfaction. That the visitor had! Fairfax had not thought about destroying the tribe's soul so directly. Yes, this fellow understood how to use power to rid the Plains of the Cheyenne.

"Even those who scatter will not bother you," said the visitor. "They have no food. They have no winter robes. They have no horses or guns to hunt with. They will surrender because they have no choice. It may not be this December day, for they will not have reached the point of starvation yet, but they will surrender soon. When they do, you will have time to rid the Plains of the scourge in any way you choose. A year from now, the Cheyenne will be out of your way completely. And then we can conclude our agreement."

Fairfax knew he had promised the man a large part of his Colorado acreage. He'd also made agreeable noises about much of the land he planned to acquire in Wyoming and Montana. With the Cheyenne out of the way, he could expand as much as he wanted and take the Montana range for horses.

He had not worried much about the size of his promise to his visitor, for it was one he had no intention of keeping. He had, however, become increasingly drawn to the idea he shared with his fellow spirit world dabblers. They believed the lands occupied by the Northern Cheyenne should belong to those who used the spirit world to their advantage and be a place where their activities would not be persecuted by the law. Of course, such an empire of conjurers and the like would elect him to sit at its head!

Rheged smiled and nodded at everything Fairfax said, knowing the bargain they'd made might well have to be enforced in blood. Still, as long as Fairfax was a willing tool, he was a useful one.

"Now," said Rheged, "did I tell you I saved you a sample of a sacred spear for your collection?"

Rides a Crow stirred. A face she did not know looked upon her. Wrapped in a buffalo robe, she was inches from a fire painfully bright against her eyes, yet she trembled from cold.

"Where?"

"I am Horse Dancing," said the man. "I am a friend of The People. You are in the camp of the Lakota, where many of your people came after your winter camp was destroyed. This is Crazy Horse's camp. You have been sleeping here many days since the Time the Living Rode with the Dead, and we feared you would join your brother."

Long Knife. Rides a Crow remembered.

"You showed up at our camp almost stiff like a spear from the cold. You spoke during your fever, but no one understood what you said. Today you are awake again, and I shall bring your grandparents to see you."

"What of Long Knife?"

"He was frozen to the horse, covered with ice. He had been dead many days when you came to us. He is on his journey to the long fork and will have his reward. Do you recall any of this?"

She recalled the night she and her brother escaped. She recalled trying to guide the horse away from the patrols. The day after she'd done so, she'd found herself in a snow-covered world of no tracks and no landmarks. She thought she had guided them toward the north, where the Lakota camp was located, but, in the snowstorm, she had nearly headed south into the thick of the army. After she finally headed north, another storm hit. Plodding through snow on the horse, she'd had a flash of guilt, for her back had been protected from the cold by the body of her brother. All she could remember was cold and her eyes closing as the snow beat down. She did not remember finding the camp.

She returned to the present. Horse Dancing was explaining what little he knew.

"You appeared on the horse with the reins dragging on the ground, as though it had been led. But we saw no footprints, save those of a wolf. You are fortunate, for in this winter little food can be found, and wolves are bold and hungry."

Rides a Crow possessed one memory of a wolf. It made her all but sit upright at the mention. No. The woods were filled with wolves. Then again, she vaguely recalled someone talking to her in words with odd sounds, but all that was part of her fever. She recalled feeling warmth somehow, and doubted she could have used the dead body of her brother for heat on such a long journey. She also remembered a thought she had along the journey that a spirit had come to save her, but the rest was snow, ice, cold, and dark.

"You are alive, Rides a Crow," Horse Dancing said. "The People are now so few, one saved life is cause for great joy. I shall return."

★ ★ ★ ★ ★

Hunting parties that returned, often with little even when they were successful, reported a strange story. The packs of hungry wolves that often stalked The People had all but vanished. There was still not enough game to feed everyone, but hunting no longer meant hunters were the prey.

The People maintained vigilance, since they kept seeing one set of tracks indicating a wolf with one injured leg remained close by. Rides a Crow wanted to tell the leaders and those who divined spirits that the wolf was not a threat, but she stilled her tongue. Unsure exactly what to share, something told her this knowledge should be kept private for now.

Still, The People grew sick and thin. They had lost their relics, their supplies, and their hope. Because soldiers had found them in a strong camp and destroyed it, many argued, the time had come to make peace. The Great Spirit had deserted them and had left The People even before soldiers burned their relics containing sacred objects.

Red Cloud had made peace and lived well. They could do the same.

Rides a Crow sometimes wondered if The People lived because of the food they found or because they refused to die and let others win the argument.

But as winter drew on, they found less and less foodstuffs. It seemed The People would either have to die or surrender. In the month the white men called March, Little Wolf and Morning Star, known better by his Sioux nickname of Dull Knife, rode to Fort Robinson to talk to the white soldier chiefs. They signed a paper that said the Northern Cheyenne could live on the grounds of the fort, as did Red Cloud. If they could not be free to roam the Plains, at least they could feed themselves. They were running out of choices.

Tears and arguments followed, but The People's strength was sapped. They would surrender.

Fairfax rubbed his hands together in all but maniacal glee. Earlier, he had sent letter after letter to President Hayes, who had replaced Grant, demanding the Northern Cheyenne be removed to the reservation packed with their southern relatives and the Arapaho. Just because some soldier made a promise ten years ago, or even this year, that they could live where they always did, that did not mean the government had to keep it. These were Indians the government was dealing with!

Now, his pale and daunting visitor informed him, the government would remove the Cheyenne to the South, to a reservation where disease was winnowing down the numbers of Arapaho and Southern Cheyenne already there. The Northern Cheyenne would march in the brutal heat of summer. More would surely fall on the way!

"You are, let us say, not alone in your concern that these Indians be removed," said Rheged, who asked to be called Mr. Wolf. His dark eyes unsettled Fairfax, who detected a man as ruthless as himself, yet with an even greater strength of spirit and a kind of wild power that made Fairfax uneasy in his presence.

Indeed, calls for the Northern Cheyenne's removal had come from others with whom Fairfax communicated, the visitor said. The spirit world and the world of men had made common cause to defeat the Cheyenne, and they had won!

"In a year, they may be half their number. In another year, a quarter. In ten years, they will be as rare as elephants," his visitor said.

But Fairfax was not a patient man. "Perhaps," he said, "we can speed that process along."

Just because they would all start walking to the Darlington

Agency in Indian Territory did not mean they would all get there, he thought.

CHAPTER FOUR

June 1877, on a forced march along the road to Indian Territory
With dust in her mouth, her nose, and her eyes, Rides a Crow plodded southward under the blazing sun in a place the white people called Kansas. She was not alone.

As far as Rides a Crow could see, lines of her people suffered and struggled to march on a wide dirt road. Soldiers forced them to keep moving, without stopping or caring if they died of thirst.

When they started their trek at Fort Robinson, in the place the whites called Nebraska, families had been grouped together and walked as one. Now they all mixed together and strung along the road for miles.

Her grandparents were at the end of the three-mile-long mass of humanity. It could not be called a line. It was more a halting, stumbling collection of pain moving slowly in dust enveloping them as they headed to the prison the soldiers were taking them to. Rides a Crow, like the other younger Northern Cheyenne captives who moved faster, now walked in front of the marchers, even though their own pace was slower than it had been the first days of the trek. They were tired.

Even their captors were becoming jaded. The insults that had marked the first days of the march had become fewer and farther between. In those days, every insult that could be hurled at The People had been. Unlike those who did not speak English, Rides a Crow knew what the insults meant. All of them.

She wanted to kill every soldier who spoke them.

When one man had likened her wizened grandmother to a cow and chided her for walking so slowly, she had been as angry at her grandfather when he begged the man's forgiveness as she was at the soldier. The warrior-grandfather she had known could have broken the man in half.

Yet she and The People had lost. Bitter to think about, few spoke of it. The Northern Cheyenne had surrendered to the white men. Despite having been told they could stay in their homes in the lands granted to them by the Great Spirit—and had signed a treaty with the white men saying so—they now meekly marched to the distant reservation of the Southern Cheyenne because soldiers were forcing them to.

This world was flat beyond the dust. They'd left their precious mountains and snow-pure waters far behind. Many said the old men who led the tribe south were wrong, that they were heading to a land of poison. Others said there would be peace and looked forward to seeing relatives they had not seen in ten years or more. Some said the great general of the white men had told them they were only going south to see if they liked the place. If they did not like it, said the whites, they could come home.

Rides a Crow harbored doubts. She respected the elders, but either they always misunderstood the whites, or the whites always lied to them. Perhaps both. The army did not guard people the way The People were being guarded if it planned to allow them to return.

A small crooked gulley to her right had caught Rides a Crow's attention several miles ago. It should hold water. Yes! The sun glinted on something. The soldiers often became lazy and drowsy as the late afternoon turned into early evening. The soldier nearest her was barely awake. She waited until he marched past. This was her chance!

Not even as wide as her hand, the tiny trickle was still water.

She put her hands in it and held the liquid to her face. She could taste dust on her lips as she watched the little stream. She scooped her hands to drink.

"Filthy Indian."

The words came from behind her, and a soldier cocked his rifle at her from five feet away.

"I am thirsty," she said.

"Too bad," replied the man. He ordered her to hold her hands out from her sides. "No tricks."

She had her hands cupped in front of her, the precious water a foot from her parched lips. If she asked if she could drink, he would refuse. She raised her hands to her mouth and gulped the water down.

She then coughed and spat out the water as the butt of the rifle came down hard, striking a blow to the center of her back. She fell, dizzy after her head hit the ground hard.

"Mistake, Injun."

"I only wanted water," she said.

"Not getting it," he said, grabbing her arm. "Ought to have just shot all of you. You killed Custer, you and the rest."

Although he was hurting her, she would not let him have the satisfaction of seeing her react. He started to drag her back to the mass of her people. She stumbled over a rock she didn't see and almost fell, nearly dragging the soldier down with her.

He stepped back and aimed the rifle at her stomach.

"I'm gonna tell them you tried to kill me. One fewer of you ain't gonna make no one unhappy. Them men walking the trail said there would be a bounty if we could prove we killed one of you. Maybe I can collect that, little girl. Right pretty hair you have!"

The smell of liquor came to her as he spoke. Many of the soldiers drank as they marched The People to their prison.

For a single blink of time, she saw her life ending there, far from home, far from everyone. Then she reached into who she was as the daughter of a warrior and launched herself at the soldier.

The gun fired. Her head filled with raw pain. Then there was nothing but darkness.

As she opened her eyes, the first streaks of a sunset greeted her. She tried to move fast. The soldier! Her head swam.

"Shhh." The voice was strange, but it sounded kind. "You have a bad wound on your head. Easy and slow."

It was a white man speaking. She could tell that much. Not a soldier, which frightened her even more. The cowboys and ranchers who hated Indians scared her more than the soldiers, whose hatred was usually kept in check by their officers. Her eyes darted. She searched for a place to run.

"Hold up a finger if you understand me," he said with a disarming smile she did not usually see whites use with Indians. She held up a finger.

"Good! I know about six words of Cheyenne that don't involve hunting buffalo, and most of those are hardly polite for a young lady of uncertain acquaintance," he said. "In case you are wondering where you are, we are about a half a mile from where you were found. There are people who will be trying to find your family, but it would help if they knew your name."

She was afraid again. Names were private. When whites knew them, they could come for you.

"I suppose I can ask if there's a family that claims a girl named Iron Skull, but there might be more than one. I'm betting they know you by another name."

She wanted to say this was not a time for jokes, but her heard hurt, too. "Rides a Crow."

"Good! With whom do you live?"

She told him.

He went away. She could hear him telling someone to ask for her family. He sounded like a man giving orders, but he did not smell of liquor and tobacco the way most soldiers did. He did not wear a uniform.

When he returned, he handed her a canteen full of cold water. She reflexively grabbed it tighter when he pulled it from her mouth.

"Not too much. You can drink it all, but slowly."

Of course. She knew that. Shame to her that a white man should remind her!

The water helped her wake up. She saw a mass of The People about a good arrow's shot away.

There were no soldiers near them. This man must be one of them or with them somehow. She did not recognize the land. It was similar to the spot where she'd sought water. All of this land was flat. It was ugly because it was not home.

"If you are looking for the late and, I am certain, unlamented Private James Mulroney, he is no longer with us," the white man said. She did not understand. Evidently her confusion showed. "By that, child, I mean he is dead."

Alarm coursed through her. Indians who killed white soldiers were hanged.

"Easy, Rides a Crow. Easy. There was a terrible accident. It seems the private discharged his gun accidentally. In doing so, he disturbed a wild animal that, sadly, killed him. He is dead as the proverbial doornail, child, which means any nasty stories and nasty things he might say died with him. Do you understand? There is nothing he can say about why you left the group."

Dead? The man was dead! The Great Spirit that protected The People did not always sleep, as the old ones often said.

"It shall be counted as miraculous that whatever could overpower and kill an armed man did not kill you. I expect someone will come to you, one of the uniforms, and ask you questions. You will need to admit you left the group, but that you did so from dizziness. Or perhaps you saw a healing plant your grandparents needed. Or you got lost, or something. I am sure you can be creative with the truth when you need to be. If you want to tell them the soldier went with you because he was not as miserable a human being as we both know he was, that is fine. If not, that is also fine. When a soldier dies, white people have to write a letter to explain the death. Paper. Paper. Paper. All they want is something they can write on paper to answer questions so that no one looks further into the matter. If you answer them, they will go away. Do you understand, Rides a Crow?"

She did. Through some stroke of luck, some animal she did not know existed had killed the man who had wanted to kill her.

She would not die. She would live. And for the first time since they had left the fort, she felt a vague glimmer that not only might she live, but that The People would live—that there was something beyond their misery awaiting them. Yet this thought was hazy, and it vanished with the next pounding ache in her head.

"They will come very soon. I know your head hurts. Speak softly, not as a crow calls, and let them think you are very upset by all of this. It is good when they think this way, for it makes them easier to fool. I must go, for it is not good if they find me."

Voices grew closer.

"Keep the canteen. And when there is trouble, recall the Day Evil Was Punished, and you shall not be alone. You shall never be alone. Recall this: It is a good day to live."

The man vanished.

A clean-shaven man in a blue uniform with the gold marks on his shoulders signifying others would listen to what he said came next. He did not look unkind, but she knew white soldiers could be kind one minute and kill Indians the next.

"I am Lieutenant Caruthers," he said. He then asked her what had happened.

She talked of seeing a rare healing plant she had seen but once before, and that, although she knew the soldiers wanted The People to stay together, she wanted to get the plant because it might help her grandmother's stomach. She said the soldier had followed her, his gun went off, and something hit her while he aimed at whatever attacked them.

"Might be the first decent thing Mulroney ever did," the man said. "How big was he?"

She started to describe the man who'd rescued her.

The lieutenant grew impatient.

"No, not him! All of you people are so simple! The wolf!"

Wolf. Now she had a flash. Something the color of some of the white man's metal when it was old and left to sit idle. Rust, they called it. And gray. No. White-faced. Thin, scraggly.

Familiar! This was knowledge to keep.

"It was fast. It leaped, and I do not recall anything else."

"It wasn't an animal of your tribe, was it? Did you do a spirit dance and summon it?"

The idea was absurd. She almost told him so, then remembered her rescuer's words.

"We have many spirits, but I do not recall this one," she said.

The answer did not seem to please the soldier. He knew, as did all army soldiers on the Plains, that Indians and animals were aligned against civilization in ways whites often failed to understand. However, Mulroney was hardly a loss. He doubted anyone would care about his death, for the man never received letters.

"Very good, then. You wait here until your family arrives, and then you must stay together with the group. You must not go off by yourself again. Do you understand?" He said the last part loudly and slowly, as though she were not very smart. The first man's words came back to her about how to appease the soldiers—for now.

She said she understood. He left her alone, but not for long.

She sensed the friendly white man's approach before he stood beside her.

"You will have to do what he said," her rescuer said.

"Who are you?" she said. "You are not a soldier or one of them."

"I am not."

"What am I to call you?"

"They call me Hunter. Your grandparents will be here soon. I shall see you again."

And he was gone.

The soldiers said there were only about two more weeks before their journey ended. She was sure they'd been saying the same thing for more than a week.

Rides a Crow was tired, as were they all, but she was among the strong ones. She had stayed with her grandparents since her incident with the soldier. On the first morning afterward, she awoke to find the canteen the man had given her filled with water. There were pieces of bread and some meat. None of them had been given meat before. On the first day, she ate it all. After that, she shared the meat with her grandparents. This became a pattern. Every night something would be left for them. Never a lot, but enough.

One night she vowed to catch the unseen benefactor and was awake until almost dawn. But in the few moments she slept, he had arrived.

Puzzled about the gifts, she scrutinized the faces of the whites traveling with the column. There was little to see except men doing a duty. As the march continued, cracks began to show in the walls of hatred the soldiers showed The People. Still, many of them looked upon the Northern Cheyenne as less than human, as though they had to guard them to ensure that the Plains that were once home to the Northern Cheyenne would not be ravaged by the old and infirm if they were to be set free upon the hunting grounds of their ancestors.

A few whites who were not soldiers traveled with the column. Many of these were missionaries, some of whom said their religion meant God loved everyone. Others said the Cheyenne were evil. The first helped the old when they were sick and tired; the second helped no one.

Men they called cowboys, who appeared toughened by war to hardness and killing, rode among the group. Even when soldiers offered kind words, these did not. They had baleful glances and called Indians names. Rides a Crow watched those especially closely.

Of all of them, soldiers and hangers-on, none seemed the least concerned about her or her grandparents. It was as though a spirit had singled them out, although she didn't know why. As long as they were captive, she feared any good intention masked a trick, because she had come to think the world was steeped in evil, and The People were so very vulnerable as they plodded toward a foreign land that was destined to be the prison of their hopes and bones.

The soldiers became increasingly angry with Flies the Hawk and Sun Raven, her grandfather and grandmother. They were very old. Rides a Crow felt guilty, because she knew the reason they went with Dull Knife and Little Wolf to surrender was fear that, without them, Rides a Crow would be hurt. They had planned to stay in the mountains and let death take its course. They had lost all of their children and other grandchildren to the soldiers. Only Rides a Crow remained to them.

She now walked with them every day. They were growing weaker. Both had been born near the time the first white men were seen in the Cheyenne lands, when no one knew what would befall The People.

She and her grandparents were not unique. There were other elders who should have been allowed to live whatever time they had left in the lands they had known from their long-distant childhoods. Once she heard soldiers and one of the missionaries arguing. The soldiers had begun making the older Indians start walking earlier and walk later than the rest, because they could not keep pace with the others.

"You will walk them to their deaths!" the missionary had exclaimed.

The soldier had shrugged aside the missionary's argument. If they died walking, it was no concern of his. Therefore, torment of the old ones continued.

Rides a Crow saw some of the soldiers talking with the tough cowboys who had come into the column. These men, she knew, were evil and wanted trouble. She did not know what they said, but she saw the way the soldiers measured the old ones after they talked. It was evil.

On the evening of a day without rain, when without the canteen that appeared full again that morning they would have had nothing to drink, a group of these men came among the oldest stragglers. The soldiers grabbed Rides a Crow and dragged her and other children who had stayed with elders apart from their aged relatives.

She fought them.

"Child." Sun Raven stepped forward with so much dignity, the men did not put their hands upon her. Rides a Crow stopped struggling. "I am bound for Seana."

Rides a Crow shivered at his mention of the place of the dead.

"They are impatient to send me, child. But the spirit is leaving me. It tells me in the morning that my time will be coming soon, and that is as it should be if the days of The People are ending. It is not the old for whom you should mourn, but those who face the evil of the day to come."

Flies a Hawk, whom Rides a Crow knew had been in the vast assemblage that fool Custer had sought to destroy, thereby bringing destruction upon himself, looked on with snapping, proud eyes. He had seen his son die and would never surrender.

She thought he, who had tried to appease the whites when the march began only to revert to his true self as the days wore on, stood straighter than his back would bear.

"If The People become only you," he said to her, "do not fear. Do not despair. Fight back, so that one day the Northern Cheyenne who will live in the generation when these soldiers are dust will know a mighty nation was torn apart by the evil visited upon it. The Custer men begged. I will not."

Fifteen others were soon grouped together. Rides a Crow and several other girls and boys were restrained by a line of armed soldiers. They saw their ancestors shoved and pushed away from the larger mass of Northern Cheyenne. She gasped as she saw a sign. The old and the men behind them were walking into a sunset that looked like the arms of a giant bird spreading yellow- and orange-colored wings to welcome them.

A small grove of trees hid what was going to happen. She heard the singing, as those stumbling with rifles at their backs sang the song that would send their spirits home. The song grew fainter as they walked. It faded as the old ones finally vanished from the children's sight.

She assumed the men, although they were not soldiers, would kill the elders the way the soldiers did. White men stood in a line and fired at people they wanted to kill until they were all dead. She had seen it happen at the fort. If they were so cruel to each other, she knew they would be equally cruel to The People. She waited to her the volley of shots that would mean her grandparents were on their spirit journey.

One gun fired. She had learned the difference between pistols and rifles. This was a pistol. Other gunshots followed, but not in the precise order of the way killings were conducted by the soldiers. These shots were random. She heard screaming, which could not come from The People. All knew, as they walked to their deaths, there could be no mercy from those filled with evil and hate. She heard more shouting and a few more shots.

Then quiet reigned. The soldiers restraining her and the other children were uneasy. Then she heard a sound she knew she would carry with her until she walked the long fork to the land of the spirits.

The People sang. The aged voices were quavering and thin, but the song of praise to the spirits for all that is good was clear to her ears.

She did not know if the soldiers or the children broke first, but soon a mix of both were running across the open space to the trees as the deep red of the sunset colored the world with blood.

All of the men who had formed the firing squad lay strewn on the ground, dead. Two of The People also lay flat, unmoving.

Flies a Hawk wore the satisfied look on his face that made him look like the grandfather she'd known as a tiny girl, when he faced down a dozen Crow warriors who had come to raid a small camp of The People.

"The spirits have spoken," he said. He touched Sun Raven on the arm. "Woman, we must go now. We shall journey together along the long fork to the Milky Way another day."

With heads high, they walked, leaning slightly into each other for support, as the rest of the elders, surrounded by incredulous and joyful children and mystified soldiers, followed. They walked slowly, but with dignity, back to the mass of The People.

Rides a Crow had to know more. She looked at the dead. Fear was writ large across the faces of the dead white men. Huge wounds had been gouged into their necks and faces. More wolves! Others had been shot. Nothing made sense. An animal that could fire a gun?

The two dead of The People had been shot. Two women; well apart.

Rides a Crow ran back to the group. Flies a Hawk explained that when they reached the trees, the soldiers had them stand facing the sunset, away from the men, who had been talking about how much money a certain man would pay for this day's work. The elders were all singing their final songs, said Flies a Hawk, as the men prepared to shoot them down. Then they heard the sounds of an animal attacking the soldiers. Shots went off from the rifles of the men, and two of the elders who had been slower than the rest to fall to the earth for safety were hit. These called out their death songs as they fell.

The men who had planned to execute them screamed and shot at something. A gun then fired from the far end of the woods. At first the elders did not realize it was firing at the soldiers.

Only when the elders rose from the ground and saw what had been done did they know all the white men were dead. As they stood, some said they saw a figure moving between them and the sunset, as though it had walked out of the sun to save them. Some said it was a man; others that it walked on four legs.

As night fell on the Day the Sun Warrior Saved the Elders, soldiers searched for traces of either an animal or a Cheyenne and found neither. As The People slept on the hard ground, soldiers came and went through their camps but still found nothing. Word of what had taken place traveled up and down the Cheyenne families, until in the morning everyone knew spirits had come to save The People from evil men.

One of the kind missionaries walked past Rides a Crow the next morning as they were preparing for the day's march.

"You can tell your grandparents they will be safe," he said. "The colonel might be superstitious, but he believes that whatever happened last night—which I think happened without his orders, because he was very angry when he found out—was a lesson for no one to leave the pack again."

He paused and looked around.

"Be careful of the men traveling with you who wear guns and are not soldiers. I was in the war, and I know when there are men who are up to something evil. Do not go with them anywhere!"

Rides a Crow took small comfort from the words. Believing in white promises was like expecting to walk on a bridge made of sparrow feathers. But that day, the pace was slower and the soldiers did not threaten the old people with bayonets.

For their part, the elderly seemed less frail, and, with renewed spirit, the column of The People moved southward to meet their Southern Cheyenne relatives in a place Rides a Crow shuddered to think would be their new prison. Yet if The People were to be prisoners, at least they would be alive.

Perhaps the Great Spirit was testing them. Perhaps there was hope at the end of the journey. For this day, the hope was enough to feed her soul. She marched.

The journey they said would soon end dragged on. Walk. Rest. Eat and drink. Walk. Sleep. Then came gunfire. A few shots. A volley!

Rides a Crow saw warriors moving to the outside of the

column of walkers, to offer some protection from whatever might be coming at them. She still walked with her grand-parents, and there were no warriors with them. She moved to the outside, vigilantly looking up and down the column to see what was going on.

It was not long before she knew.

A man she had seen but once, when they left Fort Robinson, was talking with a number of others, clearly giving them orders. When he was through, his eyes shifted to hers. She felt hate in his gaze.

The missionary who was the friendliest of the ones with them rode past. She called to him.

He told her one warrior had smuggled a rifle with him and shot a soldier before other soldiers, then shot the warrior. The column would now be searched for weapons, he said.

The soldiers were brutally methodical. They tore into the small bundles of clothes the Cheyenne people carried on bent shoulders, ripping cloth and throwing items to the ground as they searched. If they found anything that could be called a weapon, it was confiscated.

"We need our knives for meat," said one warrior, who refused to take his hand off the ornate leather sheath in which he kept his knife.

The soldier demanding the weapon cocked his rifle.

"Hand it over, or you won't ever need anything on this earth again, Custer-killer."

"Problem, soldier?"

Rides a Crow knew that voice. It had been many days, but she would know that voice if she never heard it again for a hundred winters.

The man who spoke was dressed like the scouts who rode at the edges of the column to watch for danger or prevent anyone from escaping, as well as to keep the column on the correct route to the reservation of the Southern Cheyenne. He had gray in his beard, light-brown hair, and was among the more unkempt of the marchers. However, he spoke with a voice flowing with authority.

"Who are you?"

"Indian Agent Hunter," the man replied with a touch of arrogance and an accent that was different from the rest. It made him sound superior. "Trying to get you soldiers not to kill all of my Indians before I take control."

" 'Your' Indians?"

"I am responsible. I am paid per Indian. And if you kill them, there goes my job," he said dismissively as though talking to someone who understood very little. "Is there a requirement in the army to understand nothing at all? It certainly seems so! Now, what is the matter here?"

The soldier said they were searching for weapons.

"Is the man's knife sharp or as dull as your wit, private?" Hunter asked.

"I do not know, but he should not have it. Prisoners should not have weapons."

Hunter turned to the warrior.

"May I see the knife? I shall hand it back to you when I am finished looking."

The warrior looked at Hunter, weighed him, and handed over his knife, handle first. Hunter took it from the sheath, examined it, and put it back in the cracked leather.

"That knife is Spanish-made and has probably been with him and his family a generation or more," he said condescendingly, tossing the knife back to Stone Leg.

"If you wish to take every dull, old knife from every Indian, private, you will be here all day. A child's teeth are as dangerous as that man's knife, and I don't believe you will be confiscating those either. Your orders were to search for guns. Please do that, and quickly, so we may continue to make up for lost time."

The soldier seemed uncertain.

"Do it now!" Hunter ordered. "Or do you want to walk at the back of the column until we reach the Darlington Agency and breathe everyone's dust?"

The private grudgingly gave way, but he glared with malice at Hunter as he went on to harangue his next victim.

Hunter smiled at Rides a Crow. "Ahh! A perfect assistant." He beckoned her. "Come here."

She did as Hunter asked. The man sought to determine whether the warrior, Stone Leg, could speak English well.

"He understands more than he speaks," she said. "We all do."

Stone Leg's eyes flashed at her a moment, as though accusing her of being kind to the enemy.

"Good to know. Please forgive the upcoming intrusion into your privacy, miss," he told her. "Now, if you insist on carrying weapons, a loop of rawhide is all you need. Tie it here." He held Rides a Crow by the left hip and tapped her on her inner right thigh. "They will not look under skirts. Lakota women hide parts for guns this way, as well as knives. It is the way of those who know the time is not today, but that it will come when it does."

Hunter looked at Stone Leg. "You might want to tell some of the others."

The warrior drifted into the mass of stopped Cheyenne.

"Why are you doing this?" Rides a Crow asked Hunter as he started to go. "I have seen the Indian agents. They do not look like you or act like you. You lied to me when you said you were one."

"That is unfair," he replied. "I did not lie to you. I lied to the soldier. If I was a Cheyenne, you would praise me for telling the soldier a lie he believed."

"Why did you lie to him? And why do you try to help us when white men hate us and try to kill us?"

Rides a Crow had a feeling she was being examined by the most piercing set of eyes she had ever encountered, as though everything she had ever said and done, and everything she was as a person, was being analyzed and considered.

"I cannot put it in words that flow easily, Rides a Crow," Hunter said at last. "I see you are a Spirit Walker, but you are still very young. There is good and there is evil. There is right and wrong. I cannot stop the great wrong being done by men who bring evil, see evil, and hate your people. I came to this place to be alone, for in the world of those who now come for your lands, I was one who was evil and wrong. In this place, I could be what God made me and live as that and nothing more. The People were always kind. It is a debt I will repay. And, child, it is the will of the spirits."

He tipped his hat as white men did to white women and moved off into the crowd. In a moment, he was lost to view.

In the days to come, she asked about a man named Hunter who was supposedly some kind of Indian agent, but no one knew who she was talking about.

CHAPTER FIVE

Southern Kansas, August 1877

Carter Handley was waiting. The Cheyenne exile was hardly a secret. A few hundred Indians and an armed guard of soldiers made for a hard secret to keep.

Since the Washita in '67, when the prize scalp he had coveted had been claimed by someone less drunk than he, he had been waiting for an opportunity. This was the best chance he would ever have. That man the other day had found him and told him. A reward, no less. The soldiers were thickest at the front of the herd of Indians. He could see the chiefs riding, as though they were better than the common thieves he knew the Cheyenne and every other tribe were.

At the rate they were going, he would have time. He was willing to bet that, after a day of walking, they would not offer much resistance. The old blue jacket he had worn before the army tossed him out for being drunk on duty was too small, but none of those savages would understand enough to know the difference. He had his gun and his knife. He would be ready.

Rides a Crow was very wary. A young soldier she did not know had taken a piece of a tree whose branches were scattered by lightning and carved it into a stick. He had given it to Sun Raven as a walking stick. The young man did not appear to be evil, but he was a soldier. She had met young whites in the time before the Custer battle made them all crazy, and she understood some remained good amid the many bad ones, but now there were few whites anywhere who would do anything good for a Cheyenne.

The soldier, who really seemed to be little more than a boy even though he was a few years older than she was, had tried to talk in crude sign language and then very bad English. He had blushed and stammered when Rides a Crow spoke back to him, using his language as though he were not speaking to a simple child. He looked quite young then, like a big gangling boy with a round face and blond hair, not like a man in an army that hated her people.

Her mother had insisted she learn the white language from her Lakota sister-in-law, and then later others. That way, she could tell her family what the whites said.

She wondered where her relatives were. After the Greasy Grass fight, she knew Sitting Bull kept his warriors separate from The People in an attempt to avoid bringing soldiers upon them. Still, she envied those whose families were whole. She knew that, even when the journey was over, the days of her grandparents would be few, and she would be alone after they passed.

"I speak your language very well and understand all you say," she said after deciding anyone who blushed so like a girl could not be all evil. "My grandmother accepts your gift and thanks you for it."

"I hope they like their new home," the young soldier said. "They say it is nice down there."

She wanted to tell him that the home from which the army ordered them had been perfect, but this enforced trek was not the boy's fault. He only repeated what someone else had told him.

"Do you have family there?"

She knew her grandparents had relatives in the new place,

people they had not seen in many years. They would be strangers to Rides a Crow.

"I think so," she said. She wanted to rage at him. He was her jailer, her keeper, and she was his prisoner. They were not meeting at one of the trading posts set up by the whites, where both peoples tried to be friendly. She was being taken from everything. Yet Hunter had cautioned her against attacking them.

"I'm sorry," he said, as though he understood some of what she did not say. "This must be very hard for you."

He then touched his hat and moved back into the mix of wagons and blue uniforms following The People.

Evening brought a halt to the march. As the light of day faded, Carter Handley knew his time was close. He had been stalking the column all day. His best chance would be at the rear, where a gap had opened between the old people and the rest of the Cheyenne.

He surveyed the easy pickings. In disgust, he spat a stream of tobacco juice. He didn't want some old gray head of Cheyenne hair! Then he saw the younger ones who had accompanied the elders. A couple of boys whose long, glossy hair he was determined to hang on his wall. No! Even better, he saw a girl whose hair spilled much of the way down her back.

He had watched and waited. Now was the time to strike.

The young soldier came back to Rides a Crow's family as the day's march was ending.

"Tom Ridgway," he said. "I guess I didn't . . . um . . . introduce myself."

She responded by telling him the names of her grandparents. She wondered why he had come.

"I am Rides a Crow," she said. "Sun Raven walked easier for your gift today."

Later, after he had given his gift, she realized that for a white soldier to show kindness with others watching was brave in its own way, and she should have understood.

"You may share our food."

She and her grandparents had little, but giving hospitality would even the relationship between them. If they shared their food, they would not be so in his debt for the gift.

The young man looked from side to side, as though worried someone watched them.

"That's what I came for. Here," he said, shoving something warm and damp to the touch at her.

Opening the cloth, she found some kind of cooked meat. Her finger touched it. She licked the juice as her stomach protested against not getting more than a taste.

"Let us sit to share," she said, speaking swiftly to her grandparents, who sought to maintain their impassive façade but could not help but stare at the bundle she held.

"I . . . I don't think I'm allowed to share, but . . . I thought it might . . . you know, there's not a lot but . . ."

"We thank you, Blue Eyes," Flies a Hawk spoke. "You are a brave man and a good man."

Her grandfather spoke English rarely.

"I need to go," Ridgway said. "I will bring more when I can."

"Thank you," Rides a Crow said, smiling as she walked with the man in the space between The People and the soldiers. "You are kind and brave to give to your enemies."

The young man frowned. "You aren't my enemies," he stammered. "It's just . . . well, it's just the way it is." He turned away as if embarrassed and moved quickly to the soldiers who would stand sentry for the night, who were building their fires.

She would never know what he meant.

Out of the darkness beyond, a man in a blue coat buttoned differently from the rest came up to them; a man who was older and grizzled and smelled like those who drank the poison that makes whites crazy. He pushed past Rides a Crow and knocked her sideways. She stumbled and fell with an exclamation.

"Hey, come here, Injun!" he called to Stands the Water, a girl slightly older than Rides a Crow who walked with her grandmother. The rest of her family was either dead or scattered. Unlike Rides a Crow, who chopped her hair with a knife when it grew to an annoying length, Stands the Water had let her hair grow long, presumably to attract a young man at a time when warriors were scarce.

The man pulled the girl's arm and jerked her to him. She cried out in pain. He began yanking her down a slight embankment at the edge of the trail.

Rides a Crow did not catch his next words, but the cruelty in the man's tone was unmistakable. This was no soldier!

From the ground, Rides a Crow launched herself at him. Behind her, she heard a voice call out, "Stop! Now!"

Her hands reached the man's legs, and she tried to claw at the material of his trousers. He kicked at her to shake her off, knocking her right hand loose. She tried to reach around both his legs, but she began losing any grip she had.

The voice behind her called something. Stands the Water tried to break free.

A gun fired. The man recoiled as something hit him. As he turned, Rides a Crow's world became a silent, floating place after a flash that blinded her as the gun in the man's hand exploded twice. She dropped to the ground, dizzy and disoriented as she tried to pursue him. She pushed herself up on an elbow and tried to crawl. With one knee on the ground, she attempted to bring her arms and legs together to stand.

The boom of another gun sounded like an explosion of thunder. A buffalo gun! The man in blue and Stands the Water appeared to fly as the foul man was lifted off the ground with his grip still tight around her. The two of them soon crashed down to lie in the dirt. The dazed Cheyenne girl found the grip of her captor had loosened. Stands the Water pulled herself free and sat on the ground, dazed as armed blue soldiers pointed their guns at everyone.

Rides a Crow had finally struggled to an upright position. Swaying, she staggered to the man who still lay on the ground, where part of him would rest forever, face up where he had fallen.

She saw the bloody, jagged holes made by the bullets that killed him. Sightless eyes stared up. She had seen death before. Recalling the other girl's scream after the gunfire, she turned to see if Stands the Water was hurt. Her hands clutching her chest, both knees by the unmoving body of a soldier, Stands the Water had an uncomprehending expression on her face.

Screaming soldiers demanded both girls stay still. Rides a Crow felt the sinking feeling of loss as the body was rolled over, and she looked upon the limp, lifeless face of Tom Ridgway, the young soldier whose food she had just eaten.

She started to move to him, but a soldier barred her way, threatening her with a rifle butt.

"Make way, all of you!" called a voice that demanded—and received—obedience.

Hunter.

"Are you hurt?" he asked Rides a Crow. She shook her head, not trusting her voice to betray emotion in the presence of the soldiers. Stands the Water did not answer.

"Take them back to the rest," Hunter told the soldiers. To Rides a Crow, he added, "Stay with your grandparents so I know where to find you."

Horses approached bearing officers. It was almost too dark to see. Hunter turned to deal with the officers. He knew that, in the dark, all he needed to command was a voice of authority. A lot of talk ensued, with hot and bad words volleyed back and forth. In time, with some help from the soldiers and the Cheyenne, the incident was pieced together.

"You are not hurt?" Hunter said to Rides a Crow when he found her later with her grandparents.

"No. The soldier who was killed had been kind."

Hunter thought a moment. "He was very young."

"He brought us meat."

"No one knows the man who took Stands the Water. He probably lives somewhere near and was too filled with hate to know what he was doing." Hunter sighed deeply. "Hate twists men, child. Evil touches weak souls that cannot resist, fills them with hate, and then destroys them, whether they live or die. Hate will not hold you in its jaws, child. As long as I walk. As long as I breathe."

Rides a Crow didn't understand his meaning. Her head still echoed from the gunshot near her ear. More soldiers were coming. Hunter moved away, as though seeking to avoid them. As he left, she thought the light of a fire glinted off of the barrel of a buffalo gun he carried. Then he was gone.

As Rides a Crow and her family prepared for another day of walking, she looked up to see those around her moving aside to make a path for Little Wolf, one of the leaders of The People.

Although the army had not given any of the Northern Cheyenne decent horses, Little Wolf looked every inch a leader atop the poor nag he had been given. Rides a Crow was in awe of his dignity.

"I am told there was bravery in fighting off a man who came to prey on our people," he said. "Rides a Crow, Stands the Water, step forward."

The two girls did as instructed.

"From this day, you and your grandparents will be under my

protection and travel with me."

Rides a Crow felt her grandparents' shock. Little Wolf was giving them a great honor, even if they were marching to a glorified prison.

"The food will be better, at least," muttered Flies the Eagle.

Sun Raven elbowed him.

"You will join me as a sign to our people that, even if we must bend with the wind that blows the grass, we remain The People," Little Wolf proclaimed.

Rides a Crow beheld one of the leaders of her people, a man honored for courage and wisdom. She thought he was handsome in his bearing, even as a prisoner. She wished she had the nerve to speak to him.

It took time, but eventually horses were found for the elders. Stands the Water rode with her grandmother. Rides a Crow's grandparents shared a horse. She rode with Little Wolf. She was glad. She had much to ask about their new home; and questions also about this agent, Hunter, who appeared from nowhere and whom no one seemed to know.

As they rode around the Northern Cheyenne men, women, and children being marched to the south, Rides a Crow looked out at the landscape to the west. A wolf, rusted-gray-brown with white on its muzzle, gazed back. At first, she thought she was seeing the talisman of the leader. Then she realized the wolf had focused on her.

A wolf. She recalled what had taken place at the camp near the Rosebud and what they had told her at Crazy Horse's winter camp. A wolf.

Colonel Jameson Winters hated his assignment. He would fight the Cheyenne to the death. He was a soldier, and fighting was his reason for living.

Taking them to their death in some squalid land was not to

his liking. He was under no illusions, however. Before leaving, a pale-skinned man he was told represented the president had taken him aside.

"You will escort these Indians to their new reservation, but if you must demonstrate to them that you are in charge by executing them, you are authorized to do so, no matter how many you might need to kill. The only concern regarding the number of Cheyenne who reach their new reservation is that none of them escape to fight again."

Only the connection between the man and the president prevented Winters from shooting the vile man then and there. That, and the fact that the man's very presence engendered a sick fear in Winters—a fear he could not place.

On the first day, Winters had tried to oust some men intent on whipping up hatred among the soldiers, even after he had ordered his men that their mission was to protect the Cheyenne, whether they liked it or not. That same visitor had then found him and delivered an ultimatum: keep the march going, and don't look too closely at what goes on behind him.

Winters had tried to obey and, with the march nearing its end, had managed to lose very few of his prisoners. However, he knew he was losing control of his men day by day. There had been more incidents this past day. The Cheyenne were hungry and, when not exhausted from marching, were clearly starting to mull over the idea of dying in a fight rather than dying inch by inch. He knew rumor mongers riding among the troops told tired soldiers that the Cheyenne should be shot or starved to ensure control—the very things that would prompt a violent confrontation.

Only a few more days, he told himself as he finished his prayer and was standing in his tent.

"Hello, Colonel." The tent flap opened. The click of a gun being cocked was clear.

"What do you want?"

"What you want," said the man. "You have been ordered to bring the Cheyenne to the southern reservation, and you have been told that if they die on the way, it is not your business, and that disturbs you."

"How do you know that?"

"Because I know. I also know there are men trying to stir up a fight on this march. They have become a threat and will be leaving the march. They may leave it alive and willingly or otherwise. I am certain your orders do not cover these men."

"I . . ."

"Your hands are tied, Colonel. Mine, however, are not. I shall make it clear the Cheyenne were not to blame for any losses or deaths, lest your real superiors and those who seek to use you as a cat's paw for their evil learn the truth." There was a pause. "If the Northern Cheyenne die on this march, Colonel, you will be reviled forever. You will lose not your career, but your soul. Choose carefully. Interfere with me at your peril."

"You are not Cheyenne."

"No, Colonel, but I am one of God's creatures, and those God has made and life had laid low, man shall not destroy."

"I have men who knew troopers who rode with Custer. Men will be men, whoever you are."

His visitor spoke softly. " 'Vengeance will be mine, sayeth the Lord.' "

Winters waited for more. He did not hear his visitor leave.

Hunter startled the knot of men when he approached them. Three civilians tried to slip away as he dismounted, but Hunter called to them.

"You will leave the column today," Hunter said. "You will stop telling the men to harm the Cheyenne. Before you go, you will tell me how many others like you there are, so they can follow you back to whatever sewer you emerged from."

"Someone told me you are some kind of Indian agent, but you don't look like no agent to me," said one of the men. "We were hired to do work. Gonna do it. Should be leaving their bones on this trail, 'stead of pampering them. Old Fairfax got it right, he does."

His colleagues made noises of assent.

"You will leave, or you will die," Hunter said. "If you come back, you will die. You can tell me who paid for your services, because you are not smart enough to do it on your own. Is your purchaser this Fairfax man you mention, whoever he is?"

One of the men reached out to shove Hunter to the ground as a second grabbed for his arms.

Pulling out the knife in a sheath at his waist, Hunter used it to slash the cheek of the one grabbing his arm. On the knife's return path, it sliced the left forearm of the one who shoved him. The third man thought about the gun he wore.

"Can you draw a gun faster than I can throw a knife, friend?" Hunter said.

The man lifted his hand away from the gun, making his intention clear.

"I will not warn you again. If you are with this column at the end of the day, you will be dead," Hunter said. "For I prefer to hunt in the dark."

By the end of the day, seventeen men had received warnings. None of them had been willing to tell Hunter who hired them, but one of the last men he spoke to had looked uncomfortable. In the glowering darkness, as the man had packed his possessions, Hunter sought him out.

"Describe the man. I want his name," Hunter demanded.

A portrait emerged of a man who was tall and powerfully built, with a face that looked as though it could stand up to any wind and piercing black eyes. His hair was black, and his skin white and soft, deceptive in a country where soft, white skin meant gullible Easterners. He spoke with a low voice in a different accent from those used by most men. The man who hired them had threatened some and cajoled others, the fearful hireling told Hunter, but had never given a name.

"One man told him off, and this fella, he just picked him up by the neck and threw him against a post. Broke his neck dead," the man said. "Man like that knows my name, I'm not going to go against him."

"He knew your names? Had you met?"

"Never, mister. Never. He made me shudder, like he could see all the way inside of me, as though he was not quite normal."

Hunter snorted. No, he was not. He sent the man upon his way.

In the morning, soldiers told the colonel that wolf attacks around the column had again increased. Three men were dead—all men who had joined the column after it left the fort, supposedly with the approval of someone at the Indian agency. Several other men were gone—among them all who had often walked among the soldiers urging them to mistreat the captives.

Winters kept the men moving, warning them that whatever they felt about Custer, their mission was to deliver the Cheyenne to the reservation alive, not dead. He put out word that anyone seeing the so-called Indian agent Hunter should send the man to him.

As the day ended, many reported having seen him the day before, but no one saw him that day.

Rides a Crow gazed back at the long column following the path through grasslands and rocky places as another day of travel was about to begin. She and her grandparents ate every day now, yet she wondered about those who were far at the end of the column.

"They will live," came the voice of Hunter, appearing silently beside her along with the dawn.

"Who are you?" she asked. "You are not an agent."

Hunter did not answer but talked about the Sand Hills.

"I know the place," she said. "The People go there often to hunt, and some go to hide."

"It is a place for hiding," he said. "I hid there. Now it is time for me to stop hiding. And so I am with you."

"Why?"

"I do not know, Rides a Crow. Since you are the Spirit Walker and the wise one, perhaps you should tell me."

"I have sixteen winters; I am hardly wise. I am not a Spirit Walker. Spirit Walkers are legends of The People."

"Yet you know much, have lived much, and understand much," Hunter said. "In the days ahead, the weary journey may seem like dancing, and the half-empty hole in your belly may seem like a time of plenty. The journey is not yet over, Rides a Crow. I am unsure where it leads, but, when it resumes, I will find you."

"Who are you?" she asked. "Are you a spirit?"

He looked very sad.

"I am that which I am," he replied, unwilling to use the hated word the world applied to his kind. "And you, Rides a Crow, are The People."

Three days later, as the column neared the southern reservation and increased rations had restored the strength of some, a wave of fear rose among The People. A spirit had come among them, some said, trying to kill them. It failed because the malevolent spirit was pursued by another spirit. Rides a Crow heard the talk, looked out over the plains of what they called Indian territory, and wondered what lay out of sight.

Two wolves stood, fur on end as they bared fangs inches from each other. One was gray and massive; the other the color of old metal. Smaller and grayer, it gave not an inch. Days had passed since a private challenge had been issued. Then it had been accepted. Now, on a butte rising above the Plains, the two wolves met.

"I wondered if that was you," came the thoughts of the larger werewolf as they locked baleful glances and communicated in the ways of their kind. "I thought I felt you, but it was so puny a feeling, I was not sure."

The rusted wolf let the insult pass.

"Who are The People to you, Rheged?"

"Oh. 'The People,' as if you are one of them. They are nothing. Northern Cheyenne, whatever they are, I am not interested. They are a different kind of prey, nothing more. You fret like a puling baby."

"But you are here to destroy them." Understanding glimmered in the rust-colored wolf. "You are here to do this for someone part of the group of people you call 'friends' because they have something you want."

"Clever wolf."

"Enemies of the clan are closing in, aren't they? There are only so many alleys, so many sewers, so many holes in which to hide in London. And people no longer believe, do they? Man is becoming more fearsome than all of your fears, as he invents new ways more powerful than fangs and claws. And, when he no longer believes, he no longer lives in fear, and your power fades, as it should."

"Very clever wolf. Since you must know, I am here to found a refuge, a place we will own and protect and have as ours. The power of our werewolf clan should be used to our own advantage, and in the refuge we can live like kings. Those who are inferior can either serve us or die. A man has helped to start clearing the path, but he needs assistance to remove these Indians and the spirits that have protected them."

"What you do is evil, Rheged. And so are you. You prey on the evil within people. This land deserves none of that." A pause. "I understand. The People could divine you, and your man and those who work with you. They could read the threat and prevent you from gaining the foothold you seek. You led soldiers to destroy The People's relics to wound their spirit. Now you have had them removed to make the way open for you. The foulness you wanted to bring was blocked, and now you want The People removed."

Rheged's fangs appeared to glint in what could have been a smile.

"But they will be gone, soon, Outcast. They have lost a homeland they will never see again, as well as all the relics in which they believed. They are dying every day. More will die in the place of pestilence where they are to be confined. After they all die, we shall deal with the Lakota, for they hold the key to riches, but first these Northern Cheyenne must be eliminated because they hold the spirit power of the places I want."

"And you work with one of the fools who dabbles in the other world, someone who wants this and who thinks he is ruling you when you are ruling him."

"You have never understood power, Outcast. Power is not in standing up for the weaklings you like to support, but in using the power they have over each other to make them tools of our will. In time, they may realize the hate they have for the Cheyenne made them slaves to their hate, but by then it will be too late. The one who thinks I work for him is using all the power he has with the spirit world to curse and stalk the Cheyenne until they wither and die. I am only one of his weapons. By this time next year, the mighty Northern Cheyenne will be a handful of starving weaklings begging for bread. Their

71

spirits will be dead and will not be able to control ours. There will be a refuge that is safe for us, and then we will see what it is like to have a new country to call home. Then this world will see what power truly is."

"You will fail."

"And why is that?"

"Because I will stop you."

The large wolf cocked his head.

"You could be formidable once, but you have grown soft. You are only one old wolf, and you were wounded in avenging that child. You cannot stop what is to happen. You cannot stop hunger and disease and death. Consider the hate so many feel for those Indians because of the death of Custer—a man who preened and paraded himself as though he were important and who killed as many of his own men as he did anyone else! Do you think that is normal, or have I been busy helping make the whites see evil where there was heroism? You know the answer! Admit defeat now and leave while you can, for, if you stay, I will destroy you."

"You have spread poison. Others have helped you. The poison has corroded the hearts of people who should know better. I cannot reverse everything you have done, but I can ensure the People are not drowned in a sea of hate. You will not prevail."

"Time is on my side. My benefactor would like all of this to be over instantly, but it takes a wolf to be patient, does it not?"

The larger wolf waited for a reply, then realized his antagonist was finished communicating. A gesture of contempt. Making a guttural sound, he jutted his jaw forward, stared into the unflinching eyes that dared him to attack, then turned and walked away, leaving the other wolf behind.

CHAPTER SIX

Darlington Indian Agency, December 1877

"This is a place of death!" Flies the Hawk cried, enraged.

Fears that their new home at the Darlington Agency in Indian Territory would be worse than they had been told first flared when the Southern Cheyenne made a feast for the newcomers—a feast that included stew with little to no meat in it.

The supplies The People were given would keep them alive, but barely. In the first weeks in their new home, The People were content to rest from their ordeal, and to see those who were connected by blood but from whom they had been parted for many years by many miles. In a time of loss and defeat, they felt a muted joy in seeing others who had long been all but dead.

Then fevers began to sweep the camp, and more sickness. Rides a Crow had been laid low, as had her grandparents, but within days they were healthy again.

Little Wolf and Dull Knife remonstrated with the soldiers. They wanted to hunt. The People needed food. They'd been promised cattle. They'd been promised much. They were given little.

Rides a Crow's family had quarters near Little Wolf. Rides a Crow could see their leader being worn down by talk—talk with the soldiers for food, for medicine, for guns to hunt, for everything The People needed; and then talk with The People, who condemned him for their exile, who demanded this and

73

demanded that.

More and more, he was told warriors would return to their home when the winter and the rains were over. At first, he told them to be patient. Now he heard them out in silence. Rides a Crow knew the time would come when he would no longer insist they should stay where they were. The only question for her was whether enough of The People would be alive by then to matter.

June 1878, Indian Territory

Exhaustion and defeat showed in every line of Hunter's posture. For weeks that turned into months, he had traveled the hard face of the Plains in hopes of finding the one who was working with Rheged. Left to his own, Rheged was dangerous and deadly, but Hunter knew someone who understood white settlers was orchestrating the evil taking shape.

There was no shortage of hate. A few whites had come to understand that the Cheyenne, Lakota, Crow, and other tribes were people whose rich traditions were simply different from theirs. Mostly, there was such hunger for land that pushing everyone off of it had become an all-consuming ambition of the settlers. Hunter had encountered a place in Wyoming where, once the land was free of its first people, the whites who followed then tried to kill one another. They argued over who had the rights to own a piece of land, even amid thousands of acres of land free to anyone who claimed it.

He learned about the man named Fairfax, one of those who massacred Indians at Sand Creek in 1864, but the man was not at his vast ranch in northeastern Colorado. During Hunter's visit, he sensed some foul spirit guarding the place and souls crying out for relief and vengeance, but he could not learn more.

He could not fight all evil and spend such strength as he had trying to even all scores. Rheged's clan would be a plague on a land that deserved none of it. Hunter had to stop its spread. Yet he could neither wait for this man Fairfax, nor could he look all over the country for him. He needed to return to the Indian agency to protect those he was supposed to protect. He would return.

He knew Rides a Crow and her people would be suffering soon, if they were not already. From what he had seen before the Northern Cheyenne arrived, the Darlington Agency was a place of poverty and disease. Were they better off dying by inches there than they would have been dying on the trail that took them there?

Then a voice within him replied: *Only if their journey ends there. Only then.* In that moment he understood a spirit greater than he moved the waters upon which he sailed. For he knew that if the journey did not end at the Darlington Agency, it could only end fifteen hundred miles away, in the lands of the Tongue River Valley they called home.

Around him, the world of the Northern Cheyenne was barren in the grip of frozen hope as the leading edge of hate smashed its heavy hand upon the Plains. But his thought was of something beyond hate: could the Northern Cheyenne, like the Hebrew people of the Bible, ever leave captivity behind and create a nation of their own? Perhaps freedom was a dream not only worth living for, but also dying for.

He rose and shook himself off. His journey might serve no purpose. But some path he did not understand had brought him here, had led him to The People. He would walk it where it led.

The wolf stopped his limping gait as he neared the boundary of the reservation. His spirit told him he was not alone on the

Plains. Rheged had vowed to prevent him from stopping his designs, yet the wolf had accomplished so little, he could not imagine why Rheged would stalk him.

Hunter heard the thunder in the ground: the nobility of the Plains—wild horses. The herds had moved north as the railroad had hemmed in open spaces. He had distantly seen them in the Sand Hills, galloping through on their way to freedom. The horses always gave him a thrill, because the galloping of a wild horse was like a living picture God gave man to show what power, beauty, and freedom looked like.

This was a small group of a dozen horses. Different. These were not like the rest. He could feel not only the power God gave all horses, but the further power He had given to some.

Spirit horses! His Cheyenne visitors in the Sand Hills had told him about mystical animals that galloped the Plains to keep the buffalo from ever leaving, to breed strong horses for The People, and to bring to The People the words of the Great Spirit.

"Stand, wolf." The voice in his head was as clear as if the woman speaking were inches from his ears.

As if he had a choice. A dozen horses; one wolf. He waited.

The lead horse, a glossy black mare, regarded him closely. As he blinked, the mare became a woman with coal-black hair flowing around her. Her features were pure Cheyenne, with a strong face featuring high cheekbones stretched over copper-red skin just beginning to be lined with the marks of life on the Plains. Her prominent nose and strong jaw gave her the look of an aristocrat. Well, he reasoned, in this world of the Plains, she was.

Hunter had long known that others who were more than human lived across the Plains; he sensed them from time to time as they came near his Sand Hills refuge. But he assumed they, like he, wanted to be alone.

"How can you speak inside my head? It is . . . it only happens when I am with my own kind."

"It is called Spirit Talk, wolf. It is how those of us who are of the spirit of The People communicate."

"Can I learn this?"

"I can teach you, if you are worthy."

"What do you want? I mean you no harm."

"You are the werewolf Outcast—the one we have heard about who turned from your clan across the great water and was blown by the winds of the spirits to be here for The People."

"I followed the road of that which I believe, and God or the spirits led me here."

"You now follow The People. You have dreamed a dream about The People you plan to pursue. Why?"

The answer was simple. He belonged there. And as for helping them go home, that was the vaguest of notions, as yet disconnected from reality. He was as yet unsure whether his wild notion of a Cheyenne version of Moses and the Hebrews was a true thought or a kind of madness. Phrasing that to a spirit horse was not easy.

The horse's words cut through his.

"We have seen and heard. One of us followed them south; the rest were far north, where Sitting Bull has taken his people to be away from the soldiers and where the Nez Perce are fighting the white soldiers. We came when we heard about the suffering of The People, but we came too late and went back north to save those we could. Now we are back. You have stirred the spirit world, wolf. There are those who come to oppose you, those who hate The People. There is great danger, for they want not just the lands of The People, but their lives and their souls."

"Then you must help me. This is your land, and you know its secrets. You must stay nearby."

She was clearly displeased with this command.

"Do you not know the danger you put us in by asking us to remain near men? The camps where The People will stay will hold many soldiers. We cannot evade death. Their bullets can kill us—they have killed us. And, above all, you, a stranger to the Plains, think to tell us what to do?"

"Yes, because that is why God sent me. If you did not want to be part of this, you would not be here now."

Talks to Horses stared at him as time stood still. She moved closer. Silence lengthened.

"What is it they call you?" she said at last.

"I use the name Hunter," he replied. "It makes my life simple."

"I am known as Talks to Horses. I am of The People."

"As I have heard, The People begged for spirits in their time of need. How did you come to be this way? Are you immortal, like the Sidhe?" he asked, referring to the horses of ancient Irish legends.

"Spirits that walk between worlds are born and die like all flesh, Outcast. The horses of your Irish legends were our ancestors a long time ago, but they were mortal before your legends portrayed them as being beyond death. We will talk of this as we travel, Outcast. There is a cloud seeking to cover The People, and we must be there when it arrives. Let us go, for it may already be too late. Ride on me, and we shall talk."

Once again she became a horse. His attempts to ride horses in the past had failed; they understood a wolf had no place upon their backs. He hoped spirit horses were different. He would find out.

Darlington Indian Agency, July 1878
Rides a Crow beheld what to her mind was the saddest, sorriest crop of corn she had ever seen. In these days of summer, the

stalks should have been nearing her waist, even though she was taller than during those days by the Rosebud. It seemed so long ago when the last corn crop she ever planted grew taller than she stood.

Here, the corn looked wilted under a cloudless sky as the heat made leaves droop and turn brown long before harvest time. The ground was so dry, she kicked up small clouds of dust as she walked between the rows, surveying the depths to which her people had fallen. Women and men and children had spent days planting the corn and digging the soil. For what? For nothing! If there ever was a harvest, something she doubted, it would not feed The People for very long.

"Useless!" she raged, ripping up an ankle-high, drooping, brown corn plant. "Great Spirit, cannot you hear the cries of your people?"

"Ahem."

When she glanced up, she beheld a ludicrous sight. At the far end of the row of corn stood a man in a funny little hat with the sides turned up all around, wearing a heavy, black jacket and pants she knew white people called a suit. With the suit, he wore a white shirt, a vest, and a piece of black string holding the shirt closed at the neck. Wearing shoes, not boots, she judged him to be one of the Easterners who came to the Darlington Agency.

Some of those who visited were entertaining; some wanted to teach The People white man's ways; some were missionaries; some seemed to ask many questions to no purpose and would insist the answers were important because they would write about the Northern Cheyenne for white people to read. Why should she care? What kind of people pushes another off its land and then claims it wants to be friends?

The man walked down the row, getting dust on his suit. He tried brushing it off as he went, but each time he hit the ears of corn, pollen and dust powdered even more of him. Rides a Crow tried very hard not to laugh, for white people never liked it when Indians caught them being foolish, which was often.

He perspired profusely. His face reminded her of an apple when it was ripe, being both round in form and red from heat.

She would never understand. Soldiers wore wool uniforms all year long. Those who were not soldiers wore silly clothes. Barefoot, she wore a long, cotton skirt and a thin shirt that flowed over it. If the weather felt warm to her, what must it feel like inside the little oven in which the Eastern man cooked himself all day?

"I do not mean to intrude, miss, but I could not help but hear you," he said, taking the silly hat off of his head before setting it back atop his light-brown hair slicked down with something and parted in the middle. He'd had his hair cut very short, as white men did. Sensible warriors, who understood a man had better things to do than cut his hair week after week, just let their hair grow long.

"You understand our language?" she asked in English. Some people had a gift to learn the tongues of others. She did.

"A few words," he said. "If you understand English, can we speak in that?"

"Of course," she replied. Hearing white men butcher her language was an annoyance.

"I have been visiting Darlington for the past two weeks. Philip Rockfield, of the Southwestern Connecticut Society for the Improvement of the Indians." He took his hat off again.

Rides a Crow almost giggled. Then she realized she was supposed to tell him her name. "I am called Rides a Crow."

"You don't have a real name?"

"That is my real name," she shot back angrily. "Some of your people give us names they like to call us, but those are not our names. I am named for my mother's vision. On the day I was born she saw me leading a flock of crows across the sky while the spirits painted the clouds in all the colors of the world. What is a name like Elizabeth or Victoria to that?"

"Of course. Of course," he said. "No offense intended. Your English is very good."

It should be, she thought. She had translated often since they were now forced to deal with the whites at the agency. White people were strange about names. She recalled the time a group of Northern Cheyenne young men identified themselves to a group of Eastern visitors by the various foul words they knew white people used when they were angry. The soldiers had not been amused, but the story had rippled through The People with laughter.

The man still stood there. Staring. Rides a Crow had heard of things white men called zoos, in which they would stare at animals all day. She wondered if the reservation was something like that, because whites came over and over to stare at The People.

"Ahem."

She had all but forgotten the man. Now she turned his way, pretending she cared what he would say, knowing all whites came to say something.

"The Red Label Union Suit Company is asking everyone who works with hostiles . . . um, Indians, to help them find workers for their new factory. They think it would be cheaper to build a factory out here in Dodge City, up in Kansas near the new settlements, than to ship everything across the country. The company is offering to employ young women to operate the machines used in sewing. I assume you know how to sew?"

She did, although neither sitting still to learn nor sitting still to do the work properly were areas in which she excelled. Sun Raven, even at her advanced age, could mend things faster and better than she.

"I have other work," Rides a Crow said, hoping the man would go away. She did not know or care about Dodge City, Kansas. If it was not the Tongue River Valley, it did not matter to her.

"Miss, I don't think you understand. I know you young ladies want to grow up and be squaws because you do not know any better, but the Red Label Union Suit Company offers you a chance to learn to read and write. You don't have to be ignorant your whole life! You can learn how to wear the latest fashions. You would not have to tend corn out here. You could work inside all day long, using one of the finest and newest sewing machines ever invented. The Red Label Union Suit Company is also interested in helping you learn a better way of life. The Young Ladies Academy, where you and the rest would live, will also help you to learn how to act the right way, not like . . . well, you would learn the way proper young ladies act. They would even arrange for a minister to come to teach you how to manage your moral conduct and to help you leave behind the heathen ways holding your people back. You—"

"Stop!" She stalked to within inches of his face, close enough to smell something sweet and sick emanating from him. "I had what I needed when I lived beside the Tongue River. I had the wind and the sun and the animals. Your Bible talks of a Garden of Eden. There is no railroad in that garden to kill the buffalo! You put one here in the Garden of The People. I have seen what your soldiers do. They drink and befoul themselves in every possible way, and you call *me* heathen? Do you call how whites treat Indians moral?"

Still holding the corn stalk in her hand, she began to hit the interloper across the shoulders with it.

"Who are you to tell me your machine is better than the world made for us by the Great Spirit? I do not care about your fashions! I want to live in my home without soldiers killing my family."

She kept hitting him as he backed up and put up his hands to ward off the blows.

"Take all that. Take all of the poison in your world, and keep it away from me and from my people!" The stalk finally broke, and she tossed it aside as the young man fled up the corn row and out of her sight.

Thaddeus Simpson Travers, assistant to the agent for the Darlington Indian Agency, had summoned Little Wolf. When the chief arrived, Travers made a speech about whites and Cheyenne learning the ways of peace. The other assistant agent, Paul Collins, treated Little Wolf with respect; Travers less so. Travers kept a framed photo of Custer on his desk and did his best, by the way he parted and combed his long hair and scraggly mustache, to imitate the appearance of a man who was clearly his hero.

Rides a Crow, whom the chief had brought along as he often did when dealing with whites, because she was adept at reading and speaking their language, wanted to ask when the peace lesson would be taught to white people. She felt the question wriggling on the tip of her tongue.

She shot a glance at Little Wolf and was startled to find him looking at her, wearing a slightly bemused expression on his usually solemn and careworn face. It was as if he had understood what she was thinking, or was thinking the same thing!

Travers kept talking. He paid no attention to the Indians in his office. The other man—powerfully built, with pale skin and dark, almost black hair—had paid attention. As the other man eyed her closely, Rides a Crow felt a shiver of warning, as though some spirit told her this man harbored both danger and a gift.

Yet the agent introduced him as a minister, a man of God,

who had come with a wagon of blankets for the Cheyenne. He claimed all the blankets had been made by the members of his church for the comfort of the Cheyenne, as fall was soon preparing to give way to winter.

Little Wolf accepted the gift in the name of The People. Then Rides a Crow spoke.

"Would it not be better that we use the blankets we have for the time being? Although old and threadbare, they would keep us warm during the final days of this season. Then we could use these new blankets when the cold of the winter wind blows," she said, hoping her eyes communicated one message to Little Wolf as her words spoke to everyone assembled.

She turned to the man claiming to be a minister.

"I am sure the people of your church would understand if we use thin blankets until they can be used no more. Then we can use these thick blankets in winter. Those blankets, too, were gifts of love and respect, and we wish to honor both peoples and all peoples," she said.

Though clearly unsure what Rides a Crow was doing, Little Wolf was shrewd and had come to understand the girl possessed true instincts that should be followed.

"It is so. The child speaks with the wisdom of an elder. The People will wear out the blankets we have now and then use the new ones," he said. "This gift will be needed when the weather becomes cold and our old blankets are worn through with holes. We will distribute them in a few weeks. Not now."

The agent seemed startled to find the Indians capable of planning in advance and saw it as a sign they were learning the ways of their captors. Travers readily agreed to store the blankets in a shed on the reservation until the coming of the snow.

The minister who had donated the blankets voiced a fear that those who made them would be downcast if they saw the Cheyenne walking about wrapped in old blankets when they had made them new ones.

Little Wolf then began to mutter that if whites could not let The People use a gift as they saw fit, they could take the gift back. His comment led Travers—who saw in the donation a way to reduce the amount of money he would need to spend on Indians and thereby increase the amount that would go into his pocket—to prevail upon the minister to allow the Cheyenne their way in this, because it did make sense.

Rides a Crow sensed the deep, black anger this comment provoked in the minister. It was greater than would be justified by the Cheyenne simply wanting to set new blankets aside until winter.

As they walked away from the office of the agent, Little Wolf asked his questions. "What is it you fear from this gift, little one?"

She struggled to express what she felt, then resorted to honesty.

"I am unsure. That man with the blankets was evil, Little Wolf," she said. "I cannot explain, but I have come to tell the difference between the evil ones among them and those who simply do not understand. I've learned to tell those who are clouded and misled from those who hate. That gift would not help us. I do not know why, but, if that man gives it, it is evil and is designed to hurt The People."

"And how do you come by this wisdom, Spirit Walker?"

"I do not know. Ever since the Night the Dead Rode with the Living, I have felt the spirit teaching me. Often I do not understand, but that man's evil was very clear."

Little Wolf said nothing but walked with a stronger step beside the girl. In the wearying days since the relics of The People were destroyed, he had hoped for voices from the spirits to fill the void and feared that, in the silence, the spirits had turned their backs upon The People.

He knew not what they had in mind for the girl, for him, or for the families in this foreign land, but he was now certain the spirits had not deserted The People. For the rest, he would be patient. The spirits would speak.

Rides a Crow gazed dispiritedly across the flatlands, beyond where the soldiers guarded The People. Her tribe had been allowed to hunt, but the buffalo were gone. She could not understand why the spirits took them away.

"Not them, child of thoughts, but the white hunters." Hunter. He knew it was possible the madness to slaughter was driven by something more than human greed. He also knew it did not matter now.

"Better you had let them kill us than have us die in this place," Rides a Crow spat at Hunter.

In truth, Hunter had not known what awaited the Northern Cheyenne until they had all but reached the agency. His face reflected his sober thoughts.

"Some will spend forever here with their southern relatives," he admitted. "Not all. Not you." He spoke matter-of-factly, as though talking about something already achieved.

"You must tell me what has happened since you arrived here. Spare nothing, even something you think is not important. I know you understand the spirits. There are evil ones seeking to destroy The People, but we will not let it happen. For me to help you, you must tell me all, and trust me," he said.

"Trust you? Why should a Cheyenne trust a white man?" The bitterness Rides a Crow felt as she traveled the trail south had grown worse as she saw her people mired in misery, with no hope of escaping except through death.

"Because on the Night the Dead Rode with the Living, you did not ride alone. You know this. You have been taught what is real and what is not." Hunter then described the clothing she'd worn that night, the red cloth around the wound on her foot, the horse she and her brother rode, and the route they took. "We have left behind the time when it was safe, child. You must believe."

"No white man rode with me."

"I did not say I was with you as a white man."

The possible and the impossible struggled behind the eyes staring back at him. There was only one conclusion possible.

"Those who change shape are evil spirits."

"Many," Hunter said. "Not all. Not me. Recall your journey here."

She should have known. So deep was the pain and so thick the misery, and so surrounded were they by the hate of their captors, she could not see what now seemed clear. The man was some kind of spirit—a spirit wolf—she had never imagined.

She now recalled the way the Lakota healer had looked upon her when she arrived: half in wonder that she lived, and partly in awe of something no one ever explained. The Lakota leader had been deferential in a way no Lakota man would normally be to a young Cheyenne girl. They knew she had been touched by a spirit of power!

"Why me?"

"Ask the larger spirits, child. We are their playthings. I am only . . . well, whatever I have become. But first, tell me all."

Rides a Crow saw Hunter's eyes flash with anger when she mentioned the minister's gift.

"Should you ever see this man again, you must tell me immediately, or summon me in your thoughts if I am not near. His name is Rheged. He is an agent of evil."

"You know him?"

"He is one like me, Rides a Crow, but he would sow evil. He works with a man trying to use the spirits to obliterate The People. His gift was nothing but a trap."

"How?"

"Among whites, it has long been said that infecting blankets with diseases is a way to kill Indians by exposing them to typhoid, or smallpox, or other diseases. This gift would kill The People. If that man gave The People blankets, it is only because he has poisoned the blankets."

"The blankets looked to be good and new," Rides a Crow said. "They rode high in the wagon that brought them."

"Yet you, too, felt there was evil."

Rides a Crow admitted the truth.

"I shall deal with this," said Hunter

So Rides a Crow told Hunter about The People's suffering, their illnesses, the lack of meat. She told him the young warriors were muttering that The People must leave. She said the mutterings of the angry young men were growing stronger, and that, if The People did not leave the reservation soon, they would be forced to endure another miserable winter.

When she finished, Hunter understood what Talks to Horses had meant. The spirit of The People was heading home; it would only be a matter of time before their feet would follow.

"Follow Little Wolf always," he told her. "He will be true to The People." Hunter turned to leave.

"No," Rides a Crow said. "If I am to follow you, I must know how you came to be this way. Was a curse placed upon you?"

"I do not know. The clan into which I was born has been dispersed, because the land where I come from has grown to be over populated. I was born in Wales, which is a place of high, strong mountains near England, across the vast sea between that land and this one. My parents were like me. I was not in Wales long. My kind is not welcome in many places. We lived in Ireland for a time, and in the far north of Scotland. After my parents passed, I did many things, including working for some time as a soldier. I thought the fighting would quell the rage within me. It did not. Then, by chance, I found another clan member in London. I lived with a group of my kind there, until something terrible happened."

He explained about Jenny Blue Eyes. "And so I came here, where by chance I met The People. Also by chance, the day I arrived in your camp, the soldiers attacked, and a Spirit Walker was in need."

"And now, what?" said Rides a Crow. "Do you move on again? What is it you want?"

"I do not wish to sit in the circle of The People, but to sit at the edge of the fire and know you are safe. I do not question the reason. It matters; it does. I will draw my last breath to save The People, if it should come to that," Hunter said. "It is the work I was given to do; it is the purpose that shapes the time I have left to live. I am content. And, when my duty is done, I shall sit on the far bank of the river and welcome The People when they come home to the place God has prepared for all who lived through this world."

"You talk as if your God and the Great Spirit are the same," she said.

Hunter smiled softly. "Look up, Rides a Crow." She did. "Explain to me where the sky ends."

After struggling to find words, Rides a Crow gave up the task.

"All we see and all we know is but a small piece of something so big and vast and wonderful that all of our words and thoughts and understanding can only capture a small piece of it," Hunter said. "Whatever words we use for the small piece we understand are unimportant. He who holds and loves us gave us this place to be our home. He guides us to do right, and brings us home when our time is over. He cares not for the words we use to name Him, only that we walk in His ways. You will understand. In time."

For a moment they stood in silence as the breeze bent the tall grass, and she saw her namesakes flying across the field where corn had been grown, finding the stuff of life in what was left behind.

"And I must go, for there is much work to do. I do not tell you to ignore this present pain of The People, Rides a Crow, but I beg you to believe it only becomes the end of the story if we allow it to."

Hunter walked away.

Rides a Crow smelled the stench of the fire. Flames lit up the sky from the shack where many things were stored, including the kerosene the soldiers used for their lamps. By the time men with buckets came to douse the fire, it was a danger to them. They let it burn itself out.

That the shack held blankets was not widely known. Little Wolf had not wanted The People to become dissatisfied with what they had and demand something he was uncertain whether they should have.

Rides a Crow felt Little Wolf come and stand next to her as the fire crackled and yellow tongues of flame licked high into the night.

"We will never know for sure if the man meant us evil, will we, Rides a Crow?"

"But we will know that nothing evil befell The People because of those blankets," she replied softly. "I believe the spirits like a bright fire, my chief."

She heard the older man chuckle as he moved away in the night, commenting to everyone how careless white men were that they burned down their own buildings!

Morrison Fairfax pounded the desk. His ally had assured him this latest effort to accelerate the extinction of the Cheyenne would slip through all the army's defenses. It had not. The shack was destroyed on purpose. He was certain. He had been sure the mass of men he had gathered against the Cheyenne was strong enough to wipe them out. It was only when his ally pointed out to him that an attack on the reservation would be an attack on the army that he was dissuaded from sending his own private gunmen to finish the job.

His partner was hiding something, as though he knew he had failed to carry out the simple task of pretending to be a minister. Treachery? Or was the power of this Rheged less than he tried to make it appear?

From his spies, Fairfax knew the harvest was lean, and famine would soon run rampant through the camp again. He knew the defeated Cheyenne would be inexorably weakened until they withered into a small band of curiosities the soft-hearted fools back East would come to watch, as though they were animals in a zoo.

Yet their endurance bothered Fairfax. He had dealt with the spirit world enough to know that something more than mere flesh and blood was defending the Cheyenne. He could not believe anyone was more powerful than his shadowy ally. Perhaps his ally needed an inducement to win whatever war was taking place in the spirit world. Fairfax knew it did not matter what he promised, only what he planned to deliver.

Rheged was also furious that he had been outfoxed. He had suspected the girl with Little Wolf was a Spirit Walker. Now he knew for certain. Rides a Crow would need to be eliminated. The girl had seen Rheged's face and would be on guard, but he had sent for others. They would be coming soon. Then the Outcast and his Indian friends would find out what it was like to face the full force of the clan's leaders.

Rheged knew, too, that back in London, there were some

who questioned where his leadership had taken them. The Outcast was popular with misfits like that young female Skellig, who did not understand they had been bred to kill. Rheged could not lose. He must win, no matter the cost.

Anger blended with misery in Rides a Crow as she tried to sleep in her bedding. By the score, The People had been felled by a disease white soldiers called the measles. Sick, their bodies turned red; their eyes turned to water and their throats to rocky dust at the height of the time the whites called August, when the heat beat down unmercifully.

The evil ones attacking The People had succeeded. The People were all going to die here. Rides a Crow knew this! Perhaps Hunter was not an ally, but an enemy. During the many weeks since he had talked to her of their home, the hope that had flared in her had been dampened by misery.

Then Hunter appeared, squatting over her.

"This will pass," he said. "Those who do not eat must save the rations given to them. The bread might keep. The corn will, for certain. Let nothing be wasted."

He pushed the hair, damp with sweat from her fever, off her forehead. She peered up into his eyes and saw vast pain. She also saw affection she had not known since her parents had been killed.

"Do not be in a hurry to rise, little one, for it may be many miles and many weeks before you rest. Think on the storm."

Rides a Crow recalled the first tornado at Darlington. She and many of The People stood outside to watch it, drawn by the wildness of the wind, while soldiers panicked and ran to and fro when the sky turned black. When the dark, deadly funnel had poured down from the clouds, soldiers ran and hid, even though the funnel was a mile or more away—as if the insubstantial shacks they had built would stop the winds.

Clustered in a draw offering scant protection, The People waited as the breathtaking destruction swept past and then vanished, leaving a trail of uprooted trees. Some lodges were flattened, but they could be rebuilt in a few hours, for The People knew the Great Spirit often raged across the Plains and always built their abodes lightly, lest they block its path.

After, when the rain-battered grasslands glistened in the sun, the land came to life. For once The People could see its beauty. Rainbows arched in the east, and someone from The People said all they needed to do was walk the rainbow to reach their homeland.

Hunter's meaning became clear to Rides a Crow: another storm lay ahead. This one would shake The People's world like no storm nature could produce. Escaping from Darlington would not be like walking over a rainbow so much as it would be like crossing a chasm on a thin branch with doom on both sides. She fidgeted again, trying to believe that when the coming storm ended, The People would survive.

This was his chance! Fairfax knew a man must seize opportunity. Everyone agreed that Paul Collins, one of the top agents who dealt with the Northern Cheyenne, believed he had an obligation to be kind to the savages while trying to civilize them. The telegrams flying from Indian Territory to Washington were proof of that. Fairfax had been advocating for the man's removal as part of his plan to increase the pressure on the Indians, but Washington moved slowly at best, and Collins had friends.

Collins had told everyone, including some in Fairfax's pay, that he would be leaving for a few days on some mission to Texas ranches to increase the amount of beef coming to the reservation. By going out alone, as he said he would do, he would make himself an easy target.

Any accident that might befall Collins would be blamed on marauding hostiles; Fairfax knew it. He could even have a group of witnesses claim they had ridden to the agent's aid but arrived too late. The policy of catering to the Northern Cheyenne would be discredited, and someone Fairfax knew to be of a proper mind toward the Indians could take Collins's place.

He thought of asking his ally for help. No. This was not a job for spirits; it was a job a man should handle himself. He was paying men to do work that needed doing; this was a chance for them to earn their keep. His only concern was whether he might already be too late for a messenger from Darlington to reach his ranch. His men could ride all night if they needed to. The chance to kill Collins and blame his murder on the Indians to whom Collins kowtowed was too good to lose.

As Paul Collins rode south from the Darlington camp, he knew the reservation struggled to feed too many with too little every day. The sights he saw reminded him painfully that the Indians who had surrendered to the white man were now being asked to accept starvation along with captivity.

He knew the limits of the job but would do his best. If these Indians, who had not wanted to come to the agency, could be shown they could live in peace following the white man's way, perhaps fighting between Indians and settlers could stop. He was fairly good with languages, although imperfect knowledge of Cheyenne, amid his persistence to improve, had earned him the Indian name of Talking Noises. In its own way the name was a mark of affection, because he knew the Indians appreciated his efforts to treat them as equals.

To make sure the Northern Cheyenne knew he would be gone a few days, he told them weeks ago about his plan to ride to Texas. The Indians, rightly, did not like dealing with Travers. If there were grievances and problems, Collins wanted to be sure they knew he would be back soon. They trusted few people. With good reason!

Riding alone, he left behind the cares of his job as he enjoyed the rare moments of solitude the ride offered. When he was working at the agency, he wore his Eastern suit, because he felt he should present a dignified mien to the Indians. Today, however, he wore an old shirt and jacket with a pair of cavalry trousers tucked into his boots. He kept his brown hair short and his face clean shaven, but today he did not bother attacking his whiskers. It was as close to a holiday as he was likely to get. He had a rifle and pistol, of course, but he did not anticipate trouble.

A round face and kind, brown eyes reflected Collins's inner optimism—optimism dimmed for a time by the War Between the States, but which had recovered when he came West, seeking a purpose. He'd found it now and was committed to doing right by two peoples colliding with one another like two rocks in flight.

The trail from Darlington wound around rocks poking through the dusty soil, clumps of trees enduring the heat, and small hills.

Approaching a spot where the trail swung left to pass an outcrop of rocks rising a few feet above the rest of the plains, he paused to study it and walked the horse closer to the jagged rocks.

Then the gunfire began: the crack of a rifle followed by the larger boom of a buffalo gun. Collins knew one bullet had gone whistling past him, but now he could see men in the rocks ahead rising to fire at someone else, as though he were not the only one riding. Collins drew his own rifle. Before he could fire, the buffalo gun boomed twice more. At least one of the men in the jagged rocks fell.

He could not look further, because three men emerged on horseback from behind the rocks, riding hard. They would soon reach him. Pistols fired, but the shots went wide at the distant range of fifty yards.

Refusing to run, he waited with his rifle aimed at the riders. Although he was no marksman, in fact he rarely hit his targets, he would take at least one of the would-be killers with him.

Then came the horses!

Led by a glorious black horse, a dozen horses seemed to emerge from the dirt and ride straight at the attackers. The killers' horses reared and bucked. The unsaddled wild horses then veered away from what seemed like a sure collision to circle around Collins, blocking him from firing back. A cloud of dust enveloped him, choking him. He dimly saw flashes through the haze.

Although he knew it to be impossible, he could swear he heard the horses singing a Cheyenne war song.

Then the horses were gone, galloping away as fast as they had come, the three empty-saddled beasts belonging to the killers following, as though trying desperately to catch up.

On the ground lay three lumps. Collins dismounted. The three men had been savagely killed by some wild animal. Their bodies were torn. Their faces showed fear of whatever had killed them. Moving close enough to see if he knew them, he thought one might have been around the agency, but it was hard to tell. There was nothing to say who they were. Two of them had feathers tucked in their jackets, and the third wore a Cheyenne bone bracelet. The agent looked around and saw not a soul.

Collins rode to the rocks and dismounted. Three men lay dead, all shot by a gun that had left a huge hole. That buffalo gun he had heard! Oddly enough, a bow, like those the Cheyenne sometimes used for hunting, lay there as well. Again, the men bore nothing that might identify them. Their horses, tied to trees, likewise had nothing to explain who the men were or why they had tried to waylay him.

What had been an ambush aimed at him had been thoroughly defeated. By whom? Collins called out . . . no answer. Why would anyone think he had valuables to steal? How had someone known to follow him in order to rescue him, without him knowing about them? He shivered in the summer heat. Perhaps what he carried wasn't what they sought. Perhaps it was his life they wanted. But why? If he was doing something *that* important, he wished he knew what it was. He would need to be more vigilant during the rest of his journey.

Danger lived on the Plains. He often wondered if it had existed when no one but Indians on their ponies roamed the land. He turned his horse south. He harbored no doubt that evil now surrounded him. Perhaps he could do something to ameliorate it. For certain, he needed to worry about protecting himself from it.

Fairfax Ranch, Colorado, September 1878

Fairfax and Rheged stood inches apart, each ready to reach for the other's throat as they each shifted blame because the Cheyenne had not faded away. Disease was weakening the Indians but not killing them. Although a year had passed since they were brought from their homeland to the reservation, their spirit had been slow to crumble.

Rheged had vanished for months before returning with several companions who looked as though they could slaughter children in their sleep and remain unmoved. He'd expected to secure his share of the bargain and was furious when it was not delivered. He pointed out that Fairfax's attempt on Collins's life had been ill considered and ill managed.

"Collins said there were six men; you have dozens! Six? You take the Cheyenne too lightly," Rheged said. "You cannot wish them away by snapping your fingers."

According to Fairfax, Rheged had done little to be worthy of any kind of partnership. He also said he saw no reason to keep his end of the deal if Rheged kept none of his promises.

"When we met, you made promises. You talked a fine game with your English manners and English ways, but, from what I see, the army did more than you. Perhaps I need to dissolve this partnership permanently."

The only thing checking Rheged was the knowledge that he would have no protection from the bullets of Fairfax's army of gunslingers waiting outside if he killed the old man.

As for Fairfax, he wanted this erstwhile ally slaughtered. However, like most people who try to dabble in the spirit world to create evil, he feared that what he did not know would descend upon him with a vengeance. There had to be a way.

Fairfax knew talk of the Cheyenne leaving the reservation was rampant. The army had refused to send enough troops to sufficiently guard the Indians. Then Fairfax had the idea: it mattered little if the Cheyenne actually tried to break out of the Darlington Agency. All that mattered was that they appear to pose a threat. A few raids, a few deaths. Blame would focus on the Cheyenne, who would insist they were innocent, because they were. But the army would never believe them.

Rheged agreed they would make Kansas and Indian Territory howl over the depredations they aimed to commit. He and his friends would make sure the army heard the right story. Then the Cheyenne would be suppressed once and for all.

CHAPTER SEVEN

Darlington Indian Agency, September 1878
Hunter waited for Rides a Crow beside her lodge.

"The day is almost here," he said. "Your grandparents will need your help. Prepare what they need, but make the load light enough for you to carry it all as you walk. It will be a very long walk."

"You speak in riddles."

"The People are going home," Hunter said.

Rides a Crow stared at the man. He appeared serious. Not a muscle moved on his face. His words were no joke. They were cruel.

"How can you say this? We have no food, no horses, no guides, and there are soldiers everywhere."

"I did not say it would be easy," Hunter said. "Only that it will happen. Little Wolf will come to you for counsel, for help speaking and listening, because he understands you have the spirit within you."

Rides a Crow wanted to laugh in Hunter's face. She was a girl of seventeen, not a spirit, as they spoke of in the stories. She wondered if Hunter had been drinking liquor the soldiers brewed, and it had made him crazy.

That day, Little Wolf called for her to be with him as he talked to the whites who ran the agency. He told them The People needed to go home. When they urged him to stay, he flatly refused. He told them the Darlington Agency was not a good place for the Northern Cheyenne, and that they would no longer stay there. He made no conditions or requests but presented their departure as an accomplished fact.

On the way back to their quarters, Rides a Crow asked Little Wolf how he could be so bold. She envied anyone who could say such a thing, when to her it seemed impossible, even if it was what The People dreamed of night after night.

"Will they not arrest you?"

"The whites lie when they talk, Spirit Walker. They do not know truth when it is told to them. They will think I am talking so that in a day or a week I can ask for more corn. We will never be like them. I am Cheyenne. If they discover I have spoken true and kill me for so speaking, so be it."

Three days later, Rides a Crow became excited. A few young men left the agency. Perhaps this was what Hunter had foretold. But Little Wolf said he had not sent them. He also told the agent he would not look for them, or try to make them return.

Travers then said if the men who fled did not return, soldiers would collect ten hostages. If the men still did not return, the Cheyenne food rations would be eliminated. He reminded Little Wolf the Northern Cheyenne were prisoners. The words acted like kerosene poured on a fire.

Rides a Crow felt the chief's rage. Still, Little Wolf only told the agent, once again, that he and The People would leave. He also said he would be happy to fight the soldiers, but not at the agency.

Amazed she and Little Wolf were not arrested, Rides a Crow said as much to Hunter when she saw him later.

"Your chief is a true leader," Hunter told her. "The Arapaho and Southern Cheyenne would be killed if Little Wolf fought back here, because this is not their fight. Those who run this place must now either start a war or hope your chief is like them—a man who talks big and acts small."

"That is not Little Wolf."

"Then prepare to walk fast and far, little one."

A council of The People's leaders gathered. Important men whom Rides a Crow had thought of as legends surrounded her. In awe, she wondered why Little Wolf had brought her to the gathering.

She heard Hunter speak in her mind. He had told her they would need to communicate through Spirit Talk often, because when The People went north, no white man could tag along. Hunter would be with them in the shape of a wolf, not a man.

"They will want to know how old men and children evade the sentries. The guards will be distracted," he told her. "Spirit horses will ride through the camp, and the guards will be afraid to follow them."

Hunter was right. As the leaders of the Northern Cheyenne argued, Little Wolf glanced at Rides a Crow and nodded.

Rides a Crow spoke Hunter's words. "The spirit wolf that walked with us from the homeland will walk with us to return." She added, "You all know of the Night the Elders Lived. He saved them then and will save us now."

Her words impressed the gathering.

"Yet how shall we travel?" asked one. "This is not our country."

"Has the white man changed north and turned it into south that we shall lose our way?" she riposted unprompted. Little Wolf laughed as the questioner was shamed into silence.

Rides a Crow closed her eyes a moment, as if thinking.

"Very good, child," came the thought Hunter sent her. "Toffs love a good show."

She wondered what a "toff" might be. She then repeated what he sent her: "Spirit horses will guide The People. The soldiers will follow, and the journey will not be easy, but the spirit horses will guide The People to the land The People will possess until the end of days."

In the end, although gripped with great fear that the step they were taking would leave some of them one with the earth in a place far from home, they agreed to follow Dull Knife and Little Wolf. The leaders only had to decide the right time to leave.

The People would travel with nothing but the basics: food, clothing, guns and ammunition, and anything they had brought with them south they wanted to carry on their backs home. The lodges they built would remain. Horses were required to haul tipis, and they would slow down their passage. For most, packing was the work of a few moments, because they had acquired little in the South they wished to ever see again.

As The People prepared, eating less of the meager food supply each day in order to set aside food for the journey north, a charge of excitement ran through the camp. For weeks, they talked and thought of nothing but their upcoming journey that would take them away from this place of death and disease.

Rides a Crow was amazed none of the soldiers guarding them caught the energy on the wind, which was obvious to her, and was glad the soldiers were so unaware.

Not all of those who came to the southern reservation would be leaving with them. Some were too old or sick to make the journey. Their spirits would walk with those who left, they said.

Some of The People had acquired importance on the southern reservation, due to their knack at farming or by standing with the army. One of them was Elk Running, two winters older than Rides a Crow. He had made it clear he thought she should be his wife. He had spoken of challenging Horse Walking for her two years past when The People looked forward to a future without limits. Rides a Crow had let him spew empty words. Elk Running excelled at talk and trade. He made friends with many of the whites and wanted to set up a trading post on the southern reservation.

When Little Wolf told Rides a Crow that The People would leave within days, she could barely contain her happiness. As she bustled with work to be done, Elk Running blocked her path as she moved through the camp.

"We must talk, Rides a Crow."

"I am busy, Wide Elk," she said, using the nickname given him because of his bulk. She had seen him on the road to Darlington, eating without regard to the needs of others. On those bleak days, she had rejected food so those who were in greater need could eat and live. When The People lived free, she tolerated Elk Running, for he was not unpleasant, if not handsome. Although not among the front rank of warriors, he would join the hunters. But now, she had too much to do to pay attention to him.

Grabbing her arm as she passed, Elk Running said, "I will not tolerate such disobedience. You have been in mourning, but that is past. I will talk to your grandparents, and you will move into my lodge."

His grip was strong. It hurt her.

"You will let me go, Wide Elk," she said deliberately.

"You will move into my lodge, and you will abandon this dream of going back to the old homeland," he ordered. "I know what some of you are plotting. It is not to be. The army is vast and powerful. They have singing wires that can tell soldiers many miles away where you are, and the soldiers will surround you and kill you. Many forts will send hundreds of soldiers to hunt you down. Little Wolf and Dull Knife only dream of what is past and gone forever, Rides a Crow. The way of the white man is the future. I will be prosperous here. I know their ways, and I will build a future here. You will not regret the choice to abandon this wild scheme I have heard about. You will remain here with me as my wife."

He had relaxed his grip as he talked, and she jerked her arm free.

"The spirits of our people would be ashamed to hear you talk, Wide Elk. The People were given those lands by the Great Spirit—all of them. The white man and his railroads may be coming, and the day of The People and the buffalo may be ending. But it will *not* end while The People live in this squalid place where warriors turn to stringy fat as they wait for food rations and grow cabbages. What do I care about being prosperous, when all around me I see the soul of The People shriveling in captivity?"

"You are being foolish. You always had strange ideas. You have no parents. I can convince your grandparents what I wish, and I can tell the council of elders what I please. The soldiers will back me up. Now do as I say, for a wife should be obedient."

He reached for her to take hold of her again, as though she were already his property.

Rides a Crow drew the knife from her belt, and Elk Running jumped back in surprise and alarm. She fought to control her temper.

"From the Night the Living Rode with the Dead, I have run, and run, and run away from those who hate The People," she said. "I will not take one more step except toward my home, the one the Great Spirit whom white men call God—when it suits them—has carved out for us in the land where I was born. I will fight for our lands until my last breath. If you wish to swallow dust with the ration-day beef and hear flies buzz around your head instead of the call of the eagle, then your path is set for you, but it is not mine. You are of The People, Elk Running. I do not wish to hurt you, but I shall go to no man's lodge except in the homeland of my people, and I shall not stay in this place unless I am dead. So, if you wish to stop me, you must draw your knife, and we shall fight to the death. Otherwise, let me pass, for I am a Spirit Walker and The People need me."

As she talked, the spirit radiating from her made her seem larger than life to the young man. He felt shallow and ashamed as she spoke. Saying nothing, he looked downward, as though the dusty soil held an answer for him.

Rides a Crow looked at her deflated suitor. "There is no profit to a man with a trading post if he has traded his soul," she said softly. "When the day dawns, Elk Running, I hope your spirit carries you to join us."

She did not wait for a reply but slowly moved away, leaving Elk Running behind.

Collins was rudely shaken awake.

"Who are you?" he asked his visitor. He reached for the pistol near his bed, but it had been moved.

"I am here to warn you, not harm you," said the man standing in the shadows. It was the voice of a white man, a different white man with strange accents in his speech. "If, as The People leave, you lift a finger to stop them, you will regret the day for the rest of your life."

Startled, Collins said, "If they leave, the army will kill them. This is the only place they are safe. Once they leave, they will be hunted down and exterminated. That is what many people want. I am doing the best I can for them."

"In this place they die by inches," Hunter said. "You know about good and evil. Evil is trying to kill The People. You know it even though you tell yourself you do not. Your own conscience warns you. The warning I bring is nothing you have not told yourself. You are a pawn in a greater game, and you are being used by those who seek to destroy the Northern Cheyenne."

"I have tried to do right by both peoples and by God."

"The day will come, Agent, when the eyes of the whites will be opened to the evil they are doing today. The day may take generations to arrive, but it will come. Open yours now, or I shall close them."

The visitor spoke no more. Collins realized he was gone, but he had not heard him leave. Although dawn was hours away, he did not try to sleep. He lay awake and wondered with both great fear and admiration if what his visitor had told him was taking place was truly happening.

The white man would record the time as three a.m. on the tenth day of September, 1878, when reservation officials learned that more than three hundred Northern Cheyenne had managed to slip away from the reservation undetected. The flight had begun hours earlier, but no one had told the soldiers until dawn approached, giving The People a head start, while allowing those left behind to avoid the hard edge of the soldiers' wrath by making the first report.

Sentries would later claim a herd of wild horses had been in the area, and they had been distracted trying to chase them. Others complained that reports supposedly from the agent's office about the Arapaho and carried by a man none ever recalled seeing before that night had sent men to one side of the sprawling reservation when they were in fact needed on the other. The agent's office denied sending any such message.

In his office, Collins heard the reports. His aides believed the reports affected him so much, they paralyzed him, because his first thought was not to order pursuit or wire Washington. He would have to do that, but later. His first act was to kneel in prayer. When they asked him what he was praying for, his response mystified them.

"I pray that, if these Northern Cheyenne are acting at the behest of the devil, if their ways are an abomination before the Lord, and if they flee to cause bloodshed, that the wrath of a

106

righteous God be visited upon them," he said. "I also pray that, if they are true and faithful children of God in a way unknown to me, if it is true their purpose for leaving here is to live at peace, God will hold them and protect them. May God deliver them into a land they can possess until the end of the age and ensure that, like those led by Moses to their Promised Land, they will dwell with the Lord forever."

North of the Darlington Agency, September 10, 1878
The People exulted. Few of them expected to leave Darlington without a fight. The spirit horses had picked out a path, which Hunter communicated to Rides a Crow. She then told Little Wolf about the path, which was not the most direct route. That would be the first place the soldiers searched. The spirit horses' path offered the best protection for women and children in case soldiers followed. The new path used some of an old Cheyenne trail.

For hours they walked, always looking back. As the sun rose high and then began to sink, however, no one pursued them.

The spirit horses rode back to Darlington, for they could fan out to see when and how The People would be followed. Traveling as a wolf, Hunter moved north along the route the spirit horses suggested, fearing evil would be unleashed by either those who were aware of the escape or those who followed Rheged and were, he knew, roaming the Plains to cause trouble.

Hunter had moved alone through the day and into the night, finding no trap had been prepared and that, despite his fears, no one from the north had come to block the way of The People. He wondered if the agent had alerted the army immediately, or if he had waited.

As he traveled, he smelled meat cooking, and only then realized how long it had been since last he ate. He stealthily approached the fire, which was the only light for miles of the black, flat expanse of the land. One man sat, as though unaware he was no longer alone.

"Join me, spirit wolf," said the Northern Cheyenne man sitting by the fire without turning his head. "Meat is set for you, for you must have traveled far. There is a robe for your warmth."

For a moment, Hunter felt a flood of fear. Was this a follower of Rheged? The clan leader had been quiet of late, although Hunter had sensed evil taking shape beyond the horizon. He knew The People would need to fight whatever forces Rheged could muster as well as the blue soldiers and the men summoned by Fairfax before they reached their homeland.

Yet this man radiated no evil. Taller than most Cheyenne, he possessed the build of a young warrior.

"I am known as Dead Face," the man said. "The spirit winds speak to me. I know The People are near. I felt their joy and have come to find them. I know spirit horses were near. I have heard of a wolf that went with The People. Welcome."

Hunter changed into human form and moved into the fire's glow. He slipped into the robe.

The man sitting across from him had a young warrior's body, but a face terribly scarred and lined by age. His right cheek bore the long, narrow mark of a burn, as though someone had held hot metal to his face. His left was scarred in the same manner. Both cheeks bore white marks where old gashes had been gouged.

"A bayonet," the man said. "It amused the soldiers to heat it and brand my face. Then they cut me with it. They wanted to know where The People hid. It was in the year when the white fool Fetterman died, and they wanted revenge. They thought a boy would talk, but they were wrong. They learned nothing from me. When they were through with me, my face was too hideous to be seen. It healed a little, and The People understood.

But I knew from their faces it was hard to behold me. So I have spent more time with the spirits, who judge not what is on a face, but what is behind it. I am more comfortable there."

He was silent. Hunter felt the other man's pain.

"How is it you ride now to find The People?" Hunter asked.

"I rode with Crazy Horse at the time of the Custer fight," the other man answered. "I followed him before and after, because he is in need of men who will fight and care not for their lives. In the winter, while The People were in their camp on the Rosebud, I came to find them but was captured. The soldiers talked of hanging me, of hiring me if I would vow to destroy The People, and finally of sending me to a place where bad Indians were turned to good ones. I was at Fort Robinson when Crazy Horse surrendered. Three months after they murdered him—a man stabbed him to death with a bayonet while others held his arms—I escaped. By then, The People were at the reservation with the Southern Cheyenne. I had no wish to be penned in. I rode to join Sitting Bull, for I have cousins who are Lakota. Then the spirit winds said The People were no longer going to be held for the slaughter. I have ridden as fast as I could these past days. I know The People are near. I can feel their joy and fear. I am a warrior, and my place is with my people."

Hunter asked about some the Northern Cheyenne he knew to test Dead Face. Dead Face described then all perfectly. Then he came to Rides a Crow.

The face was indeed as dead as its bearer's name proclaimed, moving not a muscle of the scarred visage. But the eyes sparkled.

"As children we were pledged. But after I was scarred, my family released hers from the pledge, so they could find a whole warrior for her. It was clear by then that I must have time away from The People. We remained friends when I visited them, for she was given a spirit gift of which she was utterly ignorant. But the spirit gift allowed her to see past the scars, as she could with the wild animals, which she would tame as pets but which would kill others who so much as looked upon them. I have thought on her. Are she and her children among those trekking north?"

"She is not married," Hunter replied. "The man she was to marry was killed at the Greasy Grass. And she is one of those coming to her homeland. She is a Spirit Walker."

Dead Face was silent for a moment. "She is your link to The People," he said, "for you are not of us and know not our ways. I understand why I feel connected to her through you."

Hunter realized that, for the better part of a year, he had been connected to the girl's spirit. For a moment he wondered if the connection was part of some plan—being exiled to find a home. But that was a thought for a different day. Today, work needed to be done. "We leave when the fire goes out," he said.

"It is not safe to travel at night," admonished Dead Face.

"For those who might seek to bar our way, it is not," replied Hunter, tearing into the meat Dead Face offered him.

By turns gleeful and enraged when he heard that the Northern Cheyenne were on the move, Morrison Fairfax's first reaction was to curse the agent and army for not slaughtering the Indians as they fled. That would have been the perfect opportunity to rid the Plains of them and their spirit champions. Then he realized the plan he had concocted to stage false attacks would be enhanced.

With the Northern Cheyenne on the loose, anything Rheged and his men did would easily be attributed to the Indians. On the Plains, out in the open, there would be time before the snow fell to exterminate them once and for all. Yes, this was not the way he had foreseen it, but he would soon reach his goal in spite of unexpected happenings! Now if only the army would throw every one of its thousands of soldiers at them!

He started scribbling off telegrams demanding people do just that. He was powerful. They would listen! If the army moved fast, the Northern Cheyenne would be history by winter.

Morning found Dead Face and Hunter moving along the irregular course of Turkey Creek to a place known locally as Turkey Springs. With The People out of sight, Hunter was free to travel as a man.

"This is the place," Hunter said.

"The place for what?" asked Dead Face.

"Did you fight soldiers very often?"

"At the Greasy Grass. I was with the party that fought against the soldiers after they attacked the village, but there was little to do. Custer's men were so few and so disorganized, it was not a battle so much as a slaughter. I fought in raids."

"I was in the British army once upon a time in a place called the Crimea. It was a terrible place." The army had been a place of refuge after Wales, after Ireland, after Scotland, and before London. "In a place called India, I learned the ground is your ally or your enemy. I believe this ground can be our ally."

Unlike the flatter land to the south, the ground around Turkey Springs was uneven.

"You know how white men fight," Hunter said. "They march in lines and fire in volleys. Look at these cedar and pine trees. Look at these rocky outcroppings that will make it impossible for them to ride in formation. Look at the higher ground there."

The light dawned on Dead Face.

"A man behind a tree or rock can have twenty men in his sights while they have no one in theirs," Dead Face replied. "And I have just the thing."

He rode one horse and led another, which carried a pair of awkwardly packed bundles. Dismounting, he walked to the second horse and showed Hunter rifles and ammunition.

"When I spent months at Fort Robinson, I learned where they kept everything. I promised if ever I was free, I would help myself to the soldiers' supplies." Something like a smile moved the dead muscles in the warrior's face. "I shall look forward to this."

Hunter left Dead Face at Turkey Springs with instructions to find the best spots to shoot at the soldiers.

"It is not important how many we wound or kill," Hunter instructed him. "We cannot lose a single warrior, because there are so few of us. The army will think it is chasing a group of women and children and a few warriors who have nothing with which to fight back. If we can hit them hard, the way a bee stings a bear on the nose, they will retreat. Although their cavalry can outrun us, if we can hurt them enough the first time they come upon us, they will give us several days' start on them."

"You do not think they will let The People go?"

Hunter thought of Rheged, of Fairfax, and of the evil hammering against the Northern Cheyenne.

"No. The men fighting The People want them all dead. The soldiers are only pawns, Dead Face. Even if they wished to let you go—for some respect fellow warriors—they cannot."

"Then it will be a fight to the death."

"It will not be one battle, Dead Face. This is not like the Custer fight. I do not know how to stop them from coming after The People. Evil and hate surround us, as do the forts of the soldiers." He stopped. To worry about tomorrow was to overlook what needed to be done in order to survive that long.

"But for now, we must focus on surviving. Prepare."

With that, he changed back to a wolf and loped off, pushing as hard as he could for fear time was not on the side of The People.

The sun broke across the jagged plain. Prairie grass swayed in the wind, pale now as the moon began to turn its hard face toward the land. The People had too few blankets, too little food, and too few weapons to fight their way all the way back to their homes. Rides a Crow recalled the awful journey of the previous summer, when they had marched in heat and dust she feared would swallow them whole.

Yet she breathed deeply this morning, for there was not one blue soldier in sight. No guards. No prison. Long Face, a warrior, had been shouted down for taking with him a wool cape from a soldier's quarters. He discarded it, even though it would have been warm on the cold nights to come.

The People wanted nothing of the army with them now. There might be death on the wind. There would be freedom. She breathed in deeply once more. The Great Spirit had created The People to live this way—free on the Plains. And if they were destined to die fighting, it would be better than living another day as prisoners.

Rides a Crow had risen in the darkness, for her day would be spent as though she were a leader—helping the oldest, soothing the fears of children, buoying the spirits of the doubtful, and always pushing them to put as much distance as possible between them and the soldiers. She knew the soldiers would come, sooner or later. She needed to connect with the spirits she could feel across the Plains—for flesh and blood would not win the race to their homeland. The People would survive only as long as their spirit refused to give in.

Turning away to begin her work, she heard and felt the drumming of hooves. At first she feared this signaled the approach of a scout for the soldiers. Despite Hunter's assurance she need not fear pursuit this day, she knew she would never feel safe until they were home.

What she saw instead of a scout was beyond anything she knew. She lost herself: stepping away from the time and space of her body to marvel at the horse approaching—one lone horse, mane whipping against the wind and outlined against the light blue of the early morning sky before being silhouetted against the sun as it drew close.

She had heard whites talk of the power and majesty of buildings and leaders and armies. This was the power and majesty of the Great Spirit, galloping free as horses had done from the dawn of time and would continue doing until the end of anything that could be called living.

The horse slowed a bit, then made a noise and picked up its speed, running fast and straight for Rides a Crow. She dimly understood she was being called, but, like hearing words when under the water of a lake, she could not understand.

The horse stopped a few feet from Rides a Crow. The girl walked to it, arm outstretched. The horse waited, as though welcoming her touch. Finally, she stroked the glossy black horse. Then she understood without fully comprehending. A spirit horse!

"He did not tell you to expect me?" came the musical Spirit Talk voice of Talks to Horses sounding inside Rides a Crow's head.

"I do not know . . . I am . . ." the girl fumbled.

"Our friend the wolf has no manners," Talks to Horses said brusquely. "Do you understand me?"

"I hear you," she said wondering how this could be.

"Stop looking at me as though I had two heads. You have sung to spirit horses for many years, Rides a Crow. Did you think we did not exist? Then why did you sing to us?"

The girl offered no reply other than a few stammered words.

"We shall have time to understand each other later, Rides a Crow. Hunter told me to look for you. The soldiers had not yet left the fort as of the night, but they will leave soon. Now they are gathering what they need for a long chase. The wolf asked

us to watch for them. The People will have another day of walking safely. I doubt there will be more than one more day after
that before the soldiers catch up. No one else is chasing you.
Tell Hunter when you see him." A pause. "And see if you can
teach him the proper way to behave!"

With that, the horse galloped away to the south, leaving Rides
a Crow wondering what had been real, what a vision, and what
perhaps a dream from a mind that had slept too little.

As The People walked, she thought about what she had been
told. They had a day to prepare. She found her grandparents.
Sun Raven once again used the stick the white soldier had given
her on the road south. Her grandparents told stories as they
walked and sang to the others. She wanted to warn them of
what was coming, and to take shelter, but she could not make
herself ruin their new happiness.

"I am near," she heard Hunter in her mind.

"The spirit horse said the soldiers are a day or so behind us,"
she said back in thoughts.

"Good."

The one word surprised her.

Hunter explained, "We shall have a reception committee
prepared."

Uncertain how to reply, she dimly understood his meaning.

"All will be well, Rides a Crow," came Hunter's thoughts.
"Their spirits lean on yours. Stay strong."

By late afternoon, Hunter was among them, walking as a
wolf. He told her what needed to be done.

"The women and children, and those who are too old to
fight, will be safe. You should stay with them."

"No."

"The People need you."

"I am not a little girl, Hunter. I am not stupid. If this battle is lost, there will be no second chance to save The People. I will not go back to the reservation. If my body mixes with the earth in this place, so be it. I will not let them try to cage my spirit. Never again."

Early the next morning, they came to Turkey Springs. Rides a Crow was helping one elderly woman up a series of steps carved into rocks by someone many generations ago. Movement was awkward because the space was small and the steps were big. Her hands on the woman's waist, Rides a Crow tried to lift her.

"Take my hands, grandmother," came a resonant, kind voice above them.

The voice could only come from one face. She turned, almost losing her grip on the woman, who slipped and was pulled to safety by Dead Face. His teeth showed in what passed for a smile.

"I regret the death of Horse Walking," Dead Face told her after pulling her, too, up to his level. "He was one of the first to fight back when the Custer men charged the village. He and Dark Hawk died as honored warriors."

She did not want to talk about the dead. "Where have you been?"

"I rode with Crazy Horse while there was a battle to fight. I was in the jail while The People were near Fort Robinson. I escaped, but The People were already at Darlington. I went to Sitting Bull and heard the spirit call to help The People. I met the spirit wolf. I have been preparing for the soldiers. Let me show you, so you can tell Little Wolf, for you stand high in his confidence."

Together they walked through the trees and rocks as Dead Face explained how rifles and ammunition were set out in places where The People would be safe, so the greatest possible damage could be inflicted on the soldiers with the least possible risk.

As they walked, Rides a Crow felt her spirit lighten. Dead Face had been her close friend as a child, and her pledged husband before he was taken and scarred. Although she understood the wounds he had suffered might make him difficult to look at—and a disfigured husband was not to be prized—she had always felt his spirit was akin to hers. She felt whole, as if something she did not even know was missing had been restored.

Dead Face looked upon the girl he knew as a friend of every animal that ever came into camp and saw how she had grown in authority and spirit. When she spoke of the homeland, he realized he also shared her dream, and that, in sharing it, there was a brightness in the day that had not been there before.

When all was said that needed to be shared, they still stood together.

"I do not know how to shoot a rifle," said Rides a Crow. "I want to learn."

"Fighting is for warriors."

"And what have I been these past months, Dead Face?"

Again his teeth flashed in what was, for him, a smile. "Then I shall teach you, if you can learn to use this better than you did the bow Long Knife made you."

Recalling the brother she had lost brought her a stab of pain. Yet she also felt joy in the memory of the bow he made her, of the thinnest wood. The bow fractured when she tried to use it. Dead Face, then known as Bear Paw, and Long Knife convinced her she had destroyed a bow handed down from her ancestors, thus horrifying her.

She laughed out loud at the memory. Others, seeing the girl who helped Little Wolf laugh as she looked over the place where they were clearly planning to fight, saw in her laughter a sign that the Northern Cheyenne were not living in fear, and they walked with greater confidence and speed.

By nightfall, the women and children had left Turkey Springs, along with those too old for the fight but who would help forage for supplies. Dull Knife led those, for he was the master at finding paths others might not follow and reading the land ahead. He and Little Wolf agreed that The People must keep moving, for, if the fight at Turkey Springs failed, and the army rolled over them, The People's dream of reaching their home would die. If it succeeded, it would buy them time to outstrip their pursuers.

Flies the Hawk had been adamant about staying. He had stolen a Sharps carbine from a soldier weeks ago and smuggled it with him on the trek. Sun Raven would not leave without him.

"His fingers are too stiff to load a gun by himself," she argued. "As with all old men, if left on his own, he will flirt with the young girls and not attend to his work. I must be with him."

Rides a Crow knew her grandparents' days were limited. If she wanted to have the freedom to die with The People instead of living as a captive, she understood she must grant her grandfather's wish.

Still, she wanted to ask for a blessing as Dead Face walked among the remaining People, posting some in places where they could shoot from cover and others in places where they would serve as the main line of defense against the soldiers. Her eyes met those of Flies the Hawk. She saw in his eyes everything she had been taught about The People, about living free and living in the path of the Great Spirit.

"It is a good day to fight," she told him.

"It is a good day to win," he replied.

CHAPTER EIGHT

Turkey Springs, September 1878

Little Wolf allowed Dead Face to speak to the assembled warriors.

"When we would fight the Shoshone or the Crow, we would charge them to show our bravery," Dead Face told the roughly one hundred warriors gathered to fight what might be the last battle of the Northern Cheyenne. "When I fought with Crazy Horse against Custer, we charged at them, for we were a swarm, and they were few. Today's fight will be very different."

There were enough guns for most of the warriors, between the good ones Dead Face had stolen and others the Cheyenne had smuggled out of the agency. Ammunition, however, was limited.

"We cannot kill all the soldiers. We want to make them turn back. White soldiers fight in different ways. The longer we hold on here, the more time the women and children will have to get far away, and the more likely it is that the soldiers will leave us," he said, looking startled as Rides a Crow appeared at his side.

"In the eyes of the Great Spirit, all of you today are heroes. The People need you to fight as the soldiers do—with caution and craftiness. When you are gone, there will be no more warriors. Let this be a glorious victory, but let it not be the last stand of the Northern Cheyenne people. The spirit guides and protects us, but, this day, we must do the work ourselves. We must remind the soldiers that they fight The People, and that

The People are mighty," she said.

One warrior raised his rifle and made an exclamation. One vowed to fight until the sun stood still. Another exclaimed, "It is a good day to die."

"No!" called out Rides a Crow, who now held her hands as wide as she could and stepped ahead of the leaders. Little Wolf and the warriors were spellbound, as though a spirit was talking. She told them what Hunter had so often told her even during days of misery when his words seemed like a mockery.

"It is a good day to live!"

Talks to Horses was the only spirit horse remaining with the warriors. The rest went ahead. That way, if the coming battle went badly, more horses besides the old and tired ones the Cheyenne were given at the agency and the ones warriors brought with them could be used. Talks to Horses told Hunter and Rides a Crow what she had seen.

"There are about twenty dozen soldiers coming," Talks to Horses said. "I did not count for certain, but they will be here this afternoon. They are coming by way of the Cimarron."

The good news was received with blank faces, because neither of them had traveled this way before. Talks to Horses explained. "The way they come will be along a path where the only standing water is so bitter, no one can drink it. Not only will the men be thirsty, but the horses will also be thirsty," she said.

Hunter added, "And thirsty horses are restive, meaning the soldiers will have to detach one man in every four to hold horses. That will be hard for them, too. Uneasy animals will make for uneasy men."

He explained the situation to Dead Face, who, like Rides a Crow, could share thoughts with him.

"In the heat, if they have not had access to fresh water in a day, they will want the water from the springs when they arrive.

If they are denied it, they will not be able to pursue us—or even remain in place—for very long. Even if our men with rifles never hit anyone, if they keep the soldiers from getting water, they will win a victory."

"They shall not drink," Dead Face said impassively, with a certainty Hunter knew meant that the army was facing a challenge far worse than anything tired soldiers could ever have dreamed of fighting.

Rides a Crow was nervous. Although she understood everything she had been told about the rugged country The People would defend, her memory flew back to the snowy camp she had been told was safe. There, The People had been defeated, never to rise again.

What if The People had, as the missionaries said, sinned and were being punished by loss of their land? What if this battle to come was to be as one-sided for the whites as the fight against Custer had been for the Lakota and Cheyenne? What if the men waiting for battle were the last flower of the Northern Cheyenne? Their deaths would fall on her head for having helped The People escape.

Earlier, while the soldiers were still far off, Dead Face had shown her how to fire a rifle. He had given her one of the new ones he'd brought and enjoined her to stay with him. She felt no anxiety coming from him, only intensity as he reminded the warriors the battle was for The People, not for their own honor.

There! The first uniforms. A gun cocked.

"Unless there is a fat rabbit in your sights, do not fire," Dead Face called out. "And if you hit it, I claim half!"

Some of the warriors chuckled.

Rides a Crow found her throat was dry. So many uniforms. More of them than of The People.

"It is not the numbers that count; it is their will to fight," came Hunter's thoughts to her. "The spirits did not bring you here only to abandon you."

The transformation in Little Wolf fascinated Rides a Crow. She knew he had almost reached sixty winters. He, like Dull Knife, had agreed long ago that few choices remained to them, other than surrender. The People had no food, no shelter, and were beset by the army at every turn. Both had come to believe that the future of The People was to live in the upside-down world created by white settlers, because that world would come to pass no matter what they did. Accusations that they had betrayed The People flew fast and furiously during the march to Darlington, and in the days of misery that followed. Although Rides a Crow had seen little of Dull Knife at the agency, she knew it took great courage for a man who was nearing seventy winters to turn his back on the comforts he might have enjoyed there in order to begin a privations-filled journey of weeks, if not months. She had seen the older chief briefly on the march, and his step appeared almost youthful.

Little Wolf was much the same. On this day, Rides a Crow knew he had spoken to every warrior, and he was the one Cheyenne who refused to take cover. Now, he looked relaxed and without a care in the world as he prepared to mount his horse.

"They will expect to talk, because they like to talk," Little Wolf told Rides a Crow. "They do not understand that I will talk their talk no longer."

"What if there is treachery?" asked one warrior as Little Wolf prepared to lead his horse to the flat land below the canyon they were defending.

"Then I will die with my face to the enemy and my soul flying in the wind," he said easily. He nodded at Rides a Crow and Dead Face and departed.

Rides a Crow saw soldiers taking positions. Then there was

Little Wolf. Voices came to her, but not in words. Then a shot. Another! A rush of warriors emerged from hiding and charged at the soldiers, who fell back firing their rifles.

Little Wolf and the Northern Cheyenne with him also fell back after a confused melee where flashes of gunfire showed through the dust and dirt, but Rides a Crow could see little.

"Stop!" Dead Face called to his men shooting. "There will be a better time."

That time came quickly. The People saw troops mounting horses.

Dead Face spoke quietly to Rides a Crow. "Aim at a rock or something else at the edge of the water. When I tell you to fire the gun, pull the trigger. Fire five times. Then stop. Reload the rifle, but do not shoot again unless I say so."

She saw his teeth flash.

"What kind of man trains his woman to be a warrior? We must talk on this later." He almost laughed as she reacted to his words. "When we are at the Tongue River, Snapping Turtle, and I need a woman in my lodge, there will be much to talk about." He used the nickname he had given her when they were children because of her refusal to let anyone win an argument in which she participated.

Before she could speak, he was gone. Rides a Crow raised the rifle to her shoulder. She saw the cavalry begin walking the horses. She watched them gather speed. For a moment, she was afraid.

"Aim as I told you!" Dead Face called out to everyone.

Rides a Crow wondered if his command was meant for only her. Focusing on a gray rock in the shape of a circle, she waited. Waited. Oh, what was happening?

"Now!"

At the edge of her vision she saw the horse entering, and she pulled the trigger over and over. Around her, the deafening noise of rifles roared.

After she finished the number of shots she was told to fire, she put the gun away. She looked across the creek to see how many soldiers had crossed it. She saw none. They had not crossed at all. Two horses lay beside the water, as did one man. The rest had retreated to where they had come, intimidated by the gunfire from the Cheyenne.

She saw Little Wolf walking from tree to tree, the most exposed man in the Cheyenne camp, encouraging the warriors.

"Is it over?" she asked Dead Face.

"It has only started," he replied.

Before darkness fell, the soldiers again tried to attack. Two parties that sought water were driven back from the spring's clear water. The warriors waited, restless. This was not how a Cheyenne warrior fought. Some of them asked if they should go to the springs and stop soldiers trying to get water under the cover of night. Dead Face said there was no need. Rides a Crow was certain he was making a mistake, but she knew not how to say that.

Then a scream from below emerged. A growl smote her ears. She almost laughed. Who needed the eyes of warriors and their weapons to guard the water when there was a different kind of hunter to do the task for them? She knew that at least three other parties seeking water were turned back.

By morning, the warriors, who rested off and on during the darkness, were ready to resume the fight. The soldiers, who had been kept awake with alarms, and who were beginning another day without water, hunkered down out of range. The aggressive posture they had projected when they arrived was clearly gone now. Yells came from their camp. Dead Face warned the warriors that the soldiers would make one last effort.

After their last attack was easily turned back, he grabbed Rides a Crow's arm and signaled for the others to join them.

"Follow me."

Even as some soldiers had attacked, others withdrew, carrying the few wounded from the first day. Dead Face led The People to a spot where they had a clear view of the soldiers, even though the range was too far for their weapons to reach.

"Take turns shooting," he told them. "Do not shoot often, and shoot when you think you can hit something. They are getting ready to run away, and if they think we will follow them, they will run faster. Do not waste ammunition, and take no chances."

A line of retreating soldiers came into view, becoming thicker now that their final charge had been repelled. The warriors wanted Rides a Crow to take the first shot as a sign of the honor they held for her.

"You are the Wise Woman with a gun," one of them told her. "You speak with the spirits and are a true Spirit Walker. You have helped save The People."

Rides a Crow crawled to the edge of a cliff. She had never killed a man. She was no warrior. Gazing down at the men who had come to obliterate her people and drag them back to their prison and kill her dreams, she realized from observing the soldiers at Darlington that white men were men like any other men. She had sought to kill in anger when she was attacked, but never like this; this felt wrong. But the soldiers had come in response to the evil being scripted, and they could not be allowed to prevail.

She closed one eye and sighted the rifle on one man riding his horse. She pulled the trigger, and, as the noise of the shot echoed around her, she saw him fall.

The warriors were both exhausted and exhilarated as the large fire burned. Although Rides a Crow guessed the soldier she shot was wounded and not dead, from the way his fellow soldiers bundled him onto a horse, the warriors with her magnified her act.

"From what I hear, you shot a man from ten miles away. At least," Hunter chided her.

"Where are you?" she thought back to him. He explained that Talks to Horses had followed the dispirited soldiers to be sure they were retreating, while he had come on the trail taken by the women and children.

"There will be more soldiers and more fights, but this fight was important," he said. "Dull Knife and the spirit horses will find a route no soldier can predict. While the soldiers search this way and that, you will keep getting closer to your home."

Home. The People had won a battle. The People were going home. That which she'd believed impossible was happening around her and through her. The spirits and The People had won a victory. Could they be strong enough to withstand everything that would next befall them? She looked up at the endless stars, as endless as the enemies they must face. Her people must be strong enough.

Rheged had been taken by surprise when the Cheyenne broke out of their agency. Soon he and those with him, after causing some depredations that could be laid at the feet of the Cheyenne, rode from ranch to ranch, from town to town, igniting flames of hate. This hate would send farmers, ranchers, soldiers, and anyone old enough to shoot a gun on the trail of the Indians.

Fairfax used his telegraph to demand that whatever fool failed to kill the Indians at Turkey Springs be driven from the army. He demanded that action be taken. Soon, across the vast Department of the Missouri commanded by Civil War failure John Pope, every fort was told to put out scouts. A dispatch of armed troopers followed every sighting of what might possibly be the Cheyenne. The army made the telegraph come alive with alarms, while railroad cars were made ready to send troopers from place to place on a moment's notice. Panic incited by Indians, who only wanted to go home, turned their innocent mission into one aiming to slaughter every settler in Kansas. Hundreds of soldiers rode and marched, waiting for their chance to butcher Indians in the name of glory.

The spirit horses, as they scouted for patrols, left their own wide trails. The army often followed those trails instead of the actual trail of The People.

As Kansas screamed for retribution against actions real and imagined, and the army scurried across the Plains, the Northern Cheyenne pressed on. The pace and strain were starting to take a toll on them. Months of poor eating and sickness had left The People unprepared for the effort to walk miles a day on limited food. Some began to believe a journey whose end might be many moons away was going to end in failure. Others were simply too physically frail to maintain the pace on a few kernels of dried corn a day. Yet, as they swallowed their doubts and fears—along with far too little food—they refused to abandon their dream that at the end of the trail, they would rest in their homeland.

Miles to the south, those who remained behind at the Darlington Agency listened to stories about the escapees with a mix of fear, joy, and envy. Stray bits of gossip came to their ears, but all they knew for certain was that, as every day passed without the Northern Cheyenne returning in chains, the band led by Dull Knife and Little Wolf gained a step closer to being free. And far from the eyes of the soldiers, both Northern and Southern Cheyenne lofted prayers to the Great Spirit to protect those walking the gauntlet the Plains had become.

Hunter felt the Indians' hunger, but in late fall, the Plains were not active with game to hunt. For him, there was no question about whether the spirits wanted The People to leave the agency. He understood this was a journey where the blood of some would seal the future for those who survived. No spirits could quell the fires raging around The People. He needed to trust in what he barely understood and hope it would not fail those who trusted him.

On this day, an impulse he could not name directed him to wander off the trail taken by The People. After walking about a half mile, his wolf nose smelled a mixture of dead animals, burned wood, and water. A doused fire! Hunter listened closely.

"You sure about this?" one man asked another.

"Heard it myself. A hundred dollars in gold for each Cheyenne you can prove you killed. Man in Colorado named Fairfax. What we got there in hides is nothing next to them Cheyenne. Fella riding the camps told me. Said there's hundreds of 'em somewhere out here. These here guns will get 'em, and we won't have to get close enough to get scalped. Don't matter if we only get a few; we can be rich!"

Hunter poked his head around the stump of a tree hit by lightning years ago. Buffalo hunters, with a haul of animal carcasses left to rot because the hunters only wanted the hides.

"Dunno, Shep," said another voice. "I hear them Cheyenne been slaughtering people. Us three against five hundred? Seems like long odds. Risky. I say we stay here and skin what we got. Won't make near as much, but we won't end up dead."

"Won't end up rich, neither."

Hunter saw the three men now: bearded hunters camping by their haul of dead animals. Not evil in and of themselves, these were simply men tempted by an offer from one who truly was evil. Fairfax would need to be dealt with, but not yet. When The People were safe enough, he could leave them and deal with Fairfax once and for all, no matter how long it took him.

The buffalo hunters kept talking. If Hunter went back to

fetch warriors, more men would die. Already, it was clear the young men who went out to find food and came back with cows, horses, and other provisions had disregarded Little Wolf's demand they not kill settlers. Survival was a brutal business. These buffalo hunters did not need to die, when there was another way.

He waited until they were gathered in one spot, having drawn a rough map in the dirt to determine where the Indians might be.

"Shep!" one man called in fear as a growling wolf stalked into the camp. The men had unsaddled their horses, and their massive buffalo guns lay on the far side of the camp. Their gun belts and pistols had been piled near the now-doused fire.

The man called Shep dashed for his pistol, but the wolf was faster than he. The hunters cringed as they heard bone crack as the wolf's jaws bit down on Shep's hand. Then the wolf released the man and stared at the two uninjured hunters. The wolf motioned toward the Plains.

One of the other men carried a knife in his boot. He and the wolf locked stares. The hunter moved quickly, but the animal was faster. By the time his hand grasped the hilt of his knife, the wolf was on him, ripping into the man's arm, then moving away out of range.

The animal again gestured toward the Plains.

"Fellas, I think this thing wants the meat," the only uninjured hunter said. His voice trembled after witnessing two men whom he knew to be fast and hard injured in an instant by an animal that could have easily killed them. "That what you want? The meat?"

The wolf waited.

The third hunter helped his two injured friends toward their horses. The wolf moved to stay between the hunters and their gear, which included their weapons and saddles. They mounted bareback. As the wolf lunged, the fearful horses bolted.

Hunter watched the men go. They might return, and perhaps bring others, but he had seen Northern Cheyenne hunting parties skin a buffalo carcass and take what they needed. The Cheyenne worked with brutal efficiency born of life on the Plains. By the time the hunters returned, if they returned, the Northern Cheyenne would be far from this place.

Rides a Crow had exchanged few words with Dull Knife and was reluctant to confront the chief, no matter what Hunter told her to do.

"You are Rides a Crow," Dull Knife said, when she moved the horse she rode to be next to him, for no longer did she walk, nor did her grandparents. "You are a Spirit Walker."

"The spirits talk to me, Morning Star," she said, using the chief's Cheyenne name and not the one given him by the Lakota and used by whites and most others. "There is a great store of buffalo meat nearby. The meat can fill the bellies of The People for many miles." She pointed to the southeast.

"How do you know this?" said Dull Knife, who knew every minute they were on the Plains without moving north was a minute when the army might catch them.

"The spirits told me. There will be heaps of dead animals beside a tree broken by lightning, near a black rock that is in the shape of a mountain and a gulley that would hold water if it was a rainy season."

He studied her for several moments. He then turned to the warriors with him.

"We shall rest here for now," he said, declaring a rare daytime halt to the march. He then appointed several warriors to go with Rides a Crow. "Go quickly and do as she tells you. If the spirits have blessed us, fire a rifle four times in succession, and we shall meet you at the place where this Spirit Walker says there is food."

The column of walkers and horses halted as Rides a Crow and her companions rode off. Word filtered through The People that the Spirit Walker had found buffalo. Soon, the group heard four gunshots.

Lowering his head for a silent moment, Dull Knife then raised it to the sky with his arms spread wide. For there to be buffalo now, when all their hunts at Darlington had proved no more buffalo existed, was clearly the work of the spirits. As Dull Knife turned the group toward the sound of the rifles, he heard behind him the chants of The People, who knew yet another miracle had been worked, and that they would not die of hunger as they walked toward home.

CHAPTER NINE

Western Kansas, September 1878

"No!"

The People had gathered by two places the white people called the Big and Little Sandy Creeks, in the place they called Kansas. The spirit horses had warned of more soldiers coming. Flies the Hawk had told Rides a Crow that he and others whose days were many planned to use the rifles they had and hold off the soldiers gaining on The People.

Sun Raven put her right arm on the left shoulder of Rides a Crow as she slowly turned the girl to face her. Rides a Crow's fists clenched at her hips as she had shouted out her reaction to the plan.

"You do know, do you not, that these warrior children never grow out of being boys?" Sun Raven said softly, swallowing with some difficulty. "Your grandfather is still trying to impress me after all of these years by showing what a brave man he is. So are the rest of them. You might change the path of the sun more easily than you can the ways of an old man who must prove he is young."

"But this is wrong! They will be killed!"

Flies the Hawk snorted.

"The soldiers' guns have been pointed at me often, and they have not killed me yet," he said.

"Little Wolf will not allow it! I will tell him not to permit it!"

"One curse of the old, Rides a Crow, is that we often do not hear what we are told," Flies the Hawk told her.

"But . . ."

"Young one, some day you will be old. The day will come when your body sings of its weariness to lie down, when it tells you your breaths are numbered, and you see in the stars the pathway to your home. That is the day you will pass on to The People how they are to remember you. We will not be remembered as those who dropped in the dirt, but the Elders Who Stopped the Soldiers. We are warriors, Rides a Crow. We have a duty to The People. When I was young, I was given many good portions of meat because I was a warrior. Now I must stand and be worthy of those days."

Rides a Crow felt the loss as though it had already happened, as though her grandfather's spirit had walked out of a lodge, and all she could do was see him through the flap as it closed. She would not weep and wail.

He was right. She was a warrior.

"Then shoot straight, Grandfather, and know that as long as the sun shines upon me and the wind blows across this place, I shall be proud to be the granddaughter of Flies the Hawk." She turned to Sun Raven. "Come, Grandmother."

Sun Raven softly raised her left hand and touched a scar on the right cheek of Rides a Crow—a scar that resulted when the girl had tried at age four to ride a horse.

"This old man's fingers are stiff and so useless that he will never be able to load the rifle, so someone will have to do it for him. He has never been able to manage without me, no matter what he tells himself. Do you not recall I have told you this before?"

Unsure of Sun Raven's meaning, Rides a Crow frowned at her grandmother.

"Oh, Granddaughter, Flies the Hawk is as helpless as a child without me when there is work to be done. It is also the way of warriors when they gather that they behave terribly, and I will not allow him to injure himself doing something stupid as if he were a boy again."

Rides a Crow knew her eyes held tears as she finally understood.

Her grandmother spoke again. "The earth is the earth, child. If we become one with this earth here in this place, it is the earth where the horses of The People rode, where the spirits of The People live, and the earth I have lived with all of these years. The People must keep moving. Coming back for those who have left behind what the earth claims as its own and whose true spirits are on their journey to the Milky Way is a foolish risk. The People have been the gift the Great Spirit gave us; it is with glad hearts we give back to The People."

Rides a Crow had nothing to say. She felt humbled in her grandparents' presence.

"Do the women plan to talk all the night through, or can the warriors get to their work?" Flies the Hawk broke in.

Rides a Crow saw his eyes gleam with wetness. She reached out to hug them both, regardless of what might be proper.

"Go with the spirits," she said as her grandparents joined a group of others—all old men, long gray, who, along with a few women who walked with them, were soon chiding each other as though they were boys.

And Rides a Crow realized that if she should live until time ended, she would never see the likes of them again as they waded into the tall grass, until it met them and soon covered them.

Soldiers once again attacked and once again were driven off. Little Wolf and Dead Face made sure warriors preserved their lives, even if doing so made victory over the soldiers less than complete.

Rides a Crow reached out to Hunter, who traveled with The People only in his wolf form for fear the Cheyenne would fire upon any white man. She told him about the elders.

"I need to know," she said. "I know, but I need to have it seen. They should be buried. I cannot say words over them. I cannot perform rituals for them. Will you do what you can for them?"

Hunter agreed. The spirit horses had not found any soldiers within three days of the Cheyenne. Thanks to the warriors who had stolen horses, most of the Northern Cheyenne could ride now, allowing them to move faster. Although he knew the soldiers and settlers vastly outnumbered the Cheyenne, he also assumed they would be dispersed over such a large area, they would never be able to bring the full brunt of their strength against the Cheyenne.

At least one more battle lay ahead. Running skirmishes would also take place in the days and weeks to come. As Dull Knife charted an irregular course through uneven ground designed to evade pursuit, however, Hunter started to believe the Cheyenne might make it out of Kansas in one piece. That is, if the gathering forces he knew Rheged and Fairfax were marshaling could be outfoxed as easily as the soldiers.

The battle at the creek had cost very few their lives. The soldiers had taken away their dead. Dead horses had been left behind.

Hunter found one of the Northern Cheyenne elders. He could not recall his Cheyenne name, but he was known as Black Hat, because he always wore a battered black cavalry hat stolen long ago. There was not a mark upon him. He had simply died while waiting for the soldiers, or while fighting. He now lay face up, his hat next to him. Hunter knelt by the body, lifted it, and put the hat back on.

He saw that the Cheyenne had dispersed themselves in a

wide half circle to slow down the soldiers. Usually, this was done by skirmishers, who would then retreat. No one in this particular half circle had left. He was not surprised to see Sun Raven and Flies the Eagle in the middle of the line. Each had a rifle; both had been shot.

Voices! Two soldiers arguing.

". . . got to get back," one said over and over.

"You know how much money these dead Injuns are worth?" his companion said.

"Hollings, they ain't worth a month in the stockade."

"Loring, quit your whining. What did you think we came here for?"

"The captain said he wanted a count of the dead ones; that's all."

"We'll give him that. He never said we couldn't take a little something for ourselves. Nobody cares what we take from them."

"Hollings! You don't rob the dead! You don't cut them up for trophies, no matter what you say that man in Colorado is offering. Robbing the dead is wrong."

"They're Indians. Did you hear Williams tell about the Easterners who pay money for the trinkets they wear? Between what we can get for their scalps or fingers and what we can get for whatever they got on 'em, we can be rich."

"They're human beings."

"They are Indians that would kill anyone as soon as look at them," said Hollings. "You know what the general said. We got to kill 'em all. All of 'em! Filthy things."

"Hollings, there's an old man and old woman here. I'm not cutting off their hair. No! Let's count them and go."

"Go back to the horses, then, if you are too squeamish to do a man's work," replied Hollings. "Don't you come around asking for a share of the take!"

Without waiting for a reply, Hollings knelt over Flies the Hawk and Sun Raven. Sun Raven wore a necklace of bones and bear claws. Hollings gave it a pull, but it did not come apart. He reached for his knife to cut the necklace off when, from the corner of his eye, he realized he was not alone.

Ten feet behind him stood a rust-colored wolf, glaring malevolently at him.

"Get out of here!" Hollings shouted, shaken to have been surprised.

The animal remained standing. Its tail did not move. Its gaze bored into the soldier. Threatening.

"You can eat them when I'm done," Hollings explained. "Just want something to remember killing Indians."

The wolf took a step closer.

"Loring!"

No answer.

Hollings still had his hand on his knife. The knife sheath he wore behind his right hip was only inches from the Colt he carried at his waist. He slowly moved his hand away from the knife and toward the gun. He kept his attention on the wolf, knowing that, if he could keep the unsuspecting animal from knowing his intentions, he might add a wolf pelt to his haul.

His hand hovered over the loop of leather keeping the holster flap fastened. He licked dry lips. One drop of sweat trailed down his right temple. The wolf still stood and watched. Now!

Loring had been leading two horses with his left hand and came back in time to see his fellow trooper fire a pistol as a wolf jumped him. He drew his own pistol and sought to find a clear shot at the animal without wounding Hollings.

The wolf's teeth found Hollings's face, and the man started screaming. The wolf swept a powerful right paw across Hollings, slamming the soldier's gun arm and sending his pistol flying into the tall grass. The jaws then closed in on the arm that had held the gun. Hollings moaned and screamed and begged.

The pounding rage within Hunter demanded he tear this man into as many pieces as possible. His teeth closed in on the man's leg and whirled him off the ground only to fling him into a ledge of rocks. He then leaped upon the man for the kill.

The wolf stopped tearing at Hollings and saw Loring, who looked back over the sights of his gun.

For a moment, there was no sound other than the flies as the wolf and the soldier stood still as statues.

Loring had an unobstructed view of the animal. Instead of firing, he watched as the wolf deliberately stepped off Hollings, who still lived. The wolf's gaze bored through Loring; the soldier could not have fired if commanded to do so. The wolf's snout shoveled under Hollings, as though pushing him toward Loring.

The cavalryman could sense the animal trying to tell him something. He understood if the wolf had wanted them dead, they would both be bleeding corpses in the grass. For a second, he shivered, as if the wolf were a spirit guarding the Indian dead, the way those legends talked about. Ridiculous! But Hollings was a fool. Whatever was going on, the only thing that made sense was to get away as quickly as possible!

Loring put the pistol away and fastened his holster. He showed the wolf his empty hands. The wolf dug some dirt with his left front paw. Loring again realized the animal was trying to communicate.

"Dig. You want me to dig?"

The wolf glared.

Loring was puzzled. Something like that. What could the creature want? What? Something to dig with? "Shovel?"

Every cavalryman carried a small spade. The wolf's head nodded. Loring went to the saddle and set the spade on the ground. The wolf had moved away from Hollings. Loring walked carefully to the injured trooper, than lifted him up and loaded him on his mount, casting glances at the baleful wolf. He took one step toward the spade, which the wolf had not touched, but a growl ended that motion. He left it where it lay.

He mounted and, leading Hollings's horse, rode off, not able to breathe deeply until he was well away from the haunted place where the Indians lay.

A week later, the cavalry rode past the Big Sandy Creek battle site. Loring had taken the raving Hollings to the infirmary, where he was kept pending confinement to the stockade and possible confinement for a fevered imagination and absurd ravings. As Loring rode past the site out of curiosity, he saw about a dozen graves and not one unburied Indian body. A wolf could not dig a grave. A wolf could not hold a spade.

Loring kept his thoughts to himself as he recalled the tales the trading post Indians told about spirits protecting their people. He thought ahead to the day in six months when his enlistment would be over, and he would no longer play a part in the drama being acted out on the Plains. He worried increasingly that not only history, but God, would find he had been acting on the side of wrong.

Thaddeus Simpson Travers believed he was a good student of human nature. He believed the leaders of the flight from the Darlington Indian Agency were hostiles. He knew they would never be brought around. Since their departure, he had worked to cultivate those he could make leaders of the remaining remnants of the Northern Cheyenne. The ones he wanted as leaders understood who was master of the Plains and also understood that serving these masters was their way to power.

Travers had been approached by a man he was certain he had last seen as a minister but who now offered him a thousand dollars to send the best and most loyal Indians to track down and eliminate their fellow Northern Cheyenne, those who, as he said, had "turned a corner." Their mission would be to kill or kidnap leaders of the fleeing Northern Cheyenne, because, once leaderless, the mass would be easy prey. The former minister made it clear he did not want the Indians to return; he wanted them left on the Plains so they could become easy victims once their leaders were out of the way. When he mentioned a young woman named Rides a Crow, who had become some kind of spirit adviser to Little Wolf, Travers knew of one Cheyenne who might have a motive to find her.

And so it was Elk Running cautiously made his way along a trail well known to the Cheyenne. During the many years since soldiers began roaming the Plains and killing any Indian on sight, a trail through the rugged parts of the country from the agency north had been established. Elk Running had never made the journey, but he knew enough about trail markers left by The People to follow the trail.

No Cheyenne would reveal the trail to a white man, and, as Elk Running traveled, he saw that Dull Knife and Little Wolf had used it here and there but often took a route he could not imagine. However, Elk Running knew The People would move north to the Tongue River Valley, so he had no need to take side trails.

More than two weeks out of Darlington, Elk Running realized he had seen no sign on the trail of either the Northern Cheyenne or even scouts for more than three days. That meant he needed to go back and walk on the flat land.

It would be dangerous to be out in the open, because the hue and cry to kill the Cheyenne was such that any lone Indian rider stood little chance of survival. Although in the pocket of his jacket he had a safe-conduct paper signed by officials at the agency, he feared a soldier or cowboy would shoot first and ask questions later.

He took pride in his efforts to move unseen and thought

about how Rides a Crow had disdainfully rejected him. She would learn!

Elk Running picked up the trail, becoming more alert as he moved through a rocky area. The Cheyenne had clearly come through here, and not long ago. Impatient, he rode his horse to where he could follow a flat trail north.

The gunshot behind him made him turn in fear. Soldiers! He had not seen them. He kicked the horse into a gallop, looking ahead at a small canyon where the rocks seemed to form a natural defense.

More shots kicked up dirt around him. The range was so great that shooting from horseback was rarely successful, but he saw the soldiers gaining each time he looked back. Gaining! He could now see the soldiers' faces. Oh, what a mistake he had made!

Then from the rocks, like magic, a group of Northern Cheyenne rose up and fired a volley at the soldiers, who immediately reined in their horses and stopped their pursuit. Elk Running was saved!

He galloped on until, around a bend in the trail, safe from the soldiers, he saw a group of Cheyenne warriors with rifles pointed at him. Leading them was the terrible Dead Face, whose scarred face revolted Elk Running. He thought the warrior had been killed in the Custer fight, for it had been years since he had seen him.

"Greetings, Elk Running."

"I have come to join you," the young man said. "I could no longer bear to be at the agency. I stole a horse and rode as far as I could. The soldiers chased me."

"Yes. They are approaching, and we are preparing for battle."

"I am here and can help."

"Good. We will find you a rifle. It will be tomorrow, I think, before the soldiers are close enough for a fight. For now, eat."

He pointed to the fire, where food would be.

Elk Running walked uneasily through the warriors, as though afraid they would smell on him what was in his heart. He thought of asking for Rides a Crow but feared that might somehow reveal his purpose. He was in luck! Rides a Crow sat by the fire, talking with Little Wolf. When she saw him, her face registered surprise. She moved to him quickly, smiling happily.

"Elk Running! Where did you come from?"

He told her his story.

"It is better to have you with us now than never," she said at the end of his story.

He hoped she would believe his lies.

Wrapped in a piece of cloth, her right hand had blood upon it. Elk Running stared at it so long, she felt the need to explain that her hand was injured in a skirmish two days ago, when she and Dead Face were on a scout and ran into some cowboys who proved more persistent than most of the cavalry.

"I must watch the horses and foodstuffs when we fight," she grumbled. "I am unable to fire a rifle with any chance of hitting anything, so I must do this when the battle comes. I can still shoot a gun and perhaps scare off soldiers who come to steal what has taken us so long to acquire, but I cannot be with the warriors because I cannot hit anything. Or so *he* says." She gestured with her chin at Dead Face, who looked at Elk Running as though he somehow smelled deceit.

Elk Running told himself it was just the man's hideous face making him nervous. When he had first met Dead Face and heard his story, he thought how stupid Dead Face must have been to accept being made ugly for life above telling the soldiers what they would surely find out anyhow.

Dead Face gave Elk Running a rifle, staring at the young man. His face showed no emotion, but Elk Running saw that he seemed reluctant to give him a gun.

"Stay with her tomorrow. If the soldiers try to circle around us, we may need an extra gun to hold them off. She is injured. You must shoot straight. Do only as she tells you. Do you understand?"

"Are you worried?" Rides a Crow asked, an interruption Elk Running was pleased she made. Dead Face made him nervous.

"We will fight as we have before," Dead Face said. "I do not know if these are the same blue soldiers or different ones. If they are the same, they may know what awaits them and try something new. We have no choice, for only by using this ground and caution can we avoid losing the few warriors we have left."

He gave Elk Running one final glance, then looked at Rides a Crow.

"It will be all right," she said. "Not everyone is made like you, which might be a good thing."

Elk Running wondered what it meant when Dead Face's teeth showed that way, but then Dead Face walked away to speak with Little Wolf. Soon the two walked to the place where the women and children would hide during the coming fight.

The barking of rifles began. Rides a Crow and Elk Running stayed by the horse herd the Cheyenne had acquired. They now had food supplies to last the coming, colder, months. Rides a Crow explained some of the adventures they'd had capturing the horses and gathering the food.

She talked of Dead Face over and over and over. Elk Running made a disparaging comment about the man's scars.

"He is a true spirit warrior," Rides a Crow said in response. "He knows we must work with the spirits and The People, for there is evil around us. When we reach the Tongue River, I will be with him in his lodge. It is where I belong. It is where I wish to be."

The words snapped Elk Running out of the dream state he

had been inhabiting, in which Rides a Crow, upon seeing how brave he was, would consent to assume her rightful place in the world and be his woman.

To scorn him and accept Dead Face? The drift in his soul to stay with the Cheyenne and never go back to the agency stopped. She would never see the Tongue River. She would never be anyone's wife but his!

"Are those soldiers?" he asked, pointing left across the broken, rock-strewn ground that offered protection for the horse herd and provisions.

"What?" She moved in front of his larger bulk to see and heard nothing when the butt of his rifle came down upon the back of her head, sending her sprawling silently into the dirt.

Elk Running pulled the knife from his belt and cut one of the ropes between trees serving as an impromptu horse pen. Hurriedly, he used the rope to tie Rides a Crow's wrists behind her. Picking the first horse that would allow him to catch it, he threw her across its back, followed with a grunting vault, and then moved out to the north. Behind him, sounds of battle raged.

Hunter felt something terribly wrong but could not guess what it was. The trap for the soldiers was working. They would be driven off. Something must have happened to Rides a Crow. His bad leg was bothering him these days and would only let him go so fast, but he moved away from where he'd been watching the soldiers attack as they tried to get to the Cheyenne camp.

The fight flared and died. Warriors again exulted at seeing the enemy thrown back. Then smoke emerged from behind them. Dead Face commanded all but a handful to stay in place in case this was a trick.

It was not.

Somehow, soldiers had dispersed the herd of horses, and fire licked at the precious food they carried to prevent hunger during the weeks ahead. Dead Face sent warriors to pull what they could from the fire, and he looked for Rides a Crow, who would never have allowed the soldiers to do this if she were alive.

The arrival of the wolf caused him further alarm.

"Where is she?" came the spirit wolf's thoughts.

"She is not here," Dead Face said. "She was watching this place with Elk Running."

"Who is that?"

"A young man who thought Rides a Crow should be his woman. He appeared yesterday. He said he escaped to join us. I did not fully trust him, but Rides a Crow was sure she could handle him. There was no time to argue."

"Send men to see if the soldiers took Rides a Crow and Elk Running. Risk no lives, but do it quickly. If the soldiers took captives, they will be somewhere near the biggest tent, for that will house the commander. I am going to look elsewhere to find her."

Hunter chose to fight at Punished Woman's Fork, because, from the south, east, and west, it was easily defended. Fighting the soldiers would have meant anyone trying to leave would have to start north. He began his hunt.

Elk Running had secured some dried meat before he left the Northern Cheyenne camp. He now ate beside a fire that helped make the dark Plains less foreboding.

Rides a Crow had not awakened since he had hit her. When he saw blood in her hair, he feared he had killed her, but the pulsing place in her neck was still active.

During the days they needed to ride before reaching the agency, she would come to understand he was the better choice for her than Dead Face. If not, he could hand her over to the soldiers to be killed. Either way, he would have the reward they offered.

Lying opposite from him on the far side of the fire, she began to stir. Elk Running found himself fighting down a lick of fear. He stayed where he was, lest this be a trick.

Groaning, Rides a Crow used her arms to try to sit up, but her hands remained tied. He had retied them after they left the place of battle. He had tied her legs as well.

No one had pursued him when he rode north for a short way before turning west and then south to find the trail that would take him back to the agency. He made camp because he was hungry and needed to eat.

"What did you do?" Rides a Crow said at last, after sitting up and trying to understand what had happened. Her head pulsed and pounded.

Elk Running explained. "You are coming back to the agency. They paid me to bring you back alive or dead, and I am doing so because you can still be my wife if you give up this silly dream of going to the Tongue River."

"I would rather die."

"Then die. If you are so stupid you cannot see the advantage of living, you ought to die. The soldiers will be happy to kill you. They say you use evil spirits to help the Cheyenne. Are you now a witch, Spirit Walker?" He mocked her openly.

"Evil has turned you against your own people because of your ambition," she said. "Did you not see, when you were with The People, that we were a strong nation again? Would you trade that for a trading post on a dusty anthill?"

"You do not understand, Rides a Crow. There will never be a Cheyenne nation again anywhere except where the agency is. Ever. It is finished. Only a few of those who marched south are marching north. You are deluded. Your dream is the evil that is doing nothing but leading to death."

"No! You are the false one, Wide Elk."

The use of his nickname angered him. Now he walked over and stood over her, making sure to stay far enough out of range if she kicked.

"You will be traveling with me for several days, woman, and you must know your place, or I will have to remind you of it." He looked down at his helpless captive. "Perhaps I should remind you of your place in the world now, so you will not cause me trouble."

"Pig," she said.

He had drawn back a leg to kick her, when he was slammed to the ground. A wolf's growl drowned out Elk Running's shout of alarm and fear. The wolf clamped its jaws around an arm and dragged the bulky young man across the dirt. Elk Running kicked and tried to struggle. For a second his leg got free. Then the snarling, snapping wolf jumped on top of him and loomed over him.

"No!" Rides a Crow called. "Hunter, no!"

The wolf waited. Drops of saliva fell on Elk Running's face. Hunter stared at Rides a Crow as the fat young man beneath him made pitiful noises.

"He is mine," Rides a Crow said grimly.

The fire crackled in the silence. Elk Running's eyes were wide with fear. So she *did* control spirits! Then the paws left his chest, and he could breathe. Gulps of air.

"Cut these ropes and find me a knife, Wide Elk," Rides a Crow said. "If you don't, I will let him have you."

"This is madness," Hunter signaled her. "Your hand is still bandaged. He deserves to die."

"He will."

The young man had not spoken since the wolf attacked him. He finally spoke after Rides a Crow stuck two knives in the ground next to each other after removing the bandage from her hand. One knife had a larger blade than the other.

"You will have this thing attack me no matter what," Elk Running said. "It is not fair."

The wolf growled.

Rides a Crow grinned an evil smile.

"He will not need to attack you if you are as great a coward as I think you are. If you do not want to fight me, you are all his."

Elk Running raced for the knives, hoping to reach them first, grab one, and throw the other at the wolf.

Rides a Crow was faster. She tripped Elk Running as he lunged for the knives, then grabbed the longer one and danced back as he spat out dirt.

"Pick it up, coward."

He did. As flames flickered dimly, he lunged. She sliced his arm as he passed. He stopped and swung at her stomach. Again, her knife flicked out and nicked him. He continued to lunge, becoming increasingly desperate as she inflicted cut after cut on his arms without incurring damage to herself.

Elk Running swung wildly at her face. Rides a Crow ducked under and sliced his bulky stomach before dancing out of range.

"End this," Hunter sent her.

"He deserves worse."

Elk Running changed tactics. He charged, hoping to wrestle her to the ground. His fat arms wrapped around her, and they tumbled to the dirt, rolling almost out of the circle of the fire's light. A high-pitched squeal followed. The wolf moved into the dimness to see the fight.

"Help get him off me," Rides a Crow said.

Hunter changed into human form and hauled Elk Running off of her, the knife still stuck in his chest. He rolled the dead man away, then used as many unstained cloths as he could find to re-bandage Rides a Crow's hand as well as wrap a deep cut on her upper left arm.

"I didn't even know he'd struck me there. You saved me," she said. "We would soon have been too far away for The People to risk following us."

"In time he would have made a mistake, and you would have killed him," Hunter replied. "He was a fool."

"An evil fool," she said. "Is there never an end to evil?"

"No," he replied flatly and completed his work of bandaging her in silence. He continued, "The People need you. Now, more than ever. Because of this man and what he did, the horses were left unguarded, and the food supplies were destroyed. The warriors gave The People another victory over the soldiers, but the wounds caused by losing the animals and food will cause The People much suffering if we cannot replace them. That will become harder to do as more and more soldiers and cowboys follow our trail," Hunter said.

"I am ashamed," Rides a Crow said. "He fooled me."

"Do not blame yourself, child," Hunter said. "Some men show evil when it infects them; some do not. Let us return to The People. Let not this shadow cloud your face. The People need to believe they have won a victory. If the damage they suffered is too great, we will find out soon enough."

Callahan Ranch, Western Kansas, October 1878

"We got one, sir."

Fairfax's men always called Rheged "sir." They treated Rheged with a mixture of fear and respect. They had seen what he could do to those who failed to obey orders. He had no complaints. He knew he could kill every last one of them if the whim overtook him, and, to judge by the current state of the hunt for the Northern Cheyenne, it just might.

The warrior, known as Owl Foot, was barely more than a

boy. He had been foraging and come to the same ranch Fairfax's men were visiting. They shot him in the ankle and then caught him as he tried to escape. They had then sent for Rheged to find out what was to happen next.

The Indian, clad in little more than the rags of the thin shirt hanging below his waist and leggings, tried to keep an impassive mask intact. His hands had been tied to the arms of a wooden chair. He eyed Rheged with defiance.

Rheged had no patience with pretense. He ground a booted foot into the boy's wounded ankle, eyes sending a message the whole time, until he was sure the boy understood.

"Tell me where they are, or I will skin you a foot at a time until you wish you were dead," Rheged threatened. He grabbed the short braids in which the boy wore his hair and pulled the boy's head close to his. "Skinning you will take me days, boy, and I will leave the choice spots for last to make sure you don't die and miss all the fun."

The boy gave no response. Rheged wanted to change on the spot and rip out his throat. Insolence! Then his rage was interrupted by one cowboy who kept clearing his throat. Rheged glared.

"Don't figger he speaks English, sir. Lot of 'em got no more than a few words."

"Don't any of you speak their language?"

No one did. To the men riding for Fairfax, learning Cheyenne was not encouraged.

"Then how do you communicate with them?"

They told Rheged there was a more or less universal sign language for some basic concepts. They would give sign language a try, but they would have to untie the boy's hands.

"Go ahead," Rheged said. "Make sure he knows I will kill him slowly and inflict as much pain as possible if he does not cooperate with us."

The boy's impassive face registered one English word he knew. The boy's hands began signing almost as soon as they were freed.

"Somethin' about you, sir," said one cowboy hesitantly. "Kid says their spirit is stronger than you; he can make buffalo appear and make them people invisible to soldiers."

"Ask him where the Northern Cheyenne are. That's all we need to know. Then we can kill him and get on with it."

The man made some signs. The boy made some in return.

"Said they got a wolf spirit no one can kill, and he is not afraid of you. Said the wolf spirit will come and rescue him. Said you ain't got the strength to hurt nobody." The man saw red blossom on Rheged's face. "Not me sayin' that, sir! The boy done it! Said you are a false spirit!"

At this, Rheged lurched forward to grab the boy by his throat.

"Sir!" one of the cowboys called. "Don't kill him! We got to get information from him first! Sir!"

The cowboys tried to wrestle Rheged away from the boy as one tried to clamp the boy's arms. The boy slid under the grasp of the cowboy reaching for him, grabbed the gun from the holster of one of the men, and blindly fired it.

Four shots came in quick succession, and three of Fairfax's men were hit. Two other men pulled their own weapons and fired, but, even before the shots rang out, Rheged had grabbed the boy by the throat and thrown him against the wall of the barn.

Even as the boy slumped with three holes in his chest, he smirked at Rheged. "You . . . evil one . . . never . . . find them," he said in fractured English through bloodstained teeth gleaming with a smile of triumph before Rheged reached him and silenced the boy with a snap of his neck.

Except for the heavy breathing of the men, none of whom dared to tell Rheged he had destroyed any chance they had of using the boy to find the Northern Cheyenne, silence filled the barn.

Rheged raged white hot. Wolf spirit! So the Outcast was leading Dull Knife and Little Wolf as they marched. Rheged would find them, and, when he did, the Outcast would learn who was the stronger.

"Well?" he growled at Fairfax's men. "Find me another one! We need to catch those Indians!"

Western Nebraska, October 1878

Talks to Horses found Hunter alone, watching the sky as the moon of the Moon's Hard Face Month neared its midpoint. The wolf silhouette stood out boldly against the flat lands of the Plains.

"You are disconsolate, spirit wolf."

"I have failed The People, Talks to Horses."

Her hooves softly thudded as she walked closer.

"They are many more days free than they would have been without you, if they would be free at all. Soldiers hunt them but do not find them. This journey was never without risk, wolf."

"Do you feel it, as well as I do? The Plains are filled with hate. Hate has poisoned so many. I know this man Fairfax works with others to create evil to fight against the spirits of The People. I am afraid he is winning, because there are more of them than there are of us. The settlers ride in search of The People; every day young men go out to steal horses and report they have had to fight, as though they must prove their manhood. Owl Foot left, never to return, and no one knows where he went. We cannot even look for him because it is too dangerous! Our pace has slowed. More foraging means less marching, and there is more foraging because I was not there to watch for the man who fooled Rides a Crow."

Talks to Horses thought a moment before replying. "Yes, the hate I feel is not normal. You are certain Fairfax has called forth some spirits?"

"I do not have proof, but the only reason there can be this much hate must be because he has called spirits."

"Hate has been powerful on these Plains since the white man first laid eyes on the land of the Indians and realized the Indians would not lie down and die so whites might own it. The line between the hate of men for their own greedy gain and hate fueled by spirits is one not even I can detect, wolf, and I have ridden these Plains all my life."

"Many are going to die, and I know not how to save them."

"How do you know this?"

He explained that about thirty Northern Cheyenne had left the group, and that the leaders were now afraid, as winter approached, that they were not likely to reach the Tongue River Valley by then. He feared many would leave The People to go separate ways. The largest group wanting to split off hoped to seek safety with Red Cloud, because their long ties with the Lakota gave them hope. Hunter feared those hopes were false.

"Soldiers will find the ones who leave. When they do—with all the hate flowing like a river in spring—they will kill them. I have heard it over and over. When the soldiers want a Cheyenne or Lakota or Oglala dead, they invent a pretext and kill him, as they did with Crazy Horse."

"Have you told this to the leaders?"

"I have told Rides a Crow, and she has spoken, but there is no way to avoid this problem. The People know that, as winter nears, shelter must be found. I also see that some demon has come upon The People."

"Demon?"

"Despair. Since the loss of their provisions, food has been scarce. We have had no gift like the buffalo we found earlier.

The eyes of The People as they walk are too often dull. I fear some force has turned their hearts and minds away from freedom and toward defeat, yet I have searched for a way to fight it and have found nothing I can fight with teeth and claws."

Talks to Horses let silence fill the moment as they watched the stars.

"You have lived how long among us?"

"I came to the Sand Hills four years ago; for the past two years I have been among The People."

"I have ridden these Plains with my herd for many years longer than you. I have learned, friend wolf, that those of us who are of the spirit have lives that are ours to live. The People will do as they do. They have walked days upon days with too little food. That they walk with little hope, spirit wolf, is not the miracle. It is that they walk at all that is the miracle."

For a moment, the horse and wolf were silent amid the hushed sounds of the night.

"I do not fully know, as many summers as I have lived, why we were made and what the Great Spirit wants us to do. There are times when the way is clear. There are times when The People are beyond our reach, for they can act only upon the things they see and turn away from the spirits. This is not always the work of evil spirits, but often the work of men. We of the spirit can do what we can, but we cannot stop The People from doing what hurts them."

"That sounds like wisdom."

"It is the lesson that comes when you love The People, and they break your heart," Talks to Horses said curtly, emotion choking off her voice. "Then their dreams and their dead cover the ground."

Talks to Horses paced. She shook herself. "This is a journey, wolf. It will end. For all your fears, I do not believe the journey will end in failure. When it does end, the herd and I will run free in some place where there are no battles. Come join us there." She paused. "I would like that."

"Such a place sounds like a dream. I would like to see it."

"I shall show it to you."

"When The People are safe."

"When they are home, wolf, and safe from those who would kill them. The People will never be safe from the greed, envy, and hate of whites who will never understand. When the day comes when nothing hooves and teeth can do can help, it will be the time to let them lead themselves. That is why the Great Spirit has you teach the Spirit Walker everything you know."

Talks to Horses made one more remark. "There is a saying I am told a spirit friend uses, saddened wolf. I am told that, when all around him are in despair, he reminds them, 'It is a good day to live.' Then let us live this day as we can."

The day came for The People to divide. One group under Dull Knife would strike out for Red Cloud's agency to seek shelter there for the winter. The other, under Little Wolf, would continue to move north toward the Tongue River Valley, although they might take refuge in the Sand Hills of Nebraska if the weather continued to be harsh.

Rides a Crow was bound for the Tongue River, as was Hunter. The spirit horses would try to keep the two bands in communication with each other if possible.

Dead Face decided to go with Dull Knife. Hunter warned him he feared the group would face battles and death. Rides a Crow spoke nothing, but her face said much. She and Dead Face had walked together for days, sometimes with hands joined, other times with his arm over her thin shoulders. Around the fire at night, he always claimed the place next to her. Dead Face spoke to them before leaving.

"When I was in jail at Fort Robinson, a missionary, a better man than most whites, told us that, in the white man's religion, the holy man who was the Son of God told The People there was nothing greater than to give up a life for the people one loves. Even if all your fears are true, Morning Star and I will walk this road, for these are the people we love. If the whites come upon us, I may be able to save lives that would perish without me."

Dead Face paused and looked upon Rides a Crow. He said softly, "We have made vows."

"I shall keep mine."

"And I mine."

Dead Face turned to the wolf. "Many of these who go to Red Cloud were ones I led in war against Custer and in battles against the Shoshone and Crow. We have tasted battle and death, spirit wolf. Let it never be said that in the greatest battle ever to face The People, Dead Face would not ride at their head."

"Go with God, my friend," Hunter sent back.

"Protect her, wolf." Dead Face turned and did not look back.

Rides a Crow's eyes followed him until the line of walking men, women, and children merged with the morning mist.

Little Wolf's band plodded north through rough ground, walking by night when they heard reports of settlers and soldiers nearby. Cold rain, sleet, and snow were now their enemies, because fires were banned except, briefly, for cooking, so that they would not give away their location.

The grim time was made worse when they learned that, in one of the blinding snowstorms, Dull Knife's party had all but collided with a cavalry unit searching for the Cheyenne and was taken to Fort Robinson. Little Wolf's band was now further divided. Some said they should have gone with Dull Knife, if the soldiers were going to take The People in and give them rations. Others said that giving rations one day did not mean the soldiers would not shoot The People the next.

Hunter led the group until they reached a spot by Wild Chokecherry Creek.

"Have The People stop here," he told Rides a Crow. By now, the snow had begun falling in earnest. Spirit horses had reported that no pursuers from the south and east were a threat to them. The cavalry from Fort Robinson had sought them but turned back because of the bad weather.

Discouraging news also came to them. The spirit horses reported that, although the soldiers at Fort Robinson had initially agreed to send the Northern Cheyenne to the Red Cloud agency at Pine Ridge in the Dakota Territory, after the Cheyenne had been in custody for several weeks, hard feelings began to grow between the groups. Then came orders from the army and from the Great Father in Washington that The People would be forced to live in the south once again.

"You will be safe here," Hunter told Rides a Crow and Talks to Horses. "Stray cattle wander here and have for years. There should be a buffalo or two as well. If the hunters are cautious, they can find game. No settlers live here, because the ground is poor for growing crops. This weather keeps others from traveling, but not me. If I can help The People break out of the fort, perhaps they can join us."

Moved almost to tears, Rides a Crow said, "I cannot lose you, too."

"I will return," he promised.

Talks to Horses went with Hunter part of the way to show him the fastest, least visible way. In four days, buildings at the fort were visible.

"This is a mistake," she said as they prepared to part. "Great evil abides there. Death resides there. Even spirit horses will not venture close, so great is its evil. When you are among them, there is nothing I can do to save you, for with so many soldiers and so many guns, my herd would be killed if I tried to help you. The captives are also tired from our journey and need rest, as do you. The whites will not send The People south in this weather. Not even white soldiers will do that."

"With so few, they could load them on their railroad and ship them like cattle," Hunter replied. "We cannot risk that."

"Then we shall wait. One of us will keep watch as closely as we dare, wolf."

"Keep most of your herd with Little Wolf's group," Hunter replied. "If the worst has happened, and we cannot save Dull Knife's group, we cannot lose Rides a Crow."

"Return, wolf," said Talks to Horses. "Too much peace and quiet might make me think that is all there is to life."

CHAPTER TEN

Fort Robinson, Nebraska, January 1879

Hunter approached with extreme caution. The fence around the fort was not high enough to stop the legs of an animal accustomed to leaping, even if that animal was old and worn. Even so, as he jumped the fence, one leg grazed the wood in a way that never would have happened a few months ago.

What he found was worse than he had feared. The leader of the white soldiers had locked The People in a cramped barracks, because they refused to agree to return to Darlington. What was worse, Morrison Fairfax was at the fort.

Although many of the soldiers had become hard in their feelings toward all Indians, others who had met the Cheyenne marching in rags from Indian Territory realized they were nothing more than men, women, and children who only wanted to live by themselves in a place that had been their home for longer than any could remember.

Fairfax had brought to the fort all the hands he'd hired, men whose hatred for the Cheyenne and whose brutal response to anyone who spoke of tolerating the Indians made the moderate men bend to the ways of the rest. From the talk Hunter heard, Fairfax was one of the many settlers who had written and wired Washington demanding the captives be forced back to the south. Fairfax also waged his spirit war against The People.

"Spirit wolf?" the thoughts of Dead Face came to him.

"I am here, spirit warrior," Hunter replied and went on to explain why he was at Fort Robinson.

Dead Face told him about their hunger and cold, now that food was forbidden them, and that Cheyenne children had to drink water made from the ice on the windows of the barracks. He told Hunter The People were prepared for one last fight.

"I am told that, on the road to Darlington, they learned how to take rifles apart and hide them. The rifles have been assembled, and we have some ammunition," Dead Face told Hunter.

"There are more than two hundred soldiers here, Dead Face. You do not even have a hundred warriors."

"If we can reach the high, rough ground, some of us will live, wolf."

"Wait until I can have spirit horses nearby, Dead Face. They can take you through the passes to Little Wolf's band. Much of the land here is flat. If soldiers catch you upon it, you will not have a chance. Wait a few more days."

Dead Face agreed. "It is hard for the children," he said. "But they will learn what it is to be Cheyenne."

Hunter had dressed himself in the uniform of a cavalry soldier, hoping that in the foul weather he would not be noticed. The heavy wool seemed bulky after the thin clothes he had worn when he traveled as a man at the edges of Little Wolf's group.

The barracks where the Cheyenne were imprisoned was heavily guarded. Hunter saw a civilian walking toward it purposefully. A soldier approached the man.

"Mr. Fairfax!" the sergeant in charge of the guards called out. Hunter could not help but stare.

So this was the man. Fairfax. Walking ten feet from Hunter. Hunter wanted to change and kill him. The blood pounded in his ears to do it and take his chances. But he waited. If the captives could starve another day for The People, he could wait to take his vengeance.

"Well?" Fairfax grumbled at the subservient soldier. "Is everything ready as I ordered it?"

The sergeant made some temporizing comment, to which Fairfax responded with anger.

"I am paying you good money. I am sick and tired of waiting. The longer we wait, the greater the chance some sniveling officer will get soft on these Indians," he said.

The sergeant replied that all was ready for the early hours of the next day.

"We will open the doors and fire once over the Indians' heads," the soldier said. "We know they have guns in there. When they use rifles to fire back, your men will be in position to shoot out the glass and then fire through the windows. My men will seal the door to ensure no one can escape. There are two guards on duty now I am unsure about. When the guards change tomorrow night, everyone will be ready to follow the orders I will give them. It will look as though they tried to riot, and we were forced to respond. Your men have to do the work, because, if there is an inquiry, I have to be able to say my men were the last to fire."

"Good!" Fairfax sneered. If his men exterminated the Cheyenne, he would not owe anything to the partner he had come to view as a liability, even though Rheged had promised to deliver Little Wolf's band by spring. However, he vowed to keep that thought close, because his partner was far too good at reading his intentions. He was also far too near for comfort.

The men then walked off and spoke in lower tones. Hunter walked the other way, later circling back to be near the barracks and keep an eye on them.

"Spirit warrior!"

"Are you ready so soon, wolf?"

"We may have to be ready soon. A man working with the soldiers plans to have all of you killed tomorrow right before dawn." He outlined Fairfax's plan.

Dead Face said the captives had been working on a plan to escape. He would determine if the escape plan was ready. "I shall seek you out. Be careful, wolf. I think there are some here at the fort who sense Spirit Talk, for I can feel them distantly in my mind."

Fairfax. He had to be able to sense the spirits.

"I shall be careful." Hunter sauntered off in the way of a trooper doing a task while taking the longest possible time to accomplish it.

Hunter wondered if letting the stabled horses loose might confuse any response to an escape and provide the Cheyenne with a horse or two, knowing their ability to mount and ride. He took a roundabout route through the buildings to avoid suspicion. Once he glanced behind him, sensing he was being followed, but this was a busy post. After months of being with friends, Hunter now felt uneasy among enemies. His nerves were getting to him. There was no danger.

Wrong.

As the object hurtling toward his head was inches away, Hunter turned. He recognized the pale, hate-filled face of the person at the end of the long-handled shovel. Then the metal resounded off his head, knocking his hat to the dirt. Rheged's second blow sent him into darkness.

Hunter awoke choking as foul, cold water splashed over him. He found himself in a place with iron bars. Jail? No. He was at Fort Robinson. His gaze darted to the window. He could not tell if it was light or dark, or snowing so much no light showed.

He heard someone talking. Then he felt the presence. Rheged slapped him hard across the face. Hunter wanted to reply in kind, but shackles bound his arms from shoulder to wrist. Something also encircled his legs. More chains.

"I sensed someone or something was here," Rheged said, squatting down next to Hunter. "I know one of those Cheyenne has some powers, but then I felt someone with real power, and there you were."

Hunter wanted to ignore him and think about how to help Dead Face and the rest who would be murdered soon.

"Let me tell you what will happen," Rheged said. "Morrison Fairfax, who has been my benefactor, has several men here who will ask you for the location of Little Wolf's band. You should be happy to know you will be the first person they have asked who will not die from their efforts, although I believe, from their enthusiasm, you may well wish you had. One Shoshone who we were sure knew the location survived his inquisition without a single unbroken bone in his legs or arms. When my inquisitors are through with you, I will indulge myself just this once. I have longed to put you out of my way once and for all. You are the spirit who helped the Cheyenne survive, and the one who turned the clan against me. When you are snuffed out like a candle, the Indians will fall as well, at least those we do not already plan to kill."

"You are wrong," Hunter rasped. "There are spirits beyond me protecting them. You will never find them. You will never hurt them."

"But I will," Rheged replied. "I left behind the old clan and its old ways when I left the old country. You had split it to the point where little Skellig—the stupid, blonde female you corrupted with your ways—was named leader while I was here. Those who are loyal to me are founding a new clan composed of those who see power as a weapon to be used. Soon, puny wolf, there will be nothing on the land your Indians think of as theirs that is not part of my empire. I will let farmers and ranchers do as they will. But their ends will be mine. The spirit war these Indians waged is all but over. The Indians will be gone soon. Very soon."

"However, you will have long since ceased to care," continued Rheged, standing. "So that you understand your position, you are in a cell whose bars are too narrow for you to escape, in any form. You might try changing, and you might even get away with it, but once you are unable to walk or move or see, it will not matter. I fear if you do change, my followers may kill you quickly out of terror, but I have told them you are mine, and they understand I mean what I say."

"Coward. You were afraid to meet as equals!"

"I find nothing interesting in taking chances, Outcast. I shall see you again one last time, but, first, you must betray your friends. That way your humiliation will be complete before I rip the life from your body inch by inch." Rheged turned away.

"He is yours now," Rheged called out to four men, each with a wooden club in his hands and death in his eyes. They entered the enclosure, merciless eyes upon Hunter.

"You could tell them now," Rheged told Hunter. "Although I hope you don't. You deserve what comes next."

Hunter remained silent.

"No response? Good. And good riddance."

The cell clanged shut behind him, and so did the door to the outside.

"Now let's get acquainted," said one of the four men. He punched Hunter in the face.

The water seeping into Hunter's mouth was tainted with his blood. From the eye not closed, he saw darkness outside. He had no idea how long he had been in the fort's stockade. He measured time in pain. If he had eaten, he would have retched it up long ago. The last blow to his head had knocked his skull against the bars, giving him a respite from the beating.

The men had asked him about Little Wolf. Over and over.

Sometimes they cajoled him, telling him the pain would end when he talked. Other times they demanded, telling him the beating and pain would only get worse. Other than moans Hunter voiced after the hardest blows, he had not responded.

"He's awake again," a bored voice said.

"Lock him in. Not rushin' my food."

The time gave Hunter the chance to try to focus his attention on the window. Outside darkness reigned, and this darkness wasn't the deep gray of winter. The lamp on the table reflected against the darkness outside.

Because he'd been imprisoned for so long, Hunter feared Dead Face and the rest of The People had already been slaughtered. Hunter had failed them. Miracles didn't exist. The best he could hope for was that Dead Face would start without him; that somehow Dead Face had realized something bad had happened. Hunter tried to frame something to send in his thoughts, but more pain than words lived in his head.

"By my watch we got a few hours," said one from outside Hunter's vision.

"Better get this done. Not missin' my chance."

The one in charge moved to the door of the cell. He looked down at Hunter on the floor.

"Don't suppose you gonna talk, are you?" he asked conversationally, looking directly at Hunter's good eye. Silence followed. "Fair enough. No sense a man working any more than he has to."

He turned to the other men. Hunter had become so little a threat, they spoke as though he were not there.

"Gonna play a game, boys. The game is to break anything a man could use. We start with the legs, then the arms. Ribs are too easy. Take turns. One shot each. You don't break something, you throw a silver dollar in the pot. Man who breaks the most gets the money. Only the first one to break a bone claims it."

165

"Ain't fair," spoke up one.

"Why not, Kelly?"

"Look at all that chain on them arms and legs. Good spots are all covered."

"Kelly's right," chimed in another voice.

"Why's he got them chains on?" Kelly asked.

"That man of Mr. Fairfax said this was a real dangerous *hombre*."

"Hardman, does this fellow look dangerous to you?"

"Come on, Hardman," added Kelly. "He's caved in and gone. Like that Shoshone."

"Well," replied Hardman, "Mr. Fairfax is paying a bonus to everyone who kills a Cheyenne tonight, and the later we get there, the fewer good spots are gonna be left. Yep. Gonna be a rush. Know Mr. Fairfax gets his pick of the trophies, but I got a mind to get me a head. One with lots of hair."

The men continued jawing.

"Here's what we'll do, boys," Hardman said at length. "That man was afraid of him getting away, so when we get in there this time, we lock the door behind us. Then we unchain him. If he puts up a fuss, Kelly, you take him down. Then we chain him up to the bars, round his middle there. Should make it easy to each get a turn. Then we can call the man giving the orders and have some supper and still be ready."

Every time the men rolled Hunter over to undo his chains, he whimpered and moaned.

"Lot of sand at the start, but it all run out of him fast," Kelly said.

"Not like that Apache," said Hardman.

"He ain't Indian," one of the others said. "Indians ain't human."

Hunter's arms were free. He retched again, even though his stomach had long been empty, and the lower half of his body twitched as he heaved.

"Gonna need a bath," one of the men said.

"Why start now?" retorted Kelly.

They all laughed as they unwound the chain from Hunter's now-still legs. He whined as they grabbed him to hold him upright on wobbly legs.

"Now we got to loop the chain around his middle, get him chained good and tight to those cell bars there, and then we can finish our chore," said Hardman.

Hunter went limp and hit the floor of the cell with a moan.

The men voiced their scorn. Not even enough of a man to take what was coming. One reflexively pulled a pistol and trained it on Hunter. Hunter, however, was on the floor, doubled over.

"What's that smell, Kelly?"

"Go get the lamp," one of them said. "I think he's dying."

"Get up," said Kelly. The men, inured to dealing out death, looked at one another as they felt a wave of panic.

Kelly peered down and tried to fight his fear. They could deal with this fuzzy-haired bastard rolling on the floor. Wait a minute. Fuzzy-haired? This was not hair, it was . . .

Fur.

Throwing off the rags of ruined clothing that had gathered around his legs, the rust-colored wolf shook himself and stared at his prey. His teeth seemed immense, and the animal seemed huge.

Kelly had the gun, but the creature had the advantage. For the first time in Hardman's life, fear paralyzed him.

"No," he said. "No. Kelly, shoot that thing!"

Kelly fired at the rust-colored wolf, but, in chorus with the gunshot, his tortured scream filled the room, ending in the choking gurgle of bloody words he never spoke. Hunter then cut down the other two men. Hardman faced the creature who was Hunter, a stout club in his hand.

"Whatever you are, you are not getting out of here alive."

He swung at the side where the wolf's eye appeared damaged. The creature dodged the blow, but barely. The impact of the club on the bars jarred Hardman's muscles.

The wolf waited. Hardman swung again, and the bars reverberated with the force of his blow. Again. Again. After one next swing, the wolf slid in the blood on the floor and lost its footing. Hardman rushed to it and bent to finish off the animal. He raised the club, which began arcing downward in a blow to crush the wolf's skull. But he tumbled to the floor when the wolf's teeth gouged his left ankle. A bone broke. The wolf dove behind Hardman, who turned in time to see the vision he would take to his death: jaws descending into his face.

Hunter lay on the floor long after Hardman was still. All the men were dead. He was not. He wasn't of much use to anyone, but he was alive.

He did not know how long he lay there, thinking about how close to death he had been. Then his mind started to function. Dead Face! He risked a message.

"Spirit warrior!"

"I have felt your pain, wolf."

"Are The People ready?"

"When they open the door, we will rush them."

"They may be distracted soon. Be ready."

Hunter wanted to send a blessing for their escape but dared not risk alerting Rheged.

The key to the cell hung at the far end almost beyond his reach. Straining despite the pain, he was able to grab the key, unlock the door, and wobble out of the cell.

He found clothes to wear. Something that would not attract attention. A soldier's overcoat hung on a hook at the far end of the building. Hunter felt sick and dizzy, but he now had all of the men's pistols tucked in his pants. He also found one rifle. They would do. Hunter kicked the table holding the burning lamp, which fell to the floor and broke. The flame did not die. Hunter waited until flame began licking at the puddle of kerosene.

Hunter staggered as the cool night air revived him. Step by step. The barracks where the Cheyenne were confined was out of firing range, but men in the dark would not know that.

"That The People will live," he prayed. "That their dream will live."

Then he opened fire.

Gunshots rang out from the fort's parade ground, where Fairfax's men camped. Hunter took aim at the fire where men had gathered, waiting for their signal to massacre the Cheyenne. One man pointed at Hunter. He was the first to die.

Guards at the barracks where the Cheyenne were penned saw winks of flame from Hunter's pistols. As soldiers moved toward the gunfire, the Cheyenne warriors locked inside pulled down the makeshift bars that turned the building into a prison and began streaming out the windows, firing their own weapons.

The soldiers took cover, then started firing back at the escaping Indians. Fairfax's men joined in until Hunter downed another. Then they turned their aim at him.

Soon they would realize they outnumbered whoever was shooting at them, Hunter knew. He considered trying to reach the stable and release the horses, for The People could not get far on foot. But the risk was too great. Soldiers now fired into the dark at shadows and imagined targets. Hunter had done what he could. It was now time to save himself.

Fort Robinson, Nebraska, January 10, 1878
Paul Collins surveyed the scene with dismay. A few soldiers had been wounded, and one had been killed. Several cowboys were dead as well.

Four men attached to Fairfax's crew had been found dead in the old stockade. It had burned as the Northern Cheyenne escaped, setting men to whisper that the Cheyenne had used some kind of magic. As it was, tales circulated that the men who were killed had been mauled by giant animals.

But what moved Collins to tears were the bodies of the Northern Cheyenne who were shot down in the response to their escape. He counted more than twenty dead bodies that had been brought in, some women and children. Many of the dead had not been merely shot. They had been shot over and over, and some had clearly been shot in the head long after they were dead.

He heard some of the troopers talking about cowboys—those would be Fairfax's men—moving among the wounded Indians to make sure they were dead. One trooper threatened to shoot one of the cowboys for trying to grab a souvenir from a corpse. As the trooper told it, a handful of warriors gave themselves up to protect the women and children in their group, but Fairfax's men tried to kill them anyhow.

"I shoot back at people who shoot at me, but these Cheyenne fought like men," he said he told the Fairfax minion. "Better men than you."

After four years fighting in the War Between the States, Collins had come west. He had been in seminary, but the war collided with his image of man and God, and he sought to leave brutality behind. He had the gift of languages and soon began working as an interpreter with the army. In the years between the Washita and Custer's defeat, Collins had come to know something of The People as well as their languages. He'd come to learn that much of the Cheyenne culture practiced virtues Eastern men honored only verbally.

He had accepted the post of a deputy agent at the Darlington Agency to help deal with the Northern Cheyenne. After a while, he realized that, as much as he knew about them, he had never fully understood that the Tongue River was not just a place on a map to them, but was part of their soul. When Little Wolf said back at the southern reservation he would prefer to die there than live anywhere else, the words weren't rhetoric, but the truth.

When the army had asked Collins to come north as an interpreter, he jumped at the chance. He hoped the courage shown by the Northern Cheyenne as they walked from Indian Territory nearly to Dakota Territory would make the army realize the Northern Cheyenne were serious.

Their escape from the barracks had not surprised him. Yesterday the Indians had been too calm, as though they had already made their plans and no longer cared what the army did. The bodies laid out made it clear that the escape had ended in freedom for some, but death for many. With no one interested in talking, no one cared about an interpreter. Collins went to the stable and found a decent horse. He could do nothing here. Maybe he could do some good out there. He had to try.

Hunter saw the man from the Darlington Agency as he passed the stall where Hunter had crawled to recover from his wounds. The man aimed to set out alone on a day when both Cheyenne and soldiers would shoot anything that moved. Guts.

From the talk Hunter overheard as troopers returned to the fort, the Cheyenne had killed mostly Fairfax's men as they escaped. More than one trooper wondered what Fairfax's men were doing by the barracks in the first place. The escapees who had survived the initial fighting had scattered, most heading for rough country around the fort, across the White River, with a large group heading northwest.

Some troopers were exhilarated by the overnight chase and the casualties they inflicted on the Cheyenne. A couple of them wondered sadly who would raise the children they brought back to the fort.

Now that The People had a head start, Hunter wasn't sure what he could do to help, but he would do what he could. He felt guilty for not trying to go with The People, but he could barely stand after he'd provided a distraction. If he'd gone with them, he would be lying with the dead. He rose and shook the hay off of his overcoat.

There were caves above the White River. Hunter would head there. He thought about trying to find Dead Face, but he was afraid any Spirit Talk would attract Rheged, who would be more than a match for him in his current condition. He would do what he could, reminding himself that, as long as Fairfax and Rheged lived, all The People were in danger.

Hunter saw soldiers everywhere. They combed the hills and caves. Some hunted for trophies; others for survivors they could rescue. There were civilians among them. Hunter knew anyone found by Fairfax's men would be killed.

The reputation of the Cheyenne as fighters served them well this day. Afraid to approach a cave that might hold one Indian, pursuers approached each possible hiding place with overwhelming force, slowing down the number of places the men could search.

Six men were gathered by the entrance to one cave, trying to talk whoever might be inside into coming out.

"Ain't gonna hurt you," one said. They grinned at one

another at the joke.

"Gettin' cold and losin' time," said one after more entreaties. "We'll just kill whatever's in there and move on. Might be another waste, like that old woman who held off the army half a day because they were so afraid they didn't know she was already half dead. Bag of rags with no hair worth havin'. Let's get this done."

Another argued he was certain from the size of the footprints the cave held at least one man. They went back to their horses, pulling out their rifles.

"Now careful, boys. If there's low-hanging rock, a bullet can bounce back out."

Four men now lined up with their rifles.

"Any old time, bo—" said the group's leader. His words were cut off by a scream when a claw raked the back of his knee, making him stumble backwards into the man next to him.

A leaping rust-colored fury then pounced on the man at the far left of the line, knocking him down. It then leaped up to tear at the side of the next man. The man on the far right swung his rifle and fired. The wolf had darted away. The bullet ripped into the group's leader as he lay on the snow clutching his injured knee.

As three of the men howled in pain, the others tried to regroup.

"Kill that!" one yelled before he, too, went down. Ferocious jaws closed upon him. Two more gunshots rang out, and then there was nothing but men moaning in pain. Soon, not even that could be heard.

Hunter then walked into the cave, hoping no one would shoot a rescuer, even if he was not human. An adolescent boy, two adolescent girls, and two small children hid as far back in the cave as they could. Their eyes filled with fear as Hunter approached.

He grunted, then turned away. At the mouth of the cave, he changed. They might not trust a white man but he could hardly speak to them as a wolf. He made one more trip to the children but did not approach too closely.

He said, "The food those men had is here. Take it. They had pistols. Take those also. Find a place where the searchers have already been. That place will be closer to the fort, but the soldiers will believe it is empty. Stay until the soldiers go away in a few days. Then follow to the east. Spirit horses will find you to guide you. When you reach the place where the earth is sand, you will find The People of Little Wolf. Bring any others you find along with you."

Hunter left the cave cautiously, afraid the men's gunshots might have alerted other searchers. He hoped he had saved five lives, but he left Fairfax's men where they had fallen. He wanted them found.

Learning that creatures prowled the hills might make the soldiers more cautious, might make them end their search before all the children, women, and wounded hiding in caves and other shelters could be found. It was not much, but it was the shred of hope to which Hunter clung as he moved across the snow to look for others he could save.

Collins rode as fast as he could. The cavalry mount was not inclined to hurry. He knew he was on the right track because he could see the trail of bloody footprints when they were not obliterated by the far larger trail of cavalry horses in pursuit.

He saw one horse moving slowly. Collins was no hand with a gun, although he could hit what he shot at most of the time. Well, some of the time. He checked his Winchester in the scabbard. It was loaded. As he neared the rider, he saw long hair flying. As he drew closer, he saw the hair was not the long, glossy, black hair of an Indian, but the light-brown hair of a woman.

Unsure what to make of this, he called out a greeting when he thought he was close enough to be heard. With the world on a hair trigger, he did not want an accident to happen. The rider stopped and waited.

"Are you lost, miss?" Collins called as he approached.

"No, but I am missing my opportunity," she said bitterly. "They gave me the worst horse possible on purpose!"

"Miss, it is dangerous to be out here alone. The Northern Cheyenne have escaped from Fort Robinson, and the army is chasing them. Where are you going?"

"After them, of course!" Collins's face must have registered his uncertainty. "I am Annie Campbell. I am a newspaper reporter. My father, Deuteronomy Campbell, publishes the *American Report* in Boston. He is a friend of the president, and he made arrangements with the army for me to write about the Cheyenne, although they all disapprove, of course! I was at the fort when the Cheyenne got away, and now I am following them."

"But you are a woman!"

"Thank you!' she said acidly. "I didn't know that."

"A woman should not—"

"There are Cheyenne women with rifles trying to save their children, Mister Whoever-you-are, so don't tell me what a woman should or should not do! I write. I draw. I wanted to paint some of the Indians. I wanted to hear why they came so far. My brother told me they were here to scalp us in our beds, but I think that is twaddle."

"Miss Campbell, I am Paul Collins. I have been serving as an interpreter—"

"Yes, I have seen you at the fort. I only reached it on the seventh. I want to catch up. I want to know what happens."

"Miss Campbell, you should know by now what happens

when soldiers fight Indians. It is not something a woman should see."

"You mean because they will kill them and cut them apart and act like brave men because fifty troopers shot an old man to death? I have heard talk like that for days. Are you one who thinks like that?"

"Miss Campbell, I do not think anything you have seen will prepare you for what is to come. Violent hatred has been unleashed, and it will not stop. Even if the Cheyenne surrender, they will probably be killed, but I am riding to see if I can get them to talk. If you need to know my political views on the Indians, I find it hard to believe that, in a country where we have declared all men free, we cannot find a way to give that same freedom to the Indians."

Campbell studied Collins as he spoke. "Well. That's more than I expected. Take me with you. I do not know where they are going, and you must know something, or you wouldn't be out here."

But he didn't know anything. He guessed that if the Cheyenne had a plan, for now all they wanted was to stay a step ahead of the army, running here, going to ground there. Finding them would not be easy. The army might be looking for quite a while.

Collins had heard of female reporters back in the East but had never met one. He read the determination in her face. She had no food, no extra clothing for the fierce winds, but he knew that she would not go back to the fort.

If the soldiers went slowly enough in their hunt for the Cheyenne, she and Collins might still catch them. Anything else would put her at too great a risk.

"We will follow the tracks for now," he told her. "But there are Indians and soldiers out here who will shoot before thinking. Stay close to me."

A begrudging assent followed. Collins clucked his horse forward.

For days, the army searched the broken White River country with its caves. Hunter helped some escapees flee, but many more were hunted down. Those who resisted were killed, although, as the hunt for the Cheyenne went on, the fever leading troopers to shoot warriors to ribbons abated.

From what Hunter had overheard from some nearby cavalrymen, Fairfax himself had been forced to leave the hunt and had taken Rheged with him. An army patrol caught them mutilating corpses, a practice that the army disliked. Fairfax then got into a gunfight with another trophy hunter, leading to a trooper being injured. The army sent everyone involved away from the fort. Fairfax had demanded to telegraph Washington, but, in the hunt for escapees, no one had time for a man so filled with himself; he became loathsome to everyone.

But if the master was gone, many of his servants remained, fueling Hunter's determination to rid the world of Fairfax's crew. He avoided groups of soldiers but trailed those of Fairfax, often with deadly results when he gave in to his rage. Because of Hunter's vengeance, Fairfax's men had taken stock of their losses and stopped looking from cave to cave. The number of Indians they found did not equal the risk of the attacks from what they believed were wild animals.

Now Fairfax's men banded together to search for the prize that had eluded them all—Dull Knife. However, more than a week after his escape, Dull Knife had not been found.

Wolves can be patient. So can evil.

Fairfax's men continued to watch and prowl even when the army had written off Dull Knife, whose illness in the weeks before his escape led them to assume the old chief was dead. Hunter had thought of several places where Dull Knife might be hiding. There were only so many caves large enough to hold a chief and those who stayed with him. Fairfax's men, Hunter was sure, had come to the same conclusion.

Dull Knife would be humiliated, tortured, and killed if he was found. Dull Knife had wanted to fight for a free people until the odds were beyond what he could face. Then he had marched north to live free or die when he was almost seventy. Hunter would not let him die if he could prevent it.

The wind howled in the moonless night as a wave of sleet hammered the White River hillside. If there was a night meant for escape, this was it.

Near one of the caves where Hunter thought Dull Knife might be hiding, his wolf eyes saw figures moving slowly. Between being careful and being crippled from days in hiding, Dull Knife's party, if it were they, would move very slowly.

Hunter reached the path they walked and waited. Soon, they came in sight. Dull Knife, one of his wives, and some of his family came into view, in thin clothes with thin blankets wrapped around them. The old chief led, holding a rifle. He stopped when he saw the wolf.

"Are you the spirit wolf who guided our path, or are you here to end our days?" the chief asked as he gazed upon the animal, which he could sense was of the spirits. His fears, however, were too great for that understanding to sink in.

One of those with Dull Knife did not stop with the rest and stumbled on frozen feet. Soon rocks tumbled upon each other. The rock fall was not loud and did not last long, but, as the only sound in the darkness, it would be heard by other ears. The wolf motioned with his head for the band to move.

"Hurry," said Dull Knife, adding a blessing as he passed the wolf.

The sleet meant fresh footprints would be easy to follow in the dark. The noise they made would be heard by someone. The question was not if those someones would come, but how soon.

Hunter thought about how to be ready. A wolf could slow down pursuers when they reached him, but a man might do the job better if he could move fast enough. Teeth lacked a gun's range!

He had barely returned from the place where he kept his supplies when he saw pursuers following Dull Knife's trail. Hunter heard hushed whispers. Through the curtain of sleet, he saw six shapes. Fairfax's men must have split up to cover multiple places, because he knew there were more men than these nearby. They moved slowly up the rugged hillside. Snow had covered the rocks, leaving a series of twisting paths the only way for men to move easily.

The group stopped. They were about fifteen yards from where Hunter concealed himself, listening hard.

". . . wants Dull Knife alive. Kill him if you have to, I guess, but the boss will skin you alive if you do."

Murmurs and laughter followed the comment.

Hunter had amassed an arsenal of rifles left behind by the Cheyenne when they were captured. He had left them stashed in several caves. Most had only a bullet or two in them, but the ones he had found from his nearest cache would suffice for tonight's work.

He aimed where the voice had spoken and fired. Exclamations of pain and surprise mingled. Three shots, and that gun was empty. The next gun held two bullets. The next one, only one. Hunter used up three more rifles, knowing from the groans he heard at least three men had been hit, perhaps more. He hoped that would be enough.

Answering gunshots sounded in the darkness, but the men were cautious. Soon, Hunter left the hillside behind. The track he found was fading fast as snow and sleet covered it. He changed to a wolf; no one in the hills wanted to follow wolf tracks! He needed to find the party and show them a path to safety. If they could reach the trees and the big hills, Dull Knife would be safe. At least the chief would live. As for his people, that was another story.

The grim reaping of Cheyenne lives continued unabated as the army pursued a dwindling band of fugitives across the rough country of northwestern Nebraska. Collins no longer talked about sparing Annie Campbell any of the horrors of what had happened, for there were too many of them.

She had showed him her notes one night when they sat beside one of the army fires. They had reached the army after three days of riding.

"Like a Greek tragedy, the Cheyenne warriors played their roles as heroes whose fate was to die," Campbell had written. "Day after day, across snow tinged with their blood, they laid down their lives for their families as their flight to freedom was ground under the hooves of cavalry horses."

The group they followed now numbered about thirty people. The pursuit had grown deadly. Even soldiers who wished the Indians would surrender and live were no longer sympathetic to fugitives who used every tree, rock, and crevice as a place from which to fire upon the soldiers following on their heels.

Campbell was writing in her diary as she prepared to leave the tent and mount her horse.

"Today is the twenty-second day of January. Tomorrow will mark two weeks since the Northern Cheyenne risked their lives to die free by escaping from Fort Robinson. I say this because I cannot imagine they expected to live. I do not know how to make anyone see how wrong this is, because it is almost too late to stop the slaughter. The Cheyenne will not stop until they reach safety or are killed trying to get there. The soldiers have chased them so long, they will never stop. One side will be murdered; the other will become murderers. If this is not tragedy, I do not know what is."

She paused. Then she added a few more lines with her pencil.

"Paul said scouts last night said Indians might be up ahead, which would make this another day of fighting. He has spent so much time trying to ask the army to let him talk to the Cheyenne before they fight. He is a good man. I hope, when he tries to talk peace, he is not caught in a crossfire. Then I think I might die."

Along Hat Creek Near Antelope Creek, Nebraska, January 22, 1879

Collins had dismounted. The flat, frozen, merciless ground north of the Hat Creek bluffs stretched before him. A natural depression stretched out for a few yards on either side of him. *The Pit,* they called it. The army was willing to give him a chance to talk to the Northern Cheyenne waiting there after he begged for the opportunity to stop the slaughter with words and not weapons.

Holding his arms out from his sides, he approached the rifle pit containing the last band of Northern Cheyenne who had yet to surrender.

Collins had the army at his back, with more than two hundred well-fed, well-mounted, and well-armed troopers against no more than about thirty men, women, and children dressed in rags, half-starved, and running low on ammunition. If it came to battle, this would be a slaughter.

He almost stumbled and fell as a man stepped out of the Pit and walked toward him: Dead Face, one of the leaders of the Cheyenne. Dead Face knew English.

"I greet you, Talking Noises," he said to Collins. "You are brave to come out here alone."

"You and everyone with you must surrender," Collins said. "The army has five soldiers for every Cheyenne. They have many guns and many bullets. You cannot hope to run farther, because they will catch you. You cannot hope to defeat them, because they will kill you. You can have peace if you surrender."

The words had the impact of dead leaves falling on a rock.

"Talking Noises, I already have peace. I have the peace of knowing I have lived these final days with the wind in my face. My eyes beheld what the Great Spirit made for us, not the inside a white man's prison. You speak of death as something from which I must run. I have lived with death since the day the soldiers did this to my face."

Collins saw women with children in the pit behind Dead Face. He also saw a row of rag-clad warriors holding rifles. Watching. Waiting. Not one face bore any hint of surrender.

"Death is nothing more than a short bridge of pain, Talking Noises, from this world to the next," Dead Face continued. "When I walk the bridge this day, I will walk it singing a song of life, Talking Noises, for I will die as a free Cheyenne. The People are alive, Talking Noises. More prison would kill The People's spirit. The stiff bodies of The People may ride with you in wagons this day, but their spirits will live free, even as the killings to come will forever fill those who kill us with shame."

Collins wanted to find a way to convince the warrior to change his course but finally realized that it was far too late for the right words, if there even were any.

"The worst the soldiers can do is kill me, Talking Noises. They cannot defeat The People."

"Dead Face, this is madness. Think of your people. They need you. You can help them find a better way."

"In a moment you must go, Talking Noises, for you are a man of peace, and this is a place for the dead. I shall turn my face to the sky. I shall sing my song. And in a day I will never see, The People will sing of the day when Dead Face and these warriors here showed they loved The People more than this life, and they will be proud. That is what they need." He paused. "Thank you for trying, Talking Noises. When your journey is done, The People will welcome you to Seana to be with us always."

The warrior lifted the rifle he had held by his side across his chest. He gave the soldiers a long look of defiance. The wind whipped the loose strands of hair that framed his face. He turned and walked with slow and measured dignity back to the Pit, which Collins knew he would never leave alive.

"Spirit wolf!"

"Spirit warrior! Where are you? I feel your danger. I am coming."

Thoughts from Dead Face came distantly, as though the warrior were as far away as the moon. Hunter was heading back towards Fort Robinson after one of the spirit horses guided Dull Knife to the home of a settler who was friendly to The People and would ensure his safety.

"The soldiers will charge the Pit in a moment, wolf. The shooting has stopped. Tell Rides a Crow I was true to my vow, that The People would live. Tell her I—"

The words stopped, and in a rush of anger, rage, and a soaring of the spirit, Hunter knew that, wherever he was, Dead Face had been under attack, but not for long.

And then he was alone.

Pale, Collins shook his head as Campbell rushed to embrace him upon his return to the army's camp. She had never seen him so wan and shaken.

"A few children. Maybe a couple of women. The rest . . ." He started to cry. "The rest—every warrior, some of the women and children . . . They are dead. Some killed ten times over. The Northern Cheyenne are dead. They lie in the pit. They are dead. They are all dead."

"No," she said. "No! Little Wolf's group is alive, Paul. There are still survivors from the breakout. Maybe Dull Knife is alive."

Collins looked as though the death in which he had immersed himself that day had sucked out the life within him. She shook him.

"Listen to me. We know—you and I know—that what was done was wrong, that if the Cheyenne were allowed to live where they wanted to live, they never would have had to die. We can't bring them back, but maybe we can make what they did have meaning."

"How?"

She swallowed. "Take me there." She silenced his objections with an upraised hand. "Let me draw the scene. Let me sketch it, this attack on the Pit. It was a massacre. Let me show Eastern people what these glorious so-called Indian Wars they like to read about really look like. You said once that if people back East knew what was being done to the Indians, right-thinking people would never accept it. Did you mean that?"

"Annie, you don't want to see—"

"No, I don't want to see it, Paul; I *have* to see it! Who else can do it? Who else will do it? No one! You just told me what Dead Face said. If soldiers shoot them all dead and nothing happens, their lives have no meaning. If they are dead and their deaths bring about something—a homeland where they want it to be for whoever is left alive—then maybe that is what they wanted their sacrifice to create."

"I don't know if anything will change."

"I don't either, Paul. But whether it changes in a hundred days or a hundred years, those Cheyenne gave up everything they had, including their lives. I can deal with being sick over what a massacre looks like if I can write about the reality of it . . . if I can change one mind."

He was quiet for so long, she assumed he had not heard a thing she'd said.

"The light will only last for a few hours," he said. "The wagons will be loaded with the dead in the morning, and then we will return to Fort Robinson. You will have to sketch very quickly."

A rust-colored wolf stood once again on the hill overlooking Fort Robinson. He had watched wagons rolling in from the west. He could tell from the way the soldiers rode that the fighting was over. He had been too late. However many Cheyenne had slipped away were free. Most were dead; the rest had been captured.

Had the escape been worth it? As if there was a choice. The People would have faced certain death at the hands of Fairfax's men. Most died in the end. Dull Knife's Cheyenne were crushed. Fairfax and Rheged were alive. As he looked for the fort, Hunter wondered if the better path would be to return to Rides a Crow and Little Wolf, or track down Rheged and Fairfax and wipe the evil they represented from the Plains, knowing it was too late for the Northern Cheyenne. Death for death. That was the world he knew.

He shook his head to clear away the noise. Some days he wondered if he would fully recover from the beating by Fairfax's men. Some days he bled from his nose. Now, as he looked out on the wind, a high-pitched noise grew, swelled, and faded as he turned to hear it. He walked down one of the paths. The noise did not stop but instead grew louder. He entered one of the small caves. The noise was real!

The cave was barely twenty feet long and curved to the left. A trail of frozen blood led inward. About halfway to the far end, the body of one of Fairfax's men lay on the cave floor, a pool of dark ice beneath him.

Huddled against the back wall of the cave sat a young woman, also dead. She had a pistol in her hand. Her body showed the red marks where two rifle shots had pierced her. She had killed the intruder but had not been strong enough to leave her grave. Behind piled rocks, where the noise was now loud, a baby cried.

For once, claws were useless. Hunter changed and lifted the child from her hiding place. She had been wrapped in a soldier's cape as well as a blanket given her by her dead mother. He scooped water from where ice had dripped and rubbed the tiny mouth. A tiny tongue moved to touch dry lips. He had asked for a direction. He had been given it.

CHAPTER ELEVEN

Sand Hills, Nebraska, January–February, 1879

Little Wolf allowed a period of mourning for the dead of Dull Knife's band, but without any of the usual customs. Clothing was too scarce to be rent. The chance of survival gave no time for any excess of ritual. None knew for sure who had died, except for Dead Face, but, from all Hunter knew, most of the warriors had sacrificed their lives and been wounded or killed.

Rides a Crow had been stoic in public but cried bitterly in private.

"He knew he went to his death," she said. "I knew, too. I could have stopped him. I should have stopped him."

Hunter let her grief flow without trying to correct her. No force of man or spirit could have prevented Dead Face from doing what he had done.

But Wrapped in a Blanket, the name given to the baby Hunter had rescued, was cause for joy all out of proportion to the baby's size. Rides a Crow, although not married, said she would care for the child, who had no known relatives in Little Wolf's band.

"Those who have no one else have me," she said. "I will take all of them, no matter how high the number should grow."

A few of the survivors Hunter had rescued arrived. Most had been lost but were guided by spirit horses to the Sand Hills. Soon, the morale of the tiny group improved when they learned Dull Knife had escaped capture and found shelter.

As Hunter moved among them, though, he saw that even

those who were most zealous about reaching the Tongue River were now seeing the cost of their dream in the faces of the dead. Rides a Crow was among the very few whose purpose did not waver.

"If not one other person walks with me, I will go alone," she said.

Hunter wondered if her words might come to pass.

Weeks later, the morose people were still going through the motions of living. It was as though the demons of hate conjured by Fairfax and those like him had sapped the will of The People to do more than exist.

"Is there a spell on The People?" Rides a Crow asked Hunter one day as she went aside from The People to speak to the wolf. "Do we face evil spirits?"

Hours later, after leaving the camp so they could speak alone, he told her there was always evil in the hearts of men, but that no conjured spell stalked the band of survivors.

He did not want to share with her the truth: that the Plains were alive with efforts of those who tried to contact spirits to raise demons, to conjure wraiths, and to poison and harden the hearts of white men against the Northern Cheyenne. It was good that most who tried to cause evil were unable to find success, but Hunter knew that, the more those who hated The People tried to raise evil spirits, the harder it would be for the Northern Cheyenne to win the spirit war in which they were engaged.

He shared the truth with Talks to Horses, who said the wilting spirit of The People needed to be revived. "The spirits reach out to help The People," she said, "but The People do not reach out in their turn."

"How do we change that? What shall I have them do? What can I do?" asked Hunter. "You understand the spirit world; I am only a freak who knows how to kill."

"Do nothing for the moment, impatient wolf," said Talks to Horses gently. "Spirit horses know how to make The People do the things they need to do while thinking the ideas come from their own minds!"

As the day ended, Rides a Crow sought out Hunter. "Find a hollow log," she commanded.

"In the dark?"

"Do you need a candle to see? Have your wolf eyes grown weak? Find one. Find two stout sticks. This is important, spirit fool!"

Hunter had no idea why she wanted the items but was relieved that she seemed to have emerged from her indecisive state. He searched, and as the dawn grew close he had dragged a small hollow log into the camp and later brought in two fat sticks about three feet long. "Are we having wood stew?" he sent as a message to Rides a Crow.

Her snapping eyes told him she had no time for his sarcasm. "Where are the spirit horses?" she asked.

"Not far," he replied. "They need to forage, and there is long grass in the next valley even with the snow."

"Tell them The People need their spirit. Tell them whatever you want, but get them here as fast as you can."

Hours later, one of the scouts yelled excitedly as the spirit horses galloped into camp, kicking the snow high as though performing. Even the most jaded and worn of The People came out to watch, for the majesty of a herd of wild spirit horses was beyond any sight to be seen on the Plains.

With The People now roused, Rides a Crow went to work.

"Slowly," she admonished Buffalo Horn, a boy who had suffered a leg wound at Punished Woman's Fork and still limped severely. She had told him he must help her. "The spirit, like a fire, must build slowly."

He tapped one of the logs gingerly, slowly, doing what he was told but not sure what this was all about.

"The spirit horses of The People have come to dance with us," she called to those looking in the direction of the noise. "They have come to bring us home. Come and dance with us; come and walk with us!"

Slowly, Rides a Crow and Talks to Horses began to move in a circle as Rides a Crow chanted.

"And the Great Warrior rode through the Darkness," she began. "And Light traveled in his footsteps. Do you believe, my people?"

A few voices softly answered her.

"And He put his Light upon The People. And the Darkness was jealous. And the Darkness sent men to steal the light. And they came upon The People and tried to send The People into Darkness. Is this not true, my people?"

More voices answered. Buffalo Horn beat louder on his improvised drum. Rides a Crow and Talks to Horses kept dancing, leading a line of high-stepping spirit horses as they plowed through the snow. Three of the younger warriors joined the dance.

"And the men used Darkness and deceit to steal land from The People, and they covered The People in Darkness and told themselves The People were smothered by Darkness and would never rise to ever see the Light again. Do you hear, my people?"

Little Wolf's voice joined those who answered.

Now Rides a Crow saw some elders join the circle, touching the spirit horses with joy and reverence as they shuffled along, grinning like children. As The People drew near, the horses began to prance, raising their hooves high as though they, too, were dancing. Buffalo Horn now pounded the hollow log faster, the dance consuming him.

Rides a Crow felt the spark take hold.

"And The People crawled out of the Darkness, and they burned the Darkness, and they set fire to it with truth and with faith and with spirit, and the fire burned in the sky and was the sun, and it set the night on fire and made the stars. Yes, my people!"

This time, a roar erupted. Rides a Crow could no longer count the dancers, some of whom now started to chant whatever the spirit told them to say.

"And The People walked over the Darkness and ground it under their bloody feet as they walked the walk of The People to their home, and the Light of The People would burn forever. Say it is so, my people!"

The drum pounded. The chanting swelled. Women with children too small to dance on their own held their babies; younger Cheyenne helped their elders join in the dance. A lone wolf's howl stretched forever as The People danced faster and stepped higher with legs that had been heavy the day before, and sang louder with spirits that had been stunned and wounded.

In rags and rapture, The People danced. And the demons within were vanquished.

There had been a thaw during which The People could have moved north. Hunter refused to hear of it. Instead, he disappeared. Then came three days of snow, covering the world in white once again. Hunter returned, snappish and anxious. As through winter would never end, the wind redoubled its ferocity and sleet beat down upon the hastily constructed lodges, keeping everyone inside whatever shelter they found.

Rides a Crow finally confronted Hunter at the meadow. It was the one place where she knew their camp was vulnerable to an attack. She had almost mentioned that when they settled there but thought Hunter knew best. Now she saw the wide open meadow with fearful eyes. Fewer than forty warriors lived in the camp, and few women or children could fill the role of warrior effectively. Hunter had recovered from his wounds at Fort Robinson, or so she thought. His disappearance worried her, for it was the only time he had left without any word to her. She needed to know what was on his mind, for The People were in her care, and she took much direction from him.

She saw his tracks in the snow. A large black rock, so massive it rose above the snow gathered all around it, lay next to him as he sat on his haunches and looked out over the meadow, like a wolf waiting for something. For no reason she could explain, she sat upon the rock.

"Good," he said in Spirit Talk. "I was hoping you would come. Yes."

Rides a Crow, anxious as the weather bore down, was amazed he seemed peaceful and relaxed on a day when the weather was about as bad as it could be. The anxiety that seemed to radiate from him during the days before had disappeared. The dance they held had revived the spirits of many, but this was the first time Hunter had not appeared careworn and anxious.

"When you look back upon these days, it will be with wonder and amazement, and a sense that life was simple," Hunter surprised her by saying.

"Look back? We may not survive."

"For these are the days when all is clear," he said. "There is good and evil; black and white. Much of life is gray, child. That is why Spirit Walkers are needed to help those who lose their way. Wrapped in a Blanket will learn to be wise as well. When the fighting is over, wisdom will be even more necessary than it is now."

"I am not wise."

"Not fully, or you would understand that the easy part is the time spent fighting and killing. The difficult part is what comes before and after."

"Why are you so calm and confident? Do you know something I do not?"

"Many things. But above all, I know that, when fighting an enemy to the death, it is well when the trap one sets is sprung, and you have helped spring this one."

Before she could reply, the open space where the ground sloped upward showed signs of movement. Hunter acted as though he could not have cared less. Rides a Crow was transfixed as wolf after wolf came into view behind the sleety, snowy weather. On this fierce day Hunter instructed her to tell Little Wolf his guards should be recalled. But here were at least fifteen wolves. Probably more.

"Why?" she asked. Hunter did not answer.

Instead, she perceived but could not share in the messages sent from the wolves at the top of the rise to Hunter.

"The spirit woman will be an added prize," Rheged thought. "I will kill her and let you watch."

"You and your collection of misfits who were thrown out by the clan should turn back," Hunter said. "Even an outcast hates to see his kind suffer. That is why I did not hunt you down at Fort Robinson."

"You were lucky. You will not be lucky again. There are nineteen of us," Rheged said. "There is you and a girl, since I assume she fights with you. If you wish to beg for mercy, I shall consider it after we have killed all the Cheyenne. You know they are defenseless."

"Rides a Crow," the wolf's message came. "Tell our friends at the top of the hill what you think of the lot of them."

She did. "I will curse you until the end of your lives, you miserable wretches," she said aloud. "You are cowards and jackals."

By chance, she had said one of the most inflammatory words

she could have used, for the enmity between wolves and jackals was deep.

Rheged waited no longer to talk or challenge. With a howl, the line of wolves began to run down the hill.

Rides a Crow had her rifle and knife. The rifle held five rounds. No more.

"It is a good day to die," she said, standing to meet the challenge.

"Stay," Hunter commanded her with authority. "Remember this day all the years of your life. And see why I tell you it is a good day to live."

He walked out a few steps ahead of her, showing no concern.

The creatures were about a third of the way down the hill when many of the animals flew into the air like magic. Some landed like broken dolls, and she heard the snapping of bones. Rides a Crow saw a rope, which had been buried in the snow. She then looked through the trees: a spirit horse held each end of the rope.

The attack faltered, but Rheged urged the animals onward.

This time, they got more than halfway to Hunter, Rheged well in front, when the snow again parted behind Rheged. This time the wolves tried to evade the rope. As they did so, Rides a Crow saw that the rope was not a mere strand of rope, but a kind of rope netting that blocked the progress of Rheged's gang. As the wolves collided with the netting, Rides a Crow heard the sound of horses galloping as the spirit horses charged, four from each direction. Wolves standing in place were trampled by the charge, as spirit horses ran them down.

"Now might be a good time for your rifle," Hunter admonished Rides a Crow.

She picked off at least two animals and wounded one more, before two survivors limped away.

Hunter remained standing. Waiting.

"You and I," said Hunter to Rheged. "If you are bold enough without the men of Fairfax or the sweepings of some street in London to do your dirty work for you."

Rides a Crow felt the hate between Hunter and Rheged as though it were a physical current. The massive Rheged charged at the smaller Hunter. Rides a Crow screamed, for it appeared certain to her that the larger Rheged would simply crush Hunter.

Rheged leaped upon Hunter, and the two animals thrashed in the snow.

Hunter darted away and bent way down on his forelegs, as puppies do when inviting play.

"Is that your best?"

Rheged's screaming howl chilled Rides a Crow to the core. She saw his teeth aiming for the neck of the rust-colored wolf, which did not move out of the way.

"Hunter!" she screamed.

Hunter heard nothing, as all the rage he contained exploded.

Rides a Crow wished she had more bullets as the larger wolf's jaws closed on the neck of the older wolf.

Then, with speed beyond what she could imagine, Hunter turned and sank his teeth into the exposed underside of Rheged's neck. Paralyzed with shock, Rides a Crow saw the death blow inflicted with more brutal efficiency than any other attack she had ever seen by any animal. The larger wolf was dead before it hit the ground.

"Others of Rheged's clan who hear me," Hunter sent out in the language of the clan. "Leave this place, leave The People alone, and I will allow you to live. Return, and you will share Rheged's fate."

He turned to Rides a Crow, ignoring the red-ringed body of the dead wolf behind him. "The People will be safe until the end of the snows," he said. "These evil spirits, who are ones of my kind that followed Rheged for what they could steal and for the joy of killing, tracked this place for days and were coming close. They knew about it from the trails taken from Fort Robinson here, tracks men would not follow but spirits could use. We do not have enough warriors to risk any Cheyenne being hurt. Those of the spirit must fight those of the spirit. I chose this spot to leave weak, and when I knew evil spirits were near, I asked that guards be brought in to be sure no Northern Cheyenne were harmed. It is not enough, Spirit Walker, merely to be stronger; it is necessary to be smarter. The spirit horses, as women, have spent weeks weaving the rope and net, knowing this day would come. I will protect you, protect The People, until an hour after my body is cold."

She realized that her ever-increasing perception of the spirit world had been the reason for her concern. Rheged's wolf allies had not only been prowling at the edge of the camp, but the edge of her mind.

For now, at least, her people were safe.

Fairfax Ranch, Colorado, January–February, 1879
Morrison Fairfax fed the newspapers into the fire. A stack of Eastern magazines would be next.

Whoever Annie Campbell was, he would deal with her. This *"American Report"* magazine she wrote for had printed article after article about the Northern Cheyenne. She included sketches supposedly taken from life that showed Cheyenne massacred in a pit as soldiers watched.

Campbell's articles were being reprinted in newspapers all across the country. How the Northern Cheyenne had died for their freedom. Rot! Weak-minded fools and other women might lose their sense when they read that kind of trash. Fairfax would have his men find her and deal with her. No! The article said she was living here in the West. His men could find her. Then he could deal with her in his own fashion.

He had come very close to eliminating the Cheyenne. The fool Indians had done some of the work themselves, even though he was certain his own plan would have worked better. He had witnessed soldiers who on one day gunned down warriors turn around the next day and give food and kindness to children. That was not the way to do things! He became disgusted with Phil Sheridan, when the general had allowed survivors of the Fort Robinson escape to take refuge at the Pine Ridge Agency. Fairfax had raged at Washington. Fools who took pity on the savages needed to be done away with. All that would take was someone with the gumption to put the remaining Indians on a cattle car to Indian Territory and be rid of them! Why could the politicians not see it? If John Chivington had only been president!

He did not know what had happened to his partner, who had vanished mysteriously after claiming he was ready to wipe out the Cheyenne and was heading to the Sand Hills of Nebraska. He felt the absence of him in his mind, as though Rheged were gone for good. The men Fairfax had left at Fort Robinson had come back to Colorado with him. When the blizzards eased, he would send them to see what had happened to his ally. This time, he would send every good man he had. The Indians might be hiding, but sooner or later they would head through the Black Hills, and Fairfax aimed to send enough men to do the job of wiping them out completely. What with Dull Knife's men having been slaughtered, there could not be many Indians left to kill.

Once he knew where Little Wolf's group was, he would go there in person to wipe them out. He had thus far relied too much on others to stop the Cheyenne. A man had to do things himself.

In the meantime, Fairfax aimed to lie low. The incident at

Fort Robinson had required some attention, because the man he'd shot had died.

Meanwhile, he had received information from one of the trusted friends in his circle about how to brew potions. He was certain he—who knew so much—could conjure up something that would obey him! When the snows melted, so would any hope the Cheyenne still possessed of surviving.

CHAPTER TWELVE

Sand Hills, Nebraska, Late February, 1879

Little Wolf's band reluctantly left its Sand Hills sanctuary. Although some white buffalo hunters and a few others had come upon The People, they had mostly remained undisturbed as they rested, ate, and recovered. Although so far no army patrol had found them, the looming end of winter meant more soldiers would search for them. In time, they would be found.

The Northern Cheyenne had no illusions about what would become of them if the cavalry found them. The disaster that had befallen Dull Knife's band left the remaining Cheyenne no less determined to press on with their march but far more fearful that few of those with whom they walked would live to reach the Tongue River Valley.

Yet on they walked and rode, knowing that every day they survived, The People had hope.

Hunter was sure Fairfax had known where Rheged was. Even if waist-deep snows now protected them, this peace would not last long. He had seen how tracks in the snow had made it easy for pursuers to follow Dull Knife's band. By the time anyone came looking for them, The People needed to be far away.

Rides a Crow, who usually walked or rode with Wrapped in a Blanket strapped to her, still felt the pain of loss. Dead Face had seemed mightier than any other man, and, if the soldiers could topple such a tree, they could kill any of them. She buried that thought deeply as she moved with The People, following a curving course through the Sioux reservation, making sure to avoid the Pine Ridge Agency, where they knew there were soldiers. Some wanted to bring Dull Knife with them or see relatives and friends who had survived the massacre and now lived at Pine Ridge. Hunter scouted the agency and urged The People to avoid it, fearing too many soldiers lived there. They moved on, screened by spirit horses that scouted for large groups of men.

Talks to Horses found them after they crossed into Dakota Territory. Most of the passes through the Black Hills were still deep with snow, but those to the southwestern corner of Dakota Territory were more easily passable. The Cheyenne sought the flattest possible route, which left them few options. Only when Talks to Horses reported to Hunter did the Cheyenne know they had been outpaced. She said a line of men waited at the western edge of the pass they were nearing.

"There are not many of them," Talks to Horses said in Spirit Talk. "They are fewer than fifty. I saw tents, but I did not see more than about thirty men, all cowboys and settlers. No soldiers. They are . . . they are evil men, Hunter. Evil hangs over them and among them."

Hunter mulled available options. Moving back through the hills to find another pass would take more time, and there was no guarantee Fairfax's men—for those thirty men could be no one else—would not find them there as well.

No, there was no way to run or find a way around them. This was the place where they needed to stand. A thrill of sorts ran down his spine. For more than two years he had done everything he could for The People. Hunter, who was created to kill, had controlled his rage for the sake of The People. The coming showdown would determine whether the Northern Cheyenne would go home or join their brothers and sisters in death. Whether Hunter's plan was good or not, he wanted revenge; he wanted to wipe Fairfax's men from the earth. He was ready!

The rugged evergreen-covered sides of the pass were more than enough cover for one stealthy scout. Fresh scars from trees cut for firewood showed Hunter that Fairfax's men had only recently camped. Soon, they would start scouting the pass to find the Cheyenne.

Yet they could not attack. Even if the Northern Cheyenne could match them gun for gun, charging the camp would kill too many attackers.

Flame grew behind the eyes of Rides a Crow as Hunter sent her his thoughts outlining his plan.

"Why me and not a warrior?"

"You are a warrior," he countered. "You have learned patience. You have learned wisdom. There will be one chance for this to succeed, Rides a Crow. If you fail, I fear there will be a slaughter. You have chafed for a chance to avenge Dead Face; this is it."

Talks to Horses was less cooperative. "We are spirit horses, Hunter. We are not warriors. When we become human, we do not shoot guns. We do not take lives. The Great Spirit made us life-givers, not death-bringers. The wolves were spirit animals who were foul and deserved what they received. I cannot do as you ask."

"For all the years you have ridden these Plains, for all the years you have watched The People, helped The People, and served the will of the Great Spirit, it comes down to this, Talks to Horses: Do you want the last free Northern Cheyenne to die so close yet so far from home, leaving no more of them on the earth, or do you want to see them in the land where they belong one last time?"

"The spirit world works as it does, wolf," was all she would say.

Little Wolf appeared doubtful when Rides a Crow told him about the plan and the predicament of The People.

"Am I being asked, spirit child, or am I being told?" Little Wolf asked her as she told him on a night when they walked out of The People's hearing range. She outlined what would happen and what was necessary and was now trying to tell from his tone whether he was bemused or offended. "If you are wrong, The People will be dead in the snow, for these who wait for us are not soldiers, but killers."

"The spirits tell us what we must do, my chief," she replied. "We have followed them for a thousand miles. This is one more step."

"Then let us take it," he replied.

She waited.

He had more to say. "When I was a young man, I walked and rode these hills without limits and never imagined what it meant not to be free. I will never be free as I was then, Rides a Crow. I do not know why, and I do not know how, but the white settlers will never leave this place. I will never ride on a buffalo hunt again. Yet, I will guide my people to the land that is theirs, and if generations to come must keep fighting in ways I may not understand, I shall rest in the earth beneath them, in the earth of our home. I cannot give my people freedom, but I can bring them home to live as freely as possible in a place where the dirt is sacred."

Little Wolf put his hands on Rides a Crow's shoulders and turned her to face him. "I believe in your spirits, and I believe in you, Spirit Walker. All shall be done as you wish."

After a day of intense work, everything was ready. As dawn

broke, Hunter was mounted on Talks to Horses. She had insisted on it.

"If this fails, my friend, no one else shall pay for your folly," she said. When he didn't respond, she shared another thought. "You are uneasy."

"There is evil there I have not yet found. I do not know how great it is, or how dark Fairfax's soul has become in seeking his way. I do not like these clothes. I do not like facing those men unarmed."

Talks to Horses snorted. The motley collection of white man's clothes The People had found for Hunter was the best they could supply. After months of mostly living as a wolf, being human was akin to throwing a sack over Hunter's senses.

"Do not shoot holes in their clothes then, wolf, and you may wear something better!" The spirit horse's snicker faded as they moved through the pass. Hunter looked behind him often, as if in panic. If Fairfax's men had scouts posted, he and Talks to Horses might already have been seen. Hunter planned to tell Fairfax's men he had sneaked away from the Cheyenne camp. He needed to look the part.

"Halt!" A rifle cocked.

"Are you a white man?" Hunter called as he lifted his arms, turning to look for the hidden speaker. "The Indians are near— the ones who escaped. It must be them!"

Two men with rifles emerged from behind trees.

"Told you I smelled smoke!" said one.

"Get this man to Lewis," said the second. "How far back are they, mister?"

"Two miles. Something like that maybe. Horse won't go fast; I must have stolen a bad one. My luck. I don't think they know I'm gone. You got many men? There's hundreds of 'em. Hundreds!"

Hunter sensed a comment from Talks to Horses but ignored it.

"Told you!" said one of the men. "There's always more of them than you think. Get this fella to Lewis."

Penfield Lewis had worked for Morrison Fairfax for ten years and been one of Fairfax's most loyal helpers in building his collection of trophies.

"Stole your clothes, did they?" he said once Hunter sat on a log by the fire.

"Stripped me bare," he replied. "I grabbed what I could, or I'd have frozen to death."

"Why didn't they kill you?"

"Told them I knew a way through the Black Hills no soldier could follow. They were thinkin' about it."

"How'd they capture you?"

"Had an elk in my sights, and I never heard 'em coming. Thought they were heading to Canada."

Lewis asked a few questions about the location of the Cheyenne camp. "They're coming this way?"

"Not sure," Hunter replied, doing his best to mimic the whites he had encountered. "They were talking about finding a way no one would follow. Couldn't tell from that talk of theirs if they know you are here. For all I know, they've scouted all the passes."

"Doubt that," Lewis replied. "Army's still warm in its forts. We're the only ones out here. We came at this from the west side. Them Indians had to get through some place."

Lewis summoned three men to the fire.

"Calvin, you go find the boss. He was planning to head north, so ride for Wyoming, Fort Laramie. Get him up here. Explain we can't wait for him, but I want him here as soon as possible. George, go find the man said he could put a spell on anyone attacking, whatever it does to them. Tell him he's about to earn his money. Will, round up the men. Leave ten men here. The rest will come with me. If we need them, I'll send a man back, but I figure if we smash their camp, they will take to the hills to get away. We'll need someone to pick off stragglers coming this way. Tell everybody: no cuttin' trophies until they're all dead. Man who does that'll get to be dead with 'em. Boss will want first pick."

He turned to Hunter. "You wait here. When we get ready, you ride to show us the camp."

"But I don't have a gun," Hunter remonstrated. "There's a lot of them. I just wanted to get away from them!"

"Don't worry," said Lewis. "If you're telling us the truth, you'll have a lot of men riding with you who know enough not to get captured by Indians. If you're lyin', you won't need a weapon, either, because, if you're lyin', you made the mistake of your life."

Rides a Crow waited impatiently as she left one side of the pass and walked to the other to take up her position where The People could see her. She knew how Hunter's trap was supposed to work. When Hunter explained it, it sounded simple. Here on the hillside, where they had dug into the snow to avoid slippery places and to hide better, the plan seemed less certain. What if Fairfax's men didn't come? What if they rode too fast? She looked around her. What if this last war party of the Northern Cheyenne—women, boys, old men, and a few warriors—was not up to the task?

Then she heard, as though it were only yesterday, what Dead Face had said to her at Turkey Springs: that the hardest part was waiting. That patience was the rule of a leader. That fear was to be swallowed. That The People were to be inspired to be brave.

She left her hiding place and stood in the pass. She lifted her voice so everyone could hear her.

"These men who come killed The People with Dull Knife. They have hounded and harried us for miles. They do not respect The People. Today, they shall learn The People are not dead, but strong. When you shoot, do not miss."

For a moment, the silence in the pass was broken by a chorus of Cheyenne warriors of all ages and sexes lifting rifles and chanting in agreement.

They were ready.

"How much farther?"

Fairfax's men were moving slowly, carefully.

"Not far after that narrow place I told you about. It's not far." Hunter tried to whine the way white men often did.

From somewhere, a rifle fired once in the direction where Hunter had been pointing. An answering gun shot twice.

"They seen us!" Hunter yelled. "I'm going back!"

"Will?"

"Sounded like a signal to me, boss. These hills, they got to have scouts."

"Go!" called Lewis. "Don't want them getting away."

"What about me?" asked Hunter.

One of the men threw him an extra rifle.

"Let's get us some Injuns, boys!" called Lewis.

Anticipating slaughter, they rode.

Rides a Crow felt the ground shake in warning as the riders approached. She wore a red piece of cloth around her head so everyone could see her. She felt their glances now. She recalled Dead Face's manner at Turkey Springs.

She raised her rifle over her head. To those within hearing, she spoke. "The whites must know Little Squirrel requires his dinner early!"

A round of chuckles echoed as those with her laughed about the warrior who, despite the fact that none of them had eaten well in months, remained the roundest Cheyenne of them all.

"As it should be!" he answered back to a chorus of hoots.

And The People stood tall and ready.

"Look! Look! I see the camp!"

Blue smoke curled up from several fires. Fairfax's riders saw tipis. They also saw a few figures in robes or covered in blankets, rushing about as though trying to strike camp and flee. A thin, ragged line of no more than about twenty men appeared to be defending the camp. As the Fairfax riders thundered closer, they saw bows in a few hands. They started to whoop and yell.

This would be easier than they had imagined.

Rides a Crow watched behind the trunk of a pine at the edge of the pass. She could see the faces of the men. The first riders were now even with her.

She stepped forward with the rifle at her shoulder. This day, she would not hide. This day, they would see The People did not need to hide.

The eyes of a rider at the edge of the group grew wide as he saw her. If his yells changed from triumph to alarm, no one heard. The alarm on his face turned to purpose as he started to shift his gun.

Rides a Crow fired and saw the man leap in his saddle as her bullet struck his chest. She did not waste another bullet on a dead man. She began firing into the group as she heard other guns behind her. She could see fear and surprise on the faces of the men now caught in a crossfire inflicted by enemies they knew would never surrender.

Screaming words and sounds in a voice that was not hers, she called the spirits to help The People wipe out these enemies.

"Down!"

She realized dimly the command had been directed at her.

One rider made a desperate attempt to ride her down. Rifles from the trees behind her fired. The rider, with a pistol in his right hand and his left hand on the reins, wobbled and reeled as bullets struck him. The horse galloped past as the empty-eyed man on its back slowly slumped forward.

Rides a Crow turned.

"Now I get my dinner!" called out Little Squirrel.

She laughed in return, feeling the power of their victory flow through her when she saw men slumped over saddles and men on the ground littering the floor of the pass.

The lead riders had passed Rides a Crow when the ambush began.

"Trick!" Lewis called out, looking around. He tried to spot the man who had lured them into the ambush, but he was not there. Then he looked ahead. The Cheyenne holding bows and arrows were now warriors holding rifles.

"Get those—" he started to say. Then rifles cracked, and the leaders of Fairfax's charge to wipe out the Cheyenne were shot down by hard-faced warriors who saw in their stand revenge for the deaths of Dull Knife and his band.

A stream of panic-stricken riders headed west through the pass to return to their camp and the safety of their comrades. The men who had stayed in camp had heard gunfire and assumed it signaled the end of the Cheyenne camp.

Hunter, who had been ignored by the riders as they attacked the Cheyenne camp, emptied a rifle as the riders passed. He was sure he hit at least one man. Then he waited. He heard no more gunfire. But he heard men yelling. Riderless horses galloped his way. He stopped those he could. They could be rides for The People.

Leading the horses he had caught, Hunter rode to the mouth of the pass. The camp had been wrecked. A few men lay on the ground, but every tent had been trampled.

"A stampede is a terrible thing," came the thoughts of Talks to Horses, sounding not the least contrite. "I believe they might run all the way home!"

The ambush had turned into a major victory for the Northern Cheyenne. In addition to horses that could give the foot-weary rides, and food that would augment their meager rations, Little Wolf's band now had guns and ammunition needed for hunting—and protection.

In the wreckage of the Fairfax camp, books on magic and spells had been found. Hunter burned them unread. Fairfax was using all of his weapons to defeat the Northern Cheyenne. Hunter feared he had not yet blunted all of those weapons.

Nineteen of the attackers had been killed. Sixteen were captured, many of them wounded—some severely. The rest of the party of forty-five had fled.

Disconsolate Fairfax survivors feared they would be slaughtered. When the fight was over, however, discipline prevented revenge killings, which might have served as a pretext for soldiers to hunt down the Cheyenne. Instead, survivors were given their dead and twelve horses to carry them away, while Rides a Crow made sure everyone who spoke to the captives made it clear she and her band were heading for Sitting Bull in Canada.

The Northern Cheyenne moved out north, keeping to the east of the Black Hills now that they had horses for The People to ride through the deeper snow. They would find a different way west. The People now moved with confidence. With hope. The Powder River lay only days away. Soon they would be home.

News that his men had found the Northern Cheyenne and that the Indians had slipped away reached Fairfax while he was visiting Fort Laramie, demanding that the army seal off the Tongue River Valley so the Indians could be stopped once and for all.

"Let me see if I understand this correctly, Mr. Fairfax," said the junior officer, whose attitude galled Fairfax. "Your men attacked the Indians in the Black Hills. Those men of yours were not defending your ranch? They just up and decided to attack the Indians instead of reporting the presence of the hostiles to the duly constituted authority?"

"Why bother? The army never does anything! You allow a marauding band of Indians to defy the law!"

The officer's brows furrowed. "Mr. Fairfax, the army is charged with providing protection for settlers and creating peaceful conditions here. We are authorized to accept the surrender of the Northern Cheyenne, not hunt them down like game to slaughter. If your men were undertaking a private war against anyone without the support of the army, they were the ones breaking the law. I have been told you killed a man over Indian trophies. We do not allow that here. Perhaps you should go home to Colorado and allow us to handle the situation. I understand you have committed vast time and labor to the protection of your state. The army will be happy to call upon you if your men are needed."

The dismissal enraged Fairfax. Who was this little wet-eared snip to tell him about Indians? As he raged, he saw on the officer's desk a copy of the magazine for which the Campbell woman had written her pro-Indian malarkey.

"You read this trash?" he said, grabbing the magazine and throwing it across the room.

"The army is aware that many citizens believe the Cheyenne might be better served with mercy than howitzers," the officer said. "Times have changed, Mr. Fairfax. I suggest you go home. An escort will be provided."

Fairfax seethed over this betrayal. Indian-lovers everywhere! He stalked out and slammed the door behind him so hard, it sounded like the bark of a gun.

CHAPTER THIRTEEN

March 1879, near the Yellowstone River, Montana Territory

The snows were melting. The Powder River glistened as they crossed it, rushing with early spring frenzy. Many of The People rode without blankets across their shoulders so they could feel the sun's warmth. The silence that had marked much of the trek now broke as older Cheyenne pointed out landmarks they recognized to their children or to anyone else near enough to hear.

Some eyes scanned for a glimpse of the Tongue River ahead. Others held tears. One of the elders recalled when he hunted with his son—a warrior who had died with Dead Face in the pit near Hat Creek after their escape from Fort Robinson.

Hunter had gone ahead when Talks to Horses reported a scouting party of soldiers. The wolf was surprised to see two civilians—a man and a woman—in the group of a dozen men, who moved at a leisurely, relaxed pace. The group also had a wagon. When he described the man leading the party to Rides a Crow, who then told Little Wolf, the Cheyenne learned the man was Captain Jack Evans, one of the few whites who had ever tried to learn the Northern Cheyenne language.

Rides a Crow rode to meet him. If all went well with her meeting, Little Wolf could meet with the soldier later. She and the rest still suspected a trick, even though the spirit horses and Hunter all agreed there was no other party of soldiers anywhere near, and the spirit horses sensed no presence of evil nearby.

The soldiers rode in a column of twos, with the civilians in the lead behind Evans. The wagon trailed the small group. The group reached a clearing where oaks and aspens blended with cedars and pines. The sounds of spring—squirrel nails on rough bark, jays complaining about everything, and woodpeckers tapping out their music—surrounded the small space that, as the soldiers watched, filled with armed Cheyenne warriors. A rust-colored wolf emerged from the trees as well, glaring intently.

"No," said Evans, as his men reached for their guns. Squinting, he saw a woman on a coal-black mare approaching. The People had searched all of their belongings for clothing and jewelry to make Rides a Crow appear as regal as possible. Around her neck, she wore the necklace Hunter had taken from her grandmother's body. Bone bracelets danced on her arm. She wore a buckskin dress and leggings. The moccasins on feet that were used to being bare were white and intricately beaded. A red cloth bound back her hair, which blew in the slight breeze.

For a moment, Evans felt a chill. By all rights, the Northern Cheyenne should be dead or dying, if not dispersed across the Plains. Yet here in front of him rode a woman who looked as though she were in command not just of herself, but of everyone around her. He felt as though he should kneel.

He dismounted and turned to Collins and Campbell. "I believe this is the moment you have been awaiting," he said. "Accompany me."

Rides a Crow maintained her seat on Talks to Horses. She knew all with her were scanning the soldiers for any movement that might be hostile. She was attuned to evil, to deceit, to danger. She felt none of that, but she would not put herself at their mercy. Not yet.

It made no sense, but Evans felt a smile he could not contain. He was seeing a miracle. These people had walked from Fort Robinson to the Darlington Agency and back again. Perhaps blood might no longer flow across the Plains.

"I am Captain Jack Evans of the U.S. Army," he said, taking off his hat. "May I introduce Paul Collins, who serves as our interpreter, and Annie Campbell, a reporter for some Eastern magazines. Miss Campbell has been looking forward to meeting the Northern Cheyenne."

"I am Rides a Crow, the daughter of Dark Hawk, who was killed at the Greasy Grass; and the granddaughter of Flies the Hawk, who was killed at Sandy Creek. I was the pledged wife of Dead Face, who was murdered at the Hat Creek pit. I was born to live in peace with all people, but the white people have killed my family and the families of others who want only to live as we wish. I am here to return to my home, for it was promised by the Great Father that The People would have a homeland given us by the Great Spirit. If you wish to talk, we may talk; if you wish to fight, we will die before we abandon our goal."

"You speak English very well," said Collins as he wondered if the figure of authority before him was the same young girl he recalled from the reservation.

"We spoke at Darlington, Talking Noises," she said. "Your words were true then. Let them be so now."

"I am authorized to accept your surrender," said Evans. Collins translated Evans's words into Cheyenne to be sure Rides a Crow understood. "My men and I can escort the band of Little Wolf to Fort Keogh. There is food in the wagon there, and more at the fort."

"No! No one is here to surrender," said Rides a Crow loudly and proudly. "We are here to go home."

Campbell scribbled furiously as Rides a Crow talked and tried to draw her image in the margin of her sketchpad.

"It is sad but it is true, Rides a Crow, that there is enmity between our peoples," said Evans. "My men can escort you to the fort, where you will be able to camp as you please nearby.

You will not be put in a barracks. But Little Wolf must surrender, and you must all give up your guns."

Rides a Crow took in the news without expression.

"Do The People not need guns to hunt? Do The People need to bow and walk in chains when they ask to live on their own land? Do we, whom no one can defeat, need to say we surrender?" She heard Dead Face in her mind. Rides a Crow stopped and waited to be sure the white man understood. Then she continued.

"The People have asked for nothing but to live on these lands. The People have never gone to the places where the Great Father's white children live in their cities to burn and kill, and The People will never do so. The People will not surrender, because The People never sought war. The People wish to go home, and, if you will walk with us, you are welcome. If you wish to bar the way, we shall have war."

Evans and Collins had a hurried, whispered conference.

"Do you understand me?" Campbell asked Rides a Crow as they talked.

"I learned English many years ago when I was a child," she replied.

"What would you say to people back in the East who wonder why you have come so far to be here? Why did you do it?"

"We were in a place of death. The spirit of The People . . . the soul of The People . . . the hearts of The People were dying. We refused to die there. We chose to die with our faces toward our home, on the land of the Great Spirit, rather than leave our people to die far from home. If the white people wish to fight the Northern Cheyenne, we shall be here. We hope to live in peace, but we will run in fear no longer. We will die before we surrender this hope. It is a good day to live, but if the white people wish it to be a day to die, we are ready to make it so."

"You will not have to die," said Collins, speaking for Evans.

"If Little Wolf will agree for his people that there will be no violence, the army will agree there will be no force used against the Northern Cheyenne. You will be allowed to camp near Fort Keogh until we can sit down together as friends to decide a permanent place for a reservation."

Rides a Crow digested the words. "No!" She bristled.

"Why not?" said Evans, clearly upset that his well-meant offer was rejected.

"The People will never agree to any place that is not ours!"

"In that case," replied Evans quickly, "let me stipulate that the permanent place will be in the Tongue River Valley." He held up his hands in a gesture of frustration. He glanced at Collins. "Make sure she knows that was what I meant! Only an idiot would send these people down south again!"

For the first time, Rides a Crow's facial expression changed slightly. The tic might have been a smile.

"She understands," Rides a Crow said to Evans. "I will tell Little Wolf we do not talk to an idiot. We will meet in this place at this time tomorrow."

She turned and slowly rode away.

Fort Keogh, at the northern edge of the Tongue River Valley, was in a state of high excitement. Rumors that the Northern Cheyenne had made it into Montana Territory had been floating in the air for days. Evans and his party had been sent out by General Nelson Miles in hopes of finding them.

Fairfax had been stunned when he reached the Black Hills to find his men dead or scattered, and the Cheyenne supposedly on their way to Canada. He had ridden to Fort Keogh in an effort to rouse the army to prevent this escape attempt, only to find that the army was waiting for the Northern Cheyenne to come to it, as though both sides should kiss and make up!

The only thing that made him stay at the fort was that he

had heard Campbell, the reporter, was there writing about a small group of Northern Cheyenne who had surrendered years ago and mistakenly been allowed to live near the fort. At the very least, he would tell her what a great wrong she was committing.

He knew Miles was far too soft on the Cheyenne, so he kept his thoughts to himself as he prowled the fort. It was there he learned about the rumor of a Cheyenne group in the area.

A courier had brought the news everyone waited for: Evans had made contact. He would be bringing in Little Wolf for talks at the fort. The news was received as though a victory had been won. Fairfax was disgusted. Then he had a thought: even if he was going to lose this war, he could still make sure the winners never enjoyed it. Hadn't he said he would have to do it all himself?

Fairfax cornered the courier. After a few drinks, the man told Fairfax everything he knew. Under the cover of darkness, Fairfax went out to do a job no one else seemed to have the guts to do.

For two days, Evans and Little Wolf talked in a tipi set up in the clearing. Rides a Crow, Collins, and Campbell were also there. Evans had Campbell keep notes to record the meetings in case Washington decided to second-guess him.

Little Wolf would talk, then think in silence for a long time. Rides a Crow knew the chief's tactic: if Evans was a man of honor, he would be able to sit calmly while his words were digested. If not, he would urge Little Wolf to agree to terms quickly. Evans passed the test.

"Bring me my gun. Be sure it is loaded," Little Wolf told Rides a Crow. She went out and returned with the rifle, noting that the soldiers watching did not look pleased, even if they did not interfere.

Little Wolf hefted the Winchester. "This gun is good at killing," he said.

"That is the purpose of a gun," said Evans calmly.

"It will kill game for The People. It will not kill any more soldiers." Little Wolf looked at Evans intently. "You are not all white men. That is a shame. We can begin peace, you and I, but it will be up to others to keep it."

He turned to Rides a Crow. "Let us tell The People."

"They know," she said.

"And what do they say?"

"That they now sleep with hope."

"Then that is enough. For today, that is enough."

Little Wolf rode between Evans and Collins as they headed back to the fort. Rides a Crow followed, riding Talks to Horses, with Campbell next to her. Soldiers were interspersed with The People. They were ordered to treat the Cheyenne with respect first and foremost. Evans had insisted upon a count to be sure that no one got lost along the way. There were one hundred twenty-three Cheyenne who had marched one thousand miles from Indian Territory to Montana.

Spirit horses rode off in all directions to search for parties of soldiers or settlers that might be a threat.

Hunter waited behind. The wolf watched the last of The People leave the clearing. There was no question in his mind that Evans was sincere. The reporter and the man with her were, as well. From the talk he had been able to overhear, the army wanted the Northern Cheyenne found, settled, and forgotten by a public that had been reading about a heroic march and a last stand. If that was true, it would mean difficulties lay ahead for the Indians. If there were no more buffalo and The People had to live on crops, it would be a major change to their lives. Festering scars from years of Plains Indian wars would linger. But at least the Northern Cheyenne would live.

What would that mean for him? Hunter would remain near for some time to be sure the Cheyenne were not clapped in irons when they reached the fort, but after that, he was not sure. Talks to Horses had painted a picture of the Plains beyond the farms and ranches. Never seeing a human for weeks. It sounded like a dream.

Then he sensed it. Some *thing* had entered the Montana woods. Something evil. It had to be Fairfax! Wolf legs could not match those of horses, but the cavalcade of soldiers and Indians was moving slowly. He could catch up. He had to!

Evans wanted to step up the pace, because it was clear a storm was near, but he did not want the Cheyenne to feel they were being pushed. Collins had been a Godsend! He and Little Wolf talked easily in Cheyenne, with both men laughing when Collins's vocabulary failed him. Collins told him about people from the Darlington Agency, and events that had taken place on the Plains and in the world since the Cheyenne had left Indian Territory eighteen months ago.

"I'm not sure how to explain changes to the Indian policy with a new president without making it sound like the Great Father is a chicken running around without a head," Collins told Evans.

"If you figure out what goes on back in Washington, let me know, too," replied Evans, who could see from Little Wolf's expression and the smile on his face after Evans spoke that the chief knew enough English to gain some sense of what was said.

Campbell had showed Rides a Crow her book of sketches. "I would like to draw you."

Then Campbell saw something was very wrong. The Cheyenne woman—no, she was a girl who could not be more than nineteen—had stopped talking and stared at the book, the index finger of her left hand reaching out to touch a page. Her face was contorted. Campbell was perplexed. She never drew anything showing Indians in a bad light, and she'd never drawn the sacred objects she had been shown on condition she never draw them!

"You knew him?" Campbell asked.

Rides a Crow was staring at a sketch of Dead Face. Campbell had drawn it after his death. Rides a Crow's hand still hovered over the image. She touched it briefly. Reverently.

"Yes. I . . ." Rides a Crow then sucked in her breath. She had come to the sketches of the Pit near Hat Creek. "This is how they died?"

Campbell nodded. "They were very brave men. Paul said he talked to that one . . ."

"To Dead Face?"

"Yes, that was his name. And Paul came home crying that such a brave man had died. Would you like Paul to tell you what he said when they met?"

"I would. He was . . . we were to be together. May I keep this?"

Campbell was unsure how to deal with Rides a Crow's request. "I like to keep all the originals. I can get you a print." The word meant nothing. Rides a Crow clearly did not understand. "I drew a final one. That was the one printed in the newspaper and the magazine. I can get you one of those, or a lithograph in color. I like to keep my drawings."

She could see the frowning Cheyenne girl working something out.

"Printed means books and paper things. People have seen this? White people?" Rides a Crow seemed upset.

"Yes, Rides a Crow. Of all the drawings I ever did, that got the largest reaction. After that drawing was printed, many people wrote in to the magazine and to the government and said that anyone willing to die that way deserved to be allowed to go home. One reason the army changed the way it acts is that people were angry about what happened at that place."

"They did not laugh at seeing dead Cheyenne?"

"Some people may have done so, because some people are very cruel. Most of the white people who saw it understood that men who had nothing had given everything for their dream of going home. That was when people began demanding that the army stop making war on your people."

"So he did not die for nothing," Rides a Crow said softly.

"No," Campbell said quickly. "He died so your people could live."

Rides a Crow had wet eyes as she looked at Campbell.

"Then I am content. He said he would keep his vow. He made one to me and one to The People. He could not keep them both."

The moment ended swiftly as Rides a Crow started at the howl of a wolf. Campbell watched her listen, as though hearing something else that was on the wind, some message somehow delivered to her. Could they really talk to animals? Rides a Crow rode Talks to Horses ahead and impulsively grabbed Evans by the shoulder.

"We must stop!"

"What! Why? What!"

"Spirit child, what is wrong?" said Little Wolf.

"Evil is stalking us," said Rides a Crow. "An evil man. I do not know if he is alone." She stopped. "He seeks to kill you and the white chief."

"Evans, get your men to form up on the sides; screen Little Wolf and his people," said Collins. "This is not a trick or a hoax or some silly fancy. I know this from Darlington. Listen to her!"

He spoke to Rides a Crow. "You must tell your people the soldiers will be riding on the side so they know they are being protected and not hurt."

Evans signaled with his hand for the cavalry to stop. The head of the column dissolved as Evans and Collins rode to give orders, and Rides a Crow went to reassure The People and to ride among them.

Fairfax had found a perfect spot in a tree. It was an effort at his age, but it would be worth it. Once the Indians got to the fort, it would be impossible to get near any of them. It was now or never. The trail to the fort wound about. There was one place along the trail where the front of the column would be all but isolated from the rear. That would give him time to fire and escape. He didn't know how many would ride at the front, but he was certain Little Wolf and Evans would be among them.

He had almost started firing when a few horses rode by—the wild ones that had galloped through his fields and, he was certain, trampled his crops for spite. The horses stopped for a moment in the clearing he had in his sights. He moved behind a huge limb and waited. The horses moved along, galloping hard and fast.

Fairfax's anger knew no bounds when the army column came in sight with Evans in the lead and a white woman behind him. That must be the reporter. He had heard at the fort she rode with the column. There! Little Wolf rode at the head of a line of scarecrows.

If he could kill the chief, the Cheyenne would believe they were being tricked. If he killed the soldier, the troops would fall upon the Indians. And if he killed the meddling scribbler, no one would spread lies about the Cheyenne ever again. They were nearing his spot. Fairfax was ready.

Hunter ran as fast as his limping gait would take him. He knew Fairfax was near. He could all but smell the man's evil. The place where the column now rode was perfect ambush country, but so was the past mile. He was almost to the front of the column as he cut through the trees.

Hauling three buffalo guns to the branches had been a chore, but it was worth it. Fairfax had two guns loaded and lying across the branches. He held the third. He cursed his luck. The soldier and the reporter had dropped back. Only Little Wolf now rode at the head of the column. But Fairfax would take what he could get. He cocked the weapon. No, wait. There was the soldier, riding hard while some Indian girl was doing the same on the other side of the small column! Riding right into his sights.

Wait. Wait. Fire!

Hunter had seen the glint of a metal barrel in a thick-limbed elm tree barren of leaves. He had one choice. He leaped as he heard the gun.

Evans fought for control of his horse. Whatever it was that had crashed into it had forced the animal to buck and rear, almost sending him into the dirt. People began yelling. A gun had boomed, but he could not see anyone firing.

Rides a Crow, who kept her rifle ready, had seen the muzzle flash and fired at the tree where the first shot came from before most of them even knew from where it came. A second shot at Little Wolf followed the first at Evans. His horse was also jostled by the wolf, and the bullet missed.

Fairfax had one shot left. As twigs rained down on his head from Rides a Crow's rifle, he took it.

Talks to Horses screamed as the massive bullet from the gun raked down her side, barely missing Rides a Crow's leg.

"No!" the girl yelled as the horse contorted in agony. She was half-thrown and dismounted as Talks to Horses spun in pain and kicked.

Three troopers rode forward, firing at the spot where Fairfax had been hiding. Two Cheyenne rode with them and did the same.

Hunter had started to find Fairfax but turned back when Talks to Horses was hit. There was blood. Far too much blood. The coal-black mare stumbled. Hunter felt its pain. Its panic. The horse moved to the trees.

"Do not let them watch me die!" she screamed at Hunter.

"Then don't die!"

But nothing but pain came from Talks to Horses.

"Get the Medicine Bundle," Hunter ordered Rides a Crow. "Meet me in the woods."

The horse staggered to the trees. Little Wolf, still stunned by the unexpected violence, meekly handed over the bundle of sacred objects when Rides a Crow asked for it. When the girl reached the trees, her heart broke. Talks to Horses was down. Hunter had become human and was holding her.

"Go!" he said brusquely. "Spirit child or not, you cannot see this. Make sure they know the shooter was Fairfax. He was trying to kill both chiefs. Go!"

Before Rides a Crow left, she bent down to touch Talks to Horses's glossy, black mane. Everyone knew what happened when a horse went down. Horses gave everything for The People. Even spirit horses died for them.

The troopers returned with a vague description of the man who had fired the buffalo guns. He had a horse ready and galloped into the trees. The troopers had not been able to catch him. Rides a Crow told Little Wolf and Evans that the man was an enemy of everyone who loved peace.

"He has tried to make our peoples enemies. He has tried to grow hate. We will not let him have his victory," she said. "He tried to kill both of you. He wants more war."

Evans watched Little Wolf with trepidation.

"I have said what I have said. When I made war with you, I prepared myself to die," Little Wolf said eventually. "I have done the same now that I have left war behind."

Both leaders walked together that evening among The People and the soldiers to ensure everyone knew that, although both men had been fired upon, neither was injured and neither would change course.

Rides a Crow sat apart that night when they made camp. She felt drained. Empty. For months she had done everything she could, and she had come to the last of her strength. It was too much. Too many had died. She no longer could do this work. She said so aloud with her arms folded over her knees and her head upon her forearms, weeping.

"Do not quit because your spirit failed, child."

A beautiful Northern Cheyenne woman with glossy, coal-black hair stood before her. The woman's right hip was red-stained and ungainly with bandages. Rides a Crow's spirit knew who the woman was even as her mind rejected the idea.

"Are you a ghost?" she asked Talks to Horses.

"If I were, my wound would not hurt," she replied, dropping a blood-stained medicine bundle at Rides a Crow's feet.

"You are alive!"

"I am hurt, child. I live, but barely. I must live this way for now, because it is all the spirit wolf knows how to heal with the gifts of the spirit. I do not know if I can ride the Plains freely and gallop as I did. I know I cannot ride with you to your home. Yet I am here so you do not give in to despair."

"How is it you live?"

"Ask me how a spirit wolf knows healing secrets of our people, and I shall tell you." Talks to Horses grimaced. "I am going. We have brought you to this place, child, and my herd

225

and I must go. Places of men are dangerous to us. I shall return to your side some day, I promise, but for now I must heal. Spirit horses heal slowly. But I will live. Do not allow The People to believe a man of hate can kill a spirit horse."

The woman turned away from the fire and walked into the night. Rides a Crow followed her with her gaze until she was indistinct. She wondered if what she saw was true, or whether, in her misery on a day that should have been a triumph, she had seen a ghost.

"I, too, must go," came Hunter's thoughts.

"Not you too!" cried Rides a Crow.

"While this man lives, the one who got away, The People are not safe. You are not safe. When his spirit no longer sweeps the Plains, I shall return."

Annie Campbell's pencil flew as she prepared the text of the article that would go by telegraph to the East. She knew she was writing history. She knew no words could capture the scene she had witnessed at Fort Keogh, but she tried.

"With the full honor of the U.S. Army, with bands playing and people cheering, and the troops giving them a salute of honor, the Northern Cheyenne came home to the Tongue River Valley today after living out the Book of Exodus on the plains of Kansas, Nebraska, Dakota, and Montana," she wrote.

"They came home in tattered clothing often stained with their blood. They came home with heads high, with tears in their eyes for those who died along the way, and with a welcome from the soldiers here at Fort Keogh, who made this occasion not the surrender some might have expected, but a celebration reflecting the respect given to a people who were denied their homeland but refused to abide the injustice, who paid in blood for their freedom. They came home proud and undefeated. They came home as heroes."

CHAPTER FOURTEEN

Fairfax Ranch, Colorado, April 1879

Life was blooming around him as Hunter waited expectantly in the tall grass. Fairfax had finally returned three days ago but had not set foot outside the house. No one else had come or gone. Hunter feared Fairfax had acquired some powers, but still he waited throughout the day. Smoke came from the chimney. In time, the smell of smoke was mixed with food. A lit kerosene lamp sat on a windowsill.

Hunter crept closer to the house, and through the windows he saw a man. An evil man. A man Hunter had to stop once and for all, because as long as Fairfax lived, he would use every ounce of his power to hurt the Northern Cheyenne.

At first light, Fairfax went to the barn. Hunter followed cautiously. The barn door stood invitingly open. A trap? Possibly. Hunter would see what sort of evil lurked there.

As soon as the wolf entered the barn, the door slammed behind him. He heard something being put into place outside. Whatever it was, the door held fast when he pushed against it.

"Well, well. You must be the spirit wolf Rheged always talked about. Did you really think, after all I have done, I was not aware of you? I realized on the day I failed to kill that miserable chief that it was you I was fighting all this time, not them. You had all those spirits on your side. I needed a few more of my own," said the voice on the far side of the door. "I am now a powerful conjurer of death. I will show you!"

The voice stopped. Hunter's eyes adjusted to the barn's dimness. Then shutters opened near one window, and he heard the sound of metal striking metal before the shutters closed again. Hinges squealed.

"I did not think you could resist the temptation to meddle," Fairfax called from outside. "I created a potion I am sure is powerful magic, because you should see what it does to these bears."

Hunter saw what appeared to be four angry grizzly bears moving towards him. He could dimly see metal bars of a cage behind them.

"When you don't feed them, they get angry," Fairfax called from outside. "But what I found is that if I give them this special drink I brewed after starving them, they become uncontrollable. It took me so many books to find out what would work, books that have knowledge men such as I can master. Unfortunately, it took a lot of dead animals to perfect my potion. The crew here did a lot of the work, but then they could not be trusted. I was afraid they would share my secret, so they joined the dead animals in the pit they dug."

He laughed.

"It has cost me everything I had, but I can now eliminate the Northern Cheyenne. I have won the spirit war, thanks to everyone who helped me create this potion! Think about it, miserable, meddling wolf. Your friends the Indians are now living in grizzly country. I suppose we will read one day how the bear spirits destroyed their homes! How tragic!"

Another round of laughter followed this statement. Hunter realized that whatever human purpose Fairfax once might have possessed in opposing the Cheyenne, it had been subsumed by a tide of pure hate and evil. Perhaps, he thought, the man was no longer sane. But he was still deadly.

Raging and growling, the bears had closed in a circle around

Hunter. Closer. Closer. The rust-colored wolf waited until they surrounded him, then leaped outside the circle, beyond the bears, and stood waiting again, as if this were a game. The bears, increasingly agitated, closed in on the wolf again, and again and again, as the animal dodged and ducked. The wolf seemed to be playing a game. The more he worked them, the angrier they grew as they collided with each other—and the closer they came to turning on one another. Finally, they had him. This time, there was no room for an escape.

Then the wolf moved. With a feint at jumping, the wolf dug its sharp, massive teeth deep into the knee of one bear. The wounded bear collapsed, while others moved forward, stomping on their former partner until it was killed. Another feint from the wolf. This time his teeth went for a bear's eyes. As the bear tried to knock the wolf loose, its huge arm hit another potion-crazed bear, knocking it flat. Blood flowed from the wounded bear's face and covered the wolf. The partially blinded bear stalked around, swinging its front paws aimlessly but viciously until another bear attacked him, killing him with one stroke.

Two creatures closed in, striking, not caring what they hit, as long as they hit something. They were beyond crazed, beyond berserk. They might destroy their muscles fighting, but they would destroy Hunter first. The few blows they landed staggered him. It was, Hunter knew, a fight to the finish, and he was going to lose it if he tried to match muscle against muscle.

He needed help. He dove between one bear's legs and ran to a pile of supplies. There! A kerosene lamp. If he could find a match, and the time to change into being a man, he could burn down the barn. That would give him room; he could get away, and eventually the bears would tire.

But the wounded bears had no intention of giving up. A paw knocked him flat. A follow-up stroke opened up a cut on his side. He gasped and dripped blood. Hunter snapped his jaws at the bears. They backed away. He tried to get away, dragging his right rear leg. He felt a paw just miss his spine, then turned and sprang, the ruse having made his pursuer less than cautious as it hunted a wounded animal. He clawed and bit into its neck. A roar came in response as he clawed something vital. He and his victim fell, with the wolf barely able to get out from under the weight of the dying bear.

The world erupted in noise. A burst of light flooded the barn. The final bear fighting Hunter turned to stare at the glare of sunlight and the silhouettes of spirit horses galloping in. This was Hunter's chance. He leaped for the neck and bit. The bear swung wildly and tried to shake off the wolf. He slammed into a wall of the barn, almost dislodging Hunter, who held on with aching jaws. One final fit of rage sent Hunter tumbling to the ground. The animal staggered to kill him but moved in slow motion. Its strength ebbed as its blood streamed from the tear left by Hunter's teeth. It finally toppled as Hunter watched, gasping.

"You are in need of what I believe the white people call a nanny," said Talks to Horses as Hunter lay on the barn floor, sides heaving from exertion. She had ridden one of the members of her herd when they followed him to Fairfax's farm and was still too weak to have joined in forcing the door. "Did you not suspect a trap? Perhaps Fairfax's magic is stronger than you think to make you so foolish. He laid a wooden beam across the door that I could not lift and even my strongest horses could barely break. You were lucky, spirit wolf."

"Fairfax has no magic," the wolf replied with deep breaths between words, "only the persistence of a truly evil man. I do not think he created a potion or anything else. I tasted nothing. I sensed nothing. He starved those bears. They would have reacted the same way, no matter what. But now it is time for him to learn the price of trying to raise evil."

"You need to rest."

"Soon." A smile of sorts passed across the wolf's bloody muzzle. Then he padded out of the barn. This particular war was not over.

Beneath his photo of John Chivington, Fairfax sat in his trophy room, chanting something evil, surrounded by the ghastly collection of relics he had amassed. Hunter did not bother to change. He needed no words for what he aimed to do. A spirit wolf could do everything that needed doing with paws that were capable of doing things paws were never intended to do.

He stood at the entrance to the room, surveying the items the evil man had collected. He waited to be noticed. Fingers, heads, jewelry, and sacred items. Hunter waited.

Finally, Fairfax, feeling Hunter's gaze, glanced over his shoulder. Blood drained from his face. He looked out the window, as though expecting help. There would be no help today.

"Perhaps we can make a deal," Fairfax said. "I have power you do not understand. You cannot make cause with the Cheyenne when you can have power for yourself."

A growl emerged from the animal stalking him.

"You will not win," Fairfax said. "There are more like me. Hundreds more. They write me, and we share spells to stop the Indians and provoke white men who normally would not care into wanting to slaughter them! If not today, tomorrow. I have already set wheels in motion you cannot stop to kill that Cheyenne girl. I have contacts high in places of power who will not allow my work to end here. You have no idea how puny your power is against mine!"

Still, Hunter waited.

Fairfax began to sweat. He looked for a useful weapon among his collection. There was a pistol he had left on his desk. Fairfax inched toward it. Slowly. The animal did not respond. Slowly. Then, moving as fast as he could, Fairfax picked up the pistol and pointed it at the wolf.

"Now who has the upper hand? I told you I will win!"

The wolf spat out six bullets. They rolled across the floor to Fairfax's transfixed gaze, as the animal slowly and surely moved in closer.

Hunter had found the kerosene jug. He also had a match. He poured kerosene over the floor, the walls, and the dead man. He found and threw every book of foul magic Fairfax owned into a heap beside the body. He threw a match in a puddle, then prayed that any spirit trapped by Fairfax and who sought a final resting place would find it.

"That spirits may rest, that The People will be safe, that evil may have the reward it deserves," he prayed.

He waited in the ranch yard with Talks to Horses until the first tongue of flame licked through the roof. The blaze smelled of death, of decay.

"Wolves are not all that bright," Talks to Horses observed. She was no longer bandaged but was bent with pain and could only exist as a human. Still, she had time to chide Hunter for his ways.

"Of course he was ready for you—or someone. You would have been killed to no purpose without us."

Hunter looked at her and smiled. "I expected you days ago."

"The life of a spirit horse is hard," she replied. "And the demands of a spirit wolf are more than should be asked of anyone."

For a space of time, they sat in companionable silence and watched the fire consume Fairfax's horde of relics. Unnoticed in the pile of papers was a list of the men Fairfax had already contacted, urging them to use every skill at their disposal to bring to ruin the Indians now camped around Fort Keogh. The notes he'd sent also said that, no matter what might happen to him, they needed to continue to put pressure on the army and politicians to rid the Plains of the Indians by any means.

Talks to Horses spoke as the flames began to dwindle.

"There are places, wolf, where no one but a few crazy white mountain men and an assortment of wild animals ever go. North. It is time for us to go. The spirit world and the world of men must be separate. It is time to let The People find their own path."

Hunter knew she was right. There would be many challenges ahead for The People, but they were not ones he could solve. Still, he was disturbed by Fairfax's words. How vast was the network of evil against the Northern Cheyenne? Only time would tell.

"We shall stop and see Rides a Crow along the way. If the peace holds and if she is well, then we shall go," said Hunter.

"They still have many hard times ahead," she cautioned. "You cannot make the way straight for them."

"I can let her know she is not alone, that she has only to think of us and we will come to help her. A spirit horse and a spirit wolf do not account for much if they leave behind those who believe in them. When their beliefs die, so shall our kind."

"Be a gloomy wolf another day. The spirit world is calm. The Northern Cheyenne are home. For now, let us go."

They each mounted one of the spirit horses, and, as the fire behind spewed a cloud of smoke and ash, they rode away from its shadow.

July 1882, Fort Keogh, Montana

Paul Collins squinted against the guttering candle as his pen scratched across the paper. His fiancée, Annie Campbell, had gone East to visit her family. They had been bombarding her with letters demanding she visit them, accompanied by some not-so-thinly veiled criticisms of her decision to stay out west after she and Paul were married. He wished he could see them try to talk her out of something she wanted to do. It was a concept he had long ago abandoned!

He stayed behind, for there was so much to be done in very little time.

Dearest Annie,

I will use the excuse of work for not writing, because I have been doing nothing but writing for days. I should not complain, because writing means one way that at least some of the Northern Cheyenne will keep their land. The idea of having them file a claim to land under the Homestead Act was brilliant. Even if they never get land as a reservation, they will have acquired it through the process the government wants homesteaders to use when they stake a claim. It is hard to believe this was the army's plan, but I think that they respect the Cheyenne in defeat. The more of them who settle along the Tongue River and file claims, the easier it might be to get all that land included in a reservation. We can hope!

It has been quiet, mostly. It is hard to believe it has been a year since Sitting Bull came back from Canada, and the Lakota are now at peace. The older Cheyenne say this is the first time in many years—since before whites found gold in the Black Hills—the army and Indians have not been actively at war. Of course, there are always problems. The young men want to hunt; they want to find buffalo herds that no longer exist and can't understand why they cannot just ride down to Kansas and hunt. There is no use explaining to them that many whites still bear a grudge for the fights that took place when the Northern Cheyenne fled from Darlington, and that going back will start new troubles. It would be easier if the government would provide enough food everyone needs to survive, but when I think of what was happening just a few years ago, we are fortunate.

Some in the army are doing all they can to ensure peace; others are still trying to subjugate the Indians. The army cannot understand why a Cheyenne warrior would want to get on a horse and ride as far as he can one day just for the joy of riding, and that same warrior cannot imagine *not* wanting to mount a horse and ride for the sheer joy of being on the Plains. Perhaps in time these two worlds will move closer. If we have the time!

I know you will do everything you can, but while you are there, please try to tell as many people as possible that the most important thing to do in order to keep the peace is to keep the promises made to the Northern Cheyenne and the other Indians. The Cheyenne are still weak from their ordeal, but when they get stronger, a trail of broken promises could lead to the same kind of defiance we saw after they escaped from Fort Robinson. Most of the Indians still believe most whites want to exterminate them. It would be nice if they were wrong.

November 1883, Tongue River Valley, Montana
Rides a Crow sat beside the river as the trees with leaves let them fall in the stiffening wind. The moon's hard face would begin freezing the narrow creeks soon. Wrapped in a Blanket toddled a safe distance from the water as she looked at a bush with red berries.

The summer had been one of conflict between whites and

The People. Perhaps the storm had broken. Perhaps this was a lull between storms.

Rides a Crow recalled Hunter's words when they were on the trail from Darlington, that those were days when everything was simple. They lived or they died. Now, there was so much talk, so many opinions and so many differences, that Rides a Crow was more than happy to claim a few minutes of time alone. She wanted to be nothing more than a woman raising orphaned children, but the times would not allow it. Little Wolf was in his self-imposed exile after killing a man who was interested in his daughter. Dull Knife, who had finally come home to the land he'd risked everything to see, had died this past year. Now The People called her a Spirit Walker and a Wise Woman, as though the spirits could help determine how best The People could restore their way of life in a world that had changed forever.

She and the child Hunter had rescued went to the river every day when evening drew close. This was her time to talk to the spirits, to mourn, to pray, to watch animals do as they had done for ten thousand years before the Cheyenne existed, and would do for ten thousand years after the Cheyenne were gone. Her gaze fixed on a sky filled with crows as they circled to find roosting places. She could lose herself in their flights.

Then she heard the small branch on the ground snap. Only shoes would snap a branch that way. She wore a knife strapped to her right thigh under her skirt. A loaded rifle lay on the ground next to her. Wrapped in a Blanket had been trained to duck and find cover on command.

Rides a Crow breathed in deeply. Tobacco?

"What have you found there, child?" she called to Wrapped in a Blanket as she turned in the direction of the rifle.

The gunshot behind her sent a bullet into the tree far above her head. Rides a Crow looked to make sure the little girl was out of the line of fire, grabbed her own rifle, and trained it on the spot where she heard thrashing in the underbrush. Muffled noises emerged as small branches cracked. At one point, she was sure she saw a man's leg kicking. There were growls and squeals. She waited. Then she lowered the gun.

A rust-colored wolf came out of the bushes. He dragged a man by the neck of his clothing to the edge of the thicket. The man was covered in his own blood.

"Do you watch my every moment?" Rides a Crow sent Hunter in Spirit Talk.

"Not those when you talk and talk and talk like a magpie," sent back the wolf. "But when you are on your own and making yourself an inviting target, yes, Rides a Crow, I always watch, for the evil ones have not yet stopped appearing. This one came the farthest of them all, for I did not sense he was a threat as easily as I did the rest of them."

"Who are they?"

"Men hired to kill the Spirit Walker of the Northern Cheyenne," he said.

Hunter explained that, before he died, Fairfax had sent letters to various people, many of whom dabbled in the spirit world, as well as others as ruthless as he was in seeking to wipe out the Indians. Fairfax wrote that the key to destroying the Northern Cheyenne was to kill Rides a Crow.

"He has been dead many years," she said. "There are others more important than I am."

"Not to those who have come to kill you."

She looked puzzled.

"Most have been easy to stop. Most were very circumspect when The People were at Fort Keogh, because the army was all around. Once you began to move south into the valley, it became harder to find and track those sent to kill you, but there have been far fewer of them."

"How many have there been?"

"This one makes nineteen of them, Rides a Crow. There was almost a year without any, and now they are coming again."

She sat silent a moment. They both knew about men who had tried to sneak into the encampment at Fort Keogh during the first weeks after their arrival. She had killed three of them herself, before the army increased the protection it gave The People.

"Why?"

"I believe that in Washington, where the whites make their laws, they are preparing to grant The People lands here as a reservation. Once that happens, no matter how hard those who hate the Indians fight against you, they will not be able to drive you from this place."

Conflicting emotions stirred within Rides a Crow. A reservation would impose a limit over what The People could have, and no reservation would be of the right size, but a reservation would at least ensure that they survived. This was something that, on the road from Darlington, would have been but a fevered dream. But that people would be so set against a reservation that they stalked The People and tried to kill her was proof the hate she thought might have ended with the death of Fairfax still lived.

"It will be a battle forever, will it not?" she said, looking at the small girl now tossing berries in the river as though there no men wanted to slaughter the Northern Cheyenne.

"Yes," Hunter said honestly. "Ten thousand buckets of water could not douse all the flames of hate that have been stirred against The People, against the Lakota, and against the other nations. The soldiers now hunt the Apache the way they once did the Northern Cheyenne. For now, Rides a Crow, the mere survival of The People is a victory. It will be left to those who follow to decide if it can be more."

She nodded, watching Wrapped in a Blanket and wondering

what world would await the child when she grew up.

"At least the man from the army who told you that you must leave for Indian Territory will not be a threat," Hunter said, seeking to dispel her gloom.

She laughed at the memory. That spring some men the whites called "peace commissioners" tried to talk The People into moving back to Indian Territory. One young man had come armed with paper after paper about the favorable nature of Indian Territory. He was fat and pompous and would not allow the leaders of the Northern Cheyenne to speak. He tried to get them to sign papers no one had read. Finally Rides a Crow lost her temper.

"If you mention taking The People anywhere but this place ever again, I will command the sprit wolf who guards The People to tear out your throat on this very spot!" she had raged. "And the spirit horses will stomp your body to dust!"

Into the shocked silence following her words of wrath came Hunter's longest possible growl from outside the tipi where they talked. Indian Territory was never mentioned again.

"Would you have done it?" she asked. "Torn out his throat?"

"He was insufferable," Hunter replied. "I do not think he would have tasted very good!"

She laughed. Hunter dragged the would-be assassin's body farther back into the brush, where Wrapped in a Blanket would not see it. Although violent death would one day invade her world, there would be plenty of time for it to arrive.

"I must leave you for a space of time," Hunter told Rides a Crow. "If we sit and wait, more of these evil men will come, along with those who stir violence. I want to stop them, and this is the time for me to go. You are safest in winter and early spring, but you must take no chances."

"Where will you go?" she said.

"You are the Spirit Walker and Wise Woman," he replied, "so

you should know. There can be but one place where the head of a snake is to be found."

March 1884, Washington, D.C.

Senator Caleb McNaughton of Nebraska gripped the head of his cane as he walked through the gusts and rain to the hotel where he kept his rooms while in Washington. He was disgusted with President Chester Arthur and the rest who said a reservation for the Northern Cheyenne should be established in Montana. If they had only left supervising Indians to the army, all this talk about coddling them would have ended long ago. Twaddle!

Had they forgotten about the depredations that took place after the horde of these Northern Cheyenne Indians escaped from Fort Robinson only five years ago? Kansas had barely recovered! A tiger does not change his stripes. He wished Morrison Fairfax had not died in that tragic and unexplained fire.

Fairfax had been a useful ally, even if the man harbored grandiose ideas about his place in the world. Fairfax had certainly been right in his final letter. Something was protecting that woman of the Northern Cheyenne, the one who was supposedly connecting the tribe to the spirit world.

Perhaps it was time to up the stakes and offer a reward for her death, or find a pretext to arrest her. Perhaps he should spend more time with the books in a locked bookcase in his room and use the same tactics others were trying against the Lakota to finish off the Northern Cheyenne. Sooner or later, whatever was now protecting them had to be beaten!

He turned the key and stopped. Fire? He smelled it and heard crackling. His orders to his staff were to have a fire ready, but he never lit it until he arrived. When he entered the room, a man stood before the fireplace.

"See now . . ."

His eyes traveled from the shaggy-headed man to the pile of books and papers near the fireplace waiting their turn to be tossed into the flames. His most private and valuable documents that had been under lock and key! His books of chants!

"Stop this!" he demanded. "I do not know who you are, but I will call the police and have you arrested."

"For burning your books on sorcery and demons?" the man asked derisively. "I think not. I doubt the newspapers would keep your penchant for demonology from their columns."

"What are you doing? Stop!"

Hunter threw more books into the flames. Smoke puffed from the old leather before a yellow tongue of fire curled around one volume.

"I expected to be home by now," Hunter said. "But this has been a longer road than I thought it would be. One of the last people you sent to kill Rides a Crow had on his person, inconveniently for you, a letter discussing who could be counted upon to ensure your safety. I had to make a few stops before I came here to talk to you."

McNaughton swallowed hard. A series of unexplained accidents had befallen several of the men who had corresponded with him and Fairfax about using demons and sorcery to defeat the Indians. McNaughton had dismissed the accidents as a coincidence. After all, many of those who communicated with the spirit world lived in ways that might well lead them to consort with violent entities.

"You cannot frighten me. I have power."

"You are a senator, and there is power in that. You are a mean, hateful man, and there is power in that, because, when you fan hate, it spreads like a forest fire out of control. But you have nothing resembling real power in the world of spirits. All you do is assist evil to walk in the world."

"Why are you here? Do you want money?"

"What would I do with money? If I wanted your purse of coins, I would have taken it and left. Forgive me for a moment. The fire is dying here." Hunter threw a load of papers into the fireplace as McNaughton groaned. He had never had the chance to read some of those, and they had been purchased in England at a great cost!

"I am here to give you a simple message. Stop everything you are doing to fight the Northern Cheyenne and any of their friends. Put an end to any plot you might have to kill Rides a Crow, the Spirit Walker."

"You cannot tell me—"

Hunter suddenly closed the distance between himself and the much larger man and grabbed the lapels of McNaughton's coat. "You will listen," he commanded. "You will listen. You will obey. Or you will die."

McNaughton tried to push Hunter away. He was taller and much heavier than Hunter, thanks to the many social dinners that were part of his routine. He was shocked when Hunter pushed him, hard, against a wall.

McNaughton waited for a better opportunity as Hunter threw more paper—the last bundle—onto the fire.

"Nothing can stop those Indians from getting what they deserve," McNaughton said. "The entire army is behind me. Sooner or later, the right moment will come, and those Indians will get what is coming to them."

"I know the president will give them a reservation this year before he leaves office," Hunter said. "If you try to stop it; if you try to strip budget money used to feed the Cheyenne; if you do anything to hurt The People—particularly if you use the evil of your spirit world against them—I will kill you."

"What makes you think I care about your threats? I have a hundred books like those elsewhere. I have friends who will help me. You are nothing!"

"As for the books you hid in your ranch in Nebraska, they burned up in a fire. As for whether I am nothing, I shall let you be the judge." Hunter took off his jacket and tossed it to the floor. McNaughton, thinking this was a prelude to a fistfight, turned and took his jacket off, removed the cufflinks from his shirt cuffs, took off his tie, and rolled up his sleeves. Then he turned around and assumed the pose of a pugilist.

His jaw dropped.

Before him stood a wolf, rust-colored and mangy, with the deadliest, most intense eyes McNaughton had ever seen. *No* he said to himself.

The wolf leaped, knocking the older man to the floor, then stood with its front paws on McNaughton's chest, staring down at him. The animal cocked its head from time to time. It then hopped off of McNaughton, who scrambled to his feet.

"No," McNaughton said. "This is impossible."

"You have been warned," Hunter said after dressing again as he moved inches away from the quaking senator. "I will find you, and I will kill you if you disobey me. You think you can play with the spirit world as if it were a toy? I can show you a very different reality!"

"I . . . I . . . I . . . There are others. Fairfax built a vast network. It began before him . . . before me. I am not responsible for all of them. The Lakota are sitting on millions in gold. The army still wants revenge for Custer, even after all these years. The railroad is going to grow. You cannot stop progress."

"I can stop you. I will, Senator. If the Northern Cheyenne are hurt, you will feel the pain."

Hunter slammed the door behind him.

★ ★ ★ ★ ★

October 1890, Lame Deer, Montana
Annie Collins watched her husband and their youngest child. They had enjoyed their years here, first when the Cheyenne camped informally by Fort Keogh under the army's protection and patrols, and even more since the Cheyenne reservation became legally established in 1884 and Paul became its agent. Being an agent was difficult for him, because he was usually in the middle of disputes between his government and the Northern Cheyenne, but it was work both he and she loved.

She picked up her pen to write her sister in Boston.

Dear Francine,

We are all well. The baby had a cough (don't they all?) but is better now. Cheyenne women lined up outside our door with remedies! It is fascinating how much they know. Do you recall the minister who said God gave us everything we need to survive and that the whole world was the Garden of Eden? Sometimes I think of that when the Cheyenne women use roots, berries, and leaves to cure their ailments.

I am glad you saw the article this summer. Cheyenne culture is so much more complex than most white people understand it to be. They are reluctant to explain their culture to outsiders, because they have become accustomed to everything they say being used against them. I wish I could write more, but I am doing less writing and more painting these days. I am trying to paint as many Cheyenne as I can, because that museum in Washington wants to display my portraits and my sketches.

We had thought of going East, but there was never a good time. Paul has to fight with the government endlessly to get the Cheyenne the basics of what they need. The men in the tribe would be happy to spend more time hunting, but since their hunts would probably end at the nearest cattle ranch now that the buffalo are all but gone, letting them hunt is not a good idea!

It is very hard on Paul. He keeps his promises, but the government does not keep theirs. Things are not as bad as when he was at Darlington, or so he says, but he has said more than once that, after the Cheyenne were no longer a threat, the government just wanted to forget them and give them no care at all. The Cheyenne, however, do not forget what they've been promised. We were afraid for a while that the army would listen to Washington when it wanted to move the Northern Cheyenne from the Tongue River Valley, or put them on the same reservation with their long-time enemies, the Crow Nation. However, the army did not want another war on its hands, so they supported the Cheyenne.

Despite that, it will be many years, I think, before the Cheyenne forget and forgive what was done to them. Last month, two Cheyenne named Head Chief and John Young Mule broke the law. I think they shot a steer on someone's ranch and then shot the rancher. They refused and refused to surrender. Then they agreed on one condition: that they could fight against the soldiers the way Dull Knife's people did. They got their way! The army lined up to take their surrender or fight. Both of them fought—two men attacking a column of soldiers in the name of honor—and both of them died. For days afterward, the young Cheyenne were calling the two men heroes who had stood tall for the Northern Cheyenne.

I have told you about the remarkable woman who helped bring the Cheyenne from Indian Territory up here.

She is now very angry with us (well, not us, but the ones we work for). Rides a Crow has left the reservation again, because of this Ghost Dance talk. I can't explain it all, but the Lakota believe if they dance a certain dance, the white men will go away, and the world will be as it was before we got here. The army thinks the Ghost Dance is being used by the Cheyenne and Lakota and others to unite all of the Plains Indians in another Indian war. When I asked Rides a Crow about the Ghost Dance, she told me, 'When people have no meat, they must eat hope instead.'

I saw her once walking along the river, talking to an animal—a wolf that must be tame because I see it around here all the time. She was talking out loud to the animal, as though it could understand her. She seemed to understand the spirits that helped her people avoid destruction were telling her she should not leave the reservation. She, however, felt a great debt to the Lakota because they had taken in the Northern Cheyenne many years ago when a camp the Cheyenne had on the Rosebud was destroyed by soldiers.

This will probably not make sense to you, but Rides a Crow believes there are people who are trying to use the spirit world to attack the Indians. I have tried to tell her that Christian people would never act this way, but when she asks me to explain why so many whites direct so much hate at her people, I confess I do not have an answer that sounds good even to me!

I am afraid for her. There's nothing wrong in how they do this dance. After all, a few years ago, all this land was theirs! How many times do we pray in church for things that those who do not believe say are foolish? But Paul said the army is taking the matter far too seriously and may precipitate a war by trying to ban the Ghost Dance.

Ever since the Ghost Dance started, young people have been drifting from reservation to reservation, spreading the news. I hope this passes without more fighting, but I fear it will not.

Please pass along my thoughts to any who remember me. Please continue to do everything you can to change the thoughts of those who believe Indian religion is mere superstition. It is only when you have lived out here among the Northern Cheyenne that you can understand their religion is not a fantasy, but part of reality people who live in brick houses on city streets can never imagine.

Sincerely,
Annie (Campbell) Collins

CHAPTER FIFTEEN

New York City, New York, January 17, 1891

Fitting his eyeglasses to his head, the doctor sat down to write. He shook his head. The young soldier had just left his office. For a moment, he wondered about what happened to men out on the Plains, where there were no buildings and streets to keep the order of civilization. He dipped the pen in the inkwell and did his duty.

Dear Colonel Wainwright:

Private Jeremiah Mackinaw was referred to me for observation and concerns about his mental instability. Private Mackinaw was among the members of the regiment who were stationed at Wounded Knee, Dakota Territory, and who participated in the December 29th battle against a marauding band of Sioux led by Big Foot.

It should be noted that many members of the cavalry unit engaged at Wounded Knee Creek have suffered short-term symptoms of mental derangement following the attack. I believe this is due to the power and noise of the Hotchkiss guns. I also believe that the effects of this type of weapon on human beings must be considered.

Many others have, in conversations with the regimental chaplains, expressed remorse over the killing of women and children that took place that day. They claim they can barely remember what they were doing, or that they were acting in some sort of haze. I believe this is due to the condemnation the slaughter received at the hands of many in the popular press, particularly one venomous female writer named Annie Campbell or Collins, whose work should be suppressed. I expect some soldiers suffer from trying to reconcile their actions with their beliefs.

My view is that few men have any real concern for the Indians and are mostly responding to what others think of them. I believe the action of the War Department in offering the Medal of Honor to several men who fought that day will help all the soldiers better understand their actions in a more positive manner.

Private Mackinaw's case is unique because of what he claims to have witnessed, in addition to his self-condemnation regarding the events of that day. I relate this at length because there have been claims spiritualists are invoking evil spirits against the Indians, when I think the truth is vastly different.

On that day, the warriors had been wisely separated from the women. When the fighting broke out, which I am certain was due to treachery on the part of the Indians, the Hotchkiss guns raked the camp holding the women and children. That was where Private Mackinaw was assigned.

Although the encampment was composed mostly of the Minneconjou band of the Sioux, there were some visitors from other tribes there trying to foment a general Indian uprising through the Ghost Dance religion.

The incident in question concerns a Northern Cheyenne woman known as Rides a Crow, who was a part of the Cheyenne fight against the army that killed many civilians in Kansas when they escaped from the southern reservation in Oklahoma in 1878. Since the Cheyenne surrendered in 1879, there were some who committed depredations or resisted the army's authority. This woman was one of them, being considered a 'Spirit Walker' by her people, as reported by the army, based on observations of spies at their reservation. She has threatened to sic spirit creatures on at least one army officer and is considered a major reason the Northern Cheyenne remain intransigent.

On the 29th, Private Mackinaw saw a woman who has since been identified as Rides a Crow holding a small girl in her arms while trying to gather her outer blanket over others as she fled the battlefield. She was called upon to halt and surrender but resisted the soldiers' entreaties.

She had been witnessed holding a rifle. Private Conrad Schlicter was with Private Mackinaw and fired his rifle, wounding Rides a Crow in the side, even though she was wearing one of the Ghost Shirts the Indians claimed would deflect bullets. She continued to try to escape, letting go of a child's hand to throw a knife at Private Schlicter. The throw went awry. The private fired again, wounding her in the face. It is here I must quote the words of Private Mackinaw to reveal the extent of his mental state.

"There was blood everywhere. She was bleeding from her face. The Ghost Shirt was red with her own blood. She looked like a monster, a horrifying creature as, with her face distorted and disfigured, she ceased her attempt to flee and turned to attack in a frenzy, clearly telling watchers she cared nothing about her own life, but craved death for us.

"She reached under her skirts to pull a long-bladed knife and advanced upon Private Schlicter and me. We were both transfixed by this vision of savagery coming to kill us. We heard screaming all around us. I know we were both calling for help, and she was screaming something. Then the woman was herself attacked. A wolf, a strange-colored wolf whose fur was blood-matted and the color of rusted metal, knocked her to the ground and stood over her as a volley of our rifle fire passed over both their heads. Blood from his fur—for we later learned he had been attacking our soldiers—dripped upon her.

"I felt, just then, some tremendous power—something otherworldly. I was afraid. I could not shoot. Private Schlicter struggled as well. The woman said something to the wolf, screaming in some language, remonstrating with the creature. Then, from behind us, Privates Oliver and Hynde emerged. For a moment I thought the wolf smiled. Then it howled a sound I hear in the night when bloody-faced dead come to me in dreams and ask why they were slain. The wolf stepped off of the woman, barked something at her with his head turned, and charged the four of us.

"The woman at first began to scream but then ran, gathering up the small child she had held, and then grabbed others and ran from the field, eventually finding a horse that took her and several of the children. The horse, which had a large bloody wound across its face, was a coal-black mare. In its pain, it lashed out with hooves and teeth and badly injured soldiers who were in its way. A volley of gunfire then raked the field. When the smoke of the guns cleared, the horse and its riders had vanished."

Private Mackinaw later said that the body of Rides a Crow was never found, and we can only assume she escaped in the confusion that followed the battle. It is possible all the Indians there that day lie dead on the Plains under the snows that came soon after the battle, although the private believes otherwise. However, we shall return to the private's testimony.

"The wolf charged Privates Oliver, Schlicter, and Hynde, and soon wounded them to the death, before turning to come for me. The wounds the wolf gouged were long and deep. The men repeatedly discharged their guns at the animal, but it did not halt. I am certain they wounded it many times, but it never stopped. It seemed almost like a Ghost Dance creature who was trying to save the woman and horse. One of the men manning the Hotchkiss guns screamed as the wolf threw the body of Private Hynde to the side. He soon unleashed fire upon the animal, which by the end of its rage of blood lust had killed several soldiers. When the gun grew silent, and the smoke of the fighting had cleared, I looked where the wolf had lain, and I could find no animal.

"Instead a man, an older man with gray hair and a grizzled beard, lay on the ground suffering from horrible wounds made by a Hotchkiss gun. What was worse, he was a white man! His eyes met mine. I knelt to hear what might pass from his lips, wondering in that moment if the man were an apparition. I had heard legends of werewolves, but until that moment believed they were only tales for the weak of mind.

" 'The People will never die,' he said, 'and you will be cursed for your work this day. Evil will never win.' He said several things more I didn't understand. He talked about horses and spirits. I believe he also spoke to the woman, for the word "crow" came from his lips. He also mentioned a dead warrior killed in the Dull Knife escape from Fort Robinson, one of those who resisted the soldiers in the Pit.

"This strange figure did not last long, nor did the battle. The fight was all but over as he breathed his last, a smile on his lips. He looked as though he were greeting someone as he stared up past me and into the sky.

" 'It is a good day to live,' he said. Then he sighed deeply as his head lolled in a way only the dead can accomplish."

These are the soldier's own words, to which he has sworn, even after reviewing them in writing. According to him, this is an accurate rendition of the events of that day. Bodies were not recovered, because, although the day was warm, a Plains blizzard was brewing. The soldiers recovered their dead and wounded and the wounded Indians they could assist and headed for shelter. Private Mackinaw was among those who went back to the battlefield a few days later to recover the frozen corpses of the Indians. He told me what he found on the spot where he claims some form of a shape-changing creature had existed. These are his words:

"There was no one there. There were no prints in the snow except those of a barefoot woman, which were only around where the body had lain, and those of a horse leading away from the scene. It was as though the man, or whatever he was, had never been there. I scoured the ground to find him, thinking someone had moved him while hunting souvenirs, but he was gone. The Cheyenne talk of a spirit wolf who guards them. I believe the spirit wolf is now roaming the world undead, and I am cursed."

Since then, Private Mackinaw has told his story about being cursed to others in his regiment, leading his commanding officer to send him to me to tell his story. His reports claiming an encounter with vague, unspecified, Cheyenne spirits have unsettled his fellow soldiers. He now holds the belief that evil spirits have infiltrated the army and settlers, and that primitive Indian spirits are fighting against them. One female reporter, Annie Campbell Collins, whose work to undercut the morale of the army has been very injurious to its efforts, has been in contact with the soldier and is trying to publish his recollections. Her report would be very damaging for the army. She should be suppressed.

It is my recommendation that Private Mackinaw be removed from the army, and his family advised that his condition may lead him to be unfit for future life without restrictions. There are institutions and asylums that may offer a better place for him if his life continues to be haunted by Wounded Knee. I further recommend, in this age of science and rational thought, that all possible efforts be accelerated to exterminate belief in spirit dances and ghost dances and such things as animals who change into men and spirits that walk. These are simply tall tales that have no place in a modern society.

Sincerely,

Dr. DeWitt Forrester, consulting physician,

New York City.

Cheyenne Indian Reservation, February 1891

"Where is he?"

The blonde visitor's conduct bordered on rudeness, but Rides a Crow had grown to understand that patience and settlers did not go together. Ever. She tried to bury the pain of her wounds and loss and deal with the stranger, a striking, wild-looking woman who radiated aggression in every movement, and who had entered her lodge as though she had a right to be there, glaring from side to side as though seeking something.

"Whom do you seek?" asked Rides a Crow.

"You do not know? You are Rides a Crow, the Spirit Walker, aren't you? He said you know everything!"

Rides a Crow had been distracted by her own pain, but now she focused entirely on the woman. The faint accent seemed familiar.

"You are this Skellig I was told years ago to expect when it was time. You were his friend in London. I should have known.

Now I understand what he meant. I'm sorry. He is gone."

"Gone? Gone where? He said I was to come here as fast as possible. That was about all he said, and I have not been able to communicate with him for more than a month now. Why would he go away? Doesn't he know it takes time to get all the way out here?"

The blonde woman stood with her mouth open as she looked around the lodge once again as if it would hold a clue. Rides a Crow let silence say what she found hard to put into words. Saying the word somehow made it real.

"He can't be dead," Skellig insisted, eventually understanding what Rides a Crow's silence signified.

"He is." Rides a Crow related the story of Wounded Knee. She rose and took Skellig by the hand, leading her to a spot by the river.

"This is my favorite spot," Rides a Crow said, sitting down on a log next to a large rock that marked the otherwise unadorned burial place, notable by the recently turned earth she showed Skellig after scraping off the snow. "I wanted him here with me."

Skellig, damp-eyed, sat on the log next to Rides a Crow.

"I think that must have been the day he reached me, that day at Wounded Knee Creek. He was so distant, so . . . something." Skellig struggled to continue. "I wondered, but he never answered half the time anyhow."

"He died saving me," Rides a Crow said. "What was his real name? He told us here his name was Hunter, but he never really told us much about himself."

"In London we called him Glyndwr, after the Welsh prince from the 1400s," Skellig said. "No one ever knew his real name. He never let anyone close to him, except you. You were closer than anyone else, I think. I know he used other names in the army. I never really knew much more than that. He was . . . I met him when I was barely more than a pup. He pretty much rescued me, because I was all on my own. You know he left London in 1874, and I never saw him again until a few years ago, but he never left me." Skellig was also wrapped in her own thoughts. "In time, I had to leave as well. So did most of the others who were left behind. We found a place in New York State in the Adirondack Mountains to be our refuge. Rheged—I assume you know about him—was so drenched in what he was doing, that the clan all but dissolved. Rheged took the worst of the crop with him."

Rides a Crow told the story of Rheged's demise at Hunter's hands. Skellig began nodding, then shaking her head in admiration as Rides a Crow told Hunter's story.

"He was clever. Always was. Rheged always thought he could outsmart him, but he never did. We knew Rheged was gone. We assumed Hunter did it, but we never knew for sure. He . . . he kept his distance. He told me once that being near him wasn't safe. He said that siding with the Northern Cheyenne meant he was living on borrowed time, but that was when his life had the most purpose. He said the spirits brought him to you."

"He told me I should expect you some day, but never why, Skellig," said Rides a Crow, not wanting to talk about Hunter in the past tense. "I am in his debt. The People are. We walk a hard road, but, without him, we might not be here at all. What is it we can do for you, and why did you come so far?"

"I am here to keep a promise. The clan I belong to will live in the refuge," she replied. "As for my mate and me, we will live here. Hunter wanted it that way. He told me there might be danger, because someone would always stalk you, and that there would be hate against the Northern Cheyenne for years to come. Hunter knew his days would be shorter than he wished, and he wanted there to be spirit wolves to guard you and The People forever."

"I do not need . . ."

Skellig lifted one eyebrow. "They say I am much like him when it comes to being stubborn. You can have me here prowling around with your blessing or without it, because I am here either way. I promise not to have too many pups, but enough to keep the family going for a few generations. And I would like your help with the spirit horses. I've never had much luck with horses. But I like it here. I understand."

"Understand what?"

"You know the person you call Hunter never had anything he could call a home in his life until he got here? When he asked me to come, he said this was not just a place where people lived. It was a place where people belonged, and there was a harmony with the spirits that did not exist anywhere else. He was right. I can feel it."

"When did he ask you to come here?"

"A few winters ago he appeared at the refuge. He had been to Washington and said he understood that, even if the battle was won, the war was not over. I didn't really understand, but I do now. He was talking about Wounded Knee, as if he knew something like that slaughter was going to happen. That's when he told me the day was coming when I would be needed here. He said the only way to stop evil was for me to get off my lazy haunches and do something about it! I didn't hear from him again until that day. The last time. The day you tell me he was killed."

"What did he say?"

"He sent his thoughts to me early that day. He said my time would come soon, and that I needed to honor my promise to come here. I heard from him again later. I didn't know what had happened, what was going on. He was different . . . wild . . . like he didn't have long to talk. Then he faded away, and I could not reach him again. I worried, but he had gone months before without sending word, so I was not sure."

"What did he say that last time?"

"He told me I had to protect you. He said The People were the spirit's children." Wet trails ran down Skellig's face. "He seemed disjointed . . . just thoughts and scrambled words. He was in pain, but he had joy, too. I know you said he was dying, but I was sure he was happy. Then he told me 'It is a good day to live.' And then he was silent."

Epilogue

October 1928, Lame Deer, Montana, Northern Cheyenne Reservation

The Wise Woman's time was near. Two days ago, she had taken to her bed. Her adopted children and their children had come to her. They hoped once more her eyes would open, but they despaired.

On this morning, not only did her eyes open, but she said she wanted to get up. She did not wait for her daughters and sons to help her. The number of her children was great, for, although she had never married, she had adopted as her own the children left without parents from the Northern Cheyenne's flight to freedom.

Her black hair had long since turned to gray and silver, and as cutting it became a chore, it was no longer hacked off but flowed down her back. The wrinkles time had etched into her skin covered her face, including the furrow from a soldier's bullet she'd received at Wounded Knee. A puckered mark in her side, one that ached through the years following Wounded Knee, showed where another bullet had come close to ending her life on the day she fought with her Lakota cousins.

She had returned to the Tongue River weeks after the Wounded Knee massacre on a travois, along with Smoky Hair, a Lakota baby girl whose origins none knew. The travois was pulled by a scarred, coal-black mare and accompanied by a small herd of horses. When the healers looked at wounds that usually left their victims dead and asked her about her treatment, Rides a Crow only talked about spirits and sent the healers on their way.

After Wounded Knee, she spoke of the need for warriors to do more than fight battles they could not win, while never giving up an inch of the Northern Cheyenne's land or a drop of its culture. She told her people the war they now faced against those who hated them would not be won in a day or with horses and rifles but would take many years. The hate had infiltrated so many places in the world around them that it could only be defeated by outlasting it. She would often rise before dawn to go to the river, where those who sought to spy upon her said she communed with spirit horses and spirit wolves.

Now, her dark eyes snapped with fire as she rose, stumbled, and then rose again as though determined to win one final battle against the body nearing the end of its days.

"I must see," Rides a Crow said with determination.

"See what, Grandmother?" asked Last Star, one of her many granddaughters.

Last Star was always at her grandmother's side during these days. She was the one of all the generations of children Rides a Crow had raised who seemed to understand when the old woman talked of visions. Last Star was Wrapped in a Blanket's daughter. She would often play with the tame wolves that greeted her grandmother, and, despite being only twelve, she had already ridden a massive, beautiful, black horse her grandmother seemed to treat more as a pet than a horse to be ridden. She had often heard Rides a Crow remark that the girl had her own gift with animals and would grow, in her own way and time, to be a Spirit Walker and help The People when Rides a Crow was no longer with them.

"The People," Rides a Crow answered.

With an arm across Last Star's shoulders, Rides a Crow

walked to the entrance of the small lodge—hers, now that all her adopted ones were grown. She could see, through the opening, many were gathered, for word had spread that she, who was revered by all leaders for her counsel, was near her time of passage.

For a moment, Rides a Crow saw a dusty trail of hobbling Cheyenne, long past their limits of endurance but refusing to give in as they marched to a place that could hold their bodies but not their spirits.

"Last Star! You must prepare me. Out, all the rest of you. Out!"

The crowd buzzed when family members who had just arrived left the lodge. One told the crowd Rides a Crow would appear shortly. The news traveled like the wind, and soon dozens upon dozens of families gathered on the land that was home eternal.

Inside the lodge, Rides a Crow spoke urgently. "The spirit will guide you," she told Last Star. "You will understand now, because it is time. When the spirit comes because I have walked my last steps, welcome it, for it will be your friend, even when all others forsake you." She paused. "And if The People face destruction, they will come, child: the spirit horses and the spirit wolves will never desert The People. The spirits do not need to be seen in our world, child, to be nearby."

"I understand."

Rides a Crow stroked the girl's raven hair, smiling at the way it had been recently sliced off in the fashion of a young girl she had known so long ago. "You do not, and may God grant you do not need to, for if The People are safe, the spirits will sleep."

She smoothed the girl's hair, lifted her chin to look her in the eyes, and told her, "Be not afraid. You are never alone."

"That is what the strange-looking wolf said in my dream last night, Grandmother. He was not like the ones we play with. He was . . ."

"Rust-colored," Rides a Crow finished for her. Then Rides a Crow smiled, a deep smile that can only come when a long and difficult journey has reached its end. "Then it is time."

Rides a Crow stretched as tall as her wounds would let her, lifted her arm from the young girl's shoulders, and stood unaided. "Open the doorway, child."

"Will you be all right, Grandmother?"

"You already know the answer, child."

Last Star felt moisture in her eyes, but she also felt a growing sense of understanding. Rides a Crow had spoken of this day often, at times with longing, at times with joy, but never with fear. She had talked of promises of the spirits she had never doubted. "Good child. Now let us go."

The crowd's buzzing stilled as Rides a Crow, one of the oldest living members of The People, stepped on the hallowed ground of the Tongue River Valley.

Gasps soon filled the silence, for, unlike the clothing she usually wore, she wore a wrinkled piece of clothing that had been in her chest for many years—a Ghost Shirt, decorated with leaping figures and ornately decorated pictures of wolves. Most of those gathered had never seen a shirt from the days of the Ghost Dance, for it and all relics of it had been outlawed by the army.

Red stains discolored her shirt where blood had flowed from her face, where it had gushed from her side, and where a spirit wolf had dripped blood on it when it had said good-bye. Rides a Crow touched those drops with reverence.

Around her head she wore a red band of cloth reeking of gunpowder. A very old bone necklace gilded her neck. Those who had known her as a grandmother and a wise woman saw for the first time the warrior princess and Spirit Walker of legend who had helped lead The People from captivity. The stories that she had set a wolf upon a peace commissioner in the 1880s when he demanded the Northern Cheyenne give up their land and move back to Indian territory seemed true. The People gathered around and believed the stories claiming she had killed men infiltrating the reservation with one shot from her rifle, no matter how far away the men were; and that she could summon a herd of wild horses from the winds by calling out their names.

Rides a Crow stepped forward, slowly but unaided, with Last Star behind her in case she was needed.

Annie Collins, the widow of the old agent, whose stiff fingers now captured images with a camera instead of pencil and paper, could not restrain her tears as Rides a Crow stood tall and proud, looking around at her People. Annie knew Rides a Crow was seeing The People one final time. She, Paul, all of them would be together again soon. Very soon.

The voice that once could ring and echo across the Plains now issued forth with the hush of a spring breeze.

"Endure, my people," called Rides A Crow. "Hold this land that is ours, which was won by the blood of our people who would not let their dreams be taken before their time. The spirits gave us this land to be ours until the day the sun shines no more in the sky. The spirits who prevented the destruction of The People will never leave us until the day we leave them. Let that day be never."

The sun shone on The People as Rides a Crow looked upon them, standing where their ancestors had hunted, enduring despite hate, enduring despite evil that could only be defeated with the help of the Spirit Warriors the Great Spirit sent to The People.

A tear came unbidden. Behind the array of generations shimmering in her vision stood a small herd of spirit horses led by a coal-black mare upon whom was mounted a man with a face more scarred and more dear than the face of any human. A thin, mangy wolf stood with them, no longer wreathed with smoke and blood. Dead Face, Hunter, and Talks to Horses had come to walk her home!

"Hold fast, my people," she said. "Hold true. You are Northern Cheyenne. Be proud. Be free." Her mind drifted to a face she had not seen for fifty years. "Be worthy of those who died as they walked, who dreamed as they died, who sacrificed their lives because they knew The People must never surrender. Fight those who even now would drain our dreams of their life."

She wobbled a step. Last Star moved forward with her hands outstretched lest Rides a Crow tumble.

"If they could not kill us at Wounded Knee . . . if they could not kill us at the Pit . . . they will never kill us." Rides a Crow gasped in a breath. "Never."

For a moment Rides a Crow saw the dust cloud from the trail to Oklahoma again. Then the smile of Little Wolf on the day they came home. Then she turned to Last Star and placed her hand upon her.

"Hear the Spirit Talk, child, and heed it."

And, with those words, the old woman took one more step, leaving behind the shade of the trees as the sun streamed in her eyes. She closed them against the brightness, and she saw the Tongue River. Beside the far bank, where the berries grew thickest, she saw a rusted wolf, sitting, wolf-patient, with a look of radiance and welcome.

"Hello, little wolf," she said aloud. Those in the world beyond her eyes muttered as they told each other the spirit of their ancestor had come to walk her home.

In her vision, the river sparkled before her. Rides a Crow put her toe into the water, which was as warm as the summer. She could hear, from the trees beyond the bank, the chanting and the singing of The People as they sang the song of home. Was that the dance they danced when everything seemed to be lost?

The wolf now stood, tail moving to the pulse of the spirits that stirred all life. Together, they had saved The People. Together, they would watch over them. Rides a Crow smiled. It had been a hard fight, but it was over. The People lived. Darkness had been defeated. She had done the job the spirits gave her to do.

In the world she was leaving, The People gathered close and reached out as her step shivered.

"It is a good day to live," she whispered softly.

A gasp.

"Oh, it is good to be home."

Behind closed eyes, Rides a Crow saw clearly. She stepped forward. The arms of The People caught the husk that had held her spirit.

As they did, the river's water rushed over her; new energy and hope flowed through her; and the song of the wolf, the song of The People, and the song of her heart became one. And all was light.

AFTERWORD AND
HISTORICAL NOTE

There are few instances in American history in which any group of people have shown the raw courage exhibited by the Northern Cheyenne who, after being forced into exile, left the Darlington Agency in Oklahoma to trek to their home in Montana, battling hunger and the elements as soldiers who vastly outnumbered them sought to capture them.

Dee Brown, whose book *Bury My Heart at Wounded Knee* should be required reading for all Americans, first introduced me to the subject. The Cheyenne Exodus, as historians often call it, was immortalized by Mari Sandoz in her novel, *Cheyenne Autumn*. Two other works, *In Dull Knife's Wake: The True Story of the Northern Cheyenne Exodus of 1878,* by Vernon R. Maddux and Albert Glenn Maddux; and *Tell Them We Are Going Home: The Odyssey of the Northern Cheyennes,* by John H. Monnett, help paint in many of the historical details this novel omits, as do numerous websites about various figures involved in the drama.

The author has made as few deviations from literal history as possible while still maintaining the pace of a narrative. Northern Cheyenne chief Little Wolf was real, although his conversations with my fictional characters were not. The same is true for Dull Knife, who is buried next to Little Wolf in Lame Deer, Montana. The Cheyenne victories over the army at Turkey Springs, Sandy Creek, and Punished Woman's Fork are also real, as is the final tragic battle of the Cheyenne escapees from Fort Robinson at the Pit near Hat Creek Bluffs.

For the rest, I have tried to look at this part of America's saga—long portrayed in Western books and movies as a morality play pitting good against evil—from a perspective that finds cruelty and evil in places we often find hard to accept, and true heroism in those to whom history often assigns the role of the loser.

There is a special joy for anyone who researches novels. For these past weeks, I have walked and ridden with the Northern Cheyenne as I sought to learn about their quest to reach their homeland. It has been a journey into a rich world with spirits at every touch and breath, and one with a deep respect for justice and honor. I do not say good-bye to them, for their courage, their words, and their culture will stay with me forever. I am the richer for the journey.

ABOUT THE AUTHOR

Rusty Davis is a Spur Award–nominated writer who writes about the rugged individualists of the West as they fight for freedom against the corrupting influences of power and wealth. He draws his inspiration from the conflicts that raged across the towns and ranches of the High Plains in a time when men and women who wanted to fight for what was theirs needed to pick up a gun—and risk their lives—to do so. Rusty is a freelance writer whose first three novels, *Wyoming Showdown, Black Wind Pass,* and *Rakeheart,* were published by Five Star. He can be reached by emailing him at rustywork777@gmail.com. Rusty is now at work on a series of novels about the Northern Cheyenne.

The employees of Five Star Publishing hope you have enjoyed this book.

Our Five Star novels explore little-known chapters from America's history, stories told from unique perspectives that will entertain a broad range of readers.

Other Five Star books are available at your local library, bookstore, all major book distributors, and directly from Five Star/Gale.

Connect with Five Star Publishing

Visit us on Facebook:
https://www.facebook.com/FiveStarCengage

Email:
FiveStar@cengage.com

For information about titles and placing orders:
(800) 223-1244
gale.orders@cengage.com

To share your comments, write to us:
Five Star Publishing
Attn: Publisher
10 Water St., Suite 310
Waterville, ME 04901